THE SINS OF THE MOTHER

THE SINS OF THE MOTHER

BY
SCOTT PRATT

WITH MARK STOUT

Thanks to Scott and Dylan Pratt. Without them, this project wouldn't have been possible. Also, to my family. They refused to let me fail and believed in me even when I lost faith in myself. And most of all to God, for protecting me and watching over me all these years, eventually making it possible for me to tell these stories.

I dedicate this book to those that have gone before, those I've served with, and those who will come after. Hold that line, brothers and sisters.

-Mark

This book, along with every book I've written and every book I'll write, is dedicated to my darling Kristy, to her unconquerable spirit, and to her inspirational courage. She lost her 11-year battle with breast cancer on June 23, 2018. She fought like a lioness to her last breath. I loved her before I was born, and I'll love her after I'm long gone.

PROLOGUE

The man had been watching them through the window for more than an hour. They were drinking champagne, snorting cocaine, watching porn and having sex on the living room couch, on the floor, on the recliner. They kept changing positions. He'd never met the young man who was having sex with his wife. He knew his name and knew he was six years younger than her. They'd been married for eight years and had two sons. He was a long-haul trucker and she was a cook at a diner in downtown Dalton, Georgia. He'd always been good to her, but he'd always wondered about her fidelity.

Now he knew for sure, and he wondered how many others there'd been over the years.

It was mid-June, warm and humid. The sky was clear. He'd parked his truck in a vacant lot about a half-mile down the road and walked to his house. He carried a Smith & Wesson Model 686 revolver. It had a six-shot capacity and was shoved in his belt beneath his T-shirt. The weapon was loaded with .357 Magnum cartridges.

The man was sober. He knew what he was about to do would constitute murder. He knew he would go to prison, most likely for the rest of his life, but he didn't care. He had loved this woman, adored her, believed in her. Now he'd learned that she was apparently nothing more than a coke whore. He felt like such a fool that he no longer cared what happened to him. His boys were in the house. He could see the faint light from the video game they were most likely playing coming through their bedroom window. He felt badly for them, for what they would undoubtedly go through, but nothing would change his course now. He was committed. The traitor and her lover had to die.

He walked around to the back of the house and up the three steps to the stoop outside the kitchen door. He pulled the pistol from his belt and his keys from his pocket. He unlocked the door and stepped quietly inside.

They didn't notice him until he was five feet away. The gun was up, pointed at the male's head.

"Get off of her," he said.

Both of them began to beg for their lives. She apologized, said it would never happen again. It was as though they were talking underwater. He could barely understand what they were saying. He didn't care what they were saying. After what he'd witnessed, their words were nothing but wind.

He shot the man first. He aimed for his testicles but may have missed an inch or so one way or the other. The man screamed and fell to the floor. As soon as he hit the ground, the woman began to scream. The husband shot her between the eyes. He walked over to her and shot her two more times, once in the heart and again in the head. The man who'd been shot in the testicles was crawling toward the front door. The husband walked up to him and shot him twice in the back of the head.

He picked up the phone and called 911, told the dispatcher there had been a shooting at his address and calmly hung up.

Then he went upstairs to check on his boys.

PART I

CHAPTER ONE

The red and blue strobes from the police and emergency vehicles gave the limp body the eerie appearance that she was dancing. She hung in front of the public library, a killer's work on display among the pillars and the art that adorned the windows. A crude noose had been fashioned from a length of nylon rope and tossed over a cross beam that ran ten feet above the ground at the library's entrance.

The scene around the body was controlled chaos. Five marked police cruisers were stationed at strategic locations on the inner perimeter, blocking likely avenues of approach and doing as much as possible to block the view of the body. News trucks from three stations were parked at different locations, all jockeying for the best vantage point. The reporters from the various stations sported their affiliate wind jackets, a thin barrier to the cool, late-autumn night in Northeast Tennessee. They milled around, awaiting any information, official or unofficial, hoping for a sound bite from someone.

A crowd of onlookers had congregated behind the trucks. Most of them had been drinking in the microbreweries that had sprung up around downtown Johnson

City. They peered at the grisly scene, talking amongst themselves in quiet contemplation beside the ambulance that would eventually act as a hearse.

Detective Lukas Miller leaned on the hood of his white, unmarked Crown Victoria and watched the paramedics go over the body. Waiting patiently was never his strong suit, but protocol was protocol. The preservation of life always trumped the investigation, but Lukas didn't think there was a chance there was any life left in the poor woman hanging from between the pillars. She was deader than four in the morning.

"Looks like a long weekend," Patrol Sgt. Don Adams said as he walked up and stood beside Lukas.

Lukas nodded, still staring at the body.

"No rest for the weary, I guess," Adams said.

"The wicked aren't resting, either. Who found her?"

"Officer Cragg, I believe. He was on routine patrol and noticed something odd from the parking lot. So, he went to check it out and found her. Coffee?" Adams held up a cup with a red stir stick through the lip.

"Yeah, thanks. Do any of your guys recognize her?"

Lukas eagerly accepted the hot drink and took a sip, glad for the warmth it offered.

"Not that I know of," Adams said, "but I'll bet it's one of our regulars."

Someone called Lukas's name from behind him.

A young officer Lukas didn't recognize walked up quickly. He was nodding as he spoke into his radio. He broke off and addressed Lukas, "Detective Miller, we just got a call from headquarters."

"And?"

"Sir, I hate to make the situation worse, but Captain Hunter has ordered that nothing be done to the scene until a detective from Kingsport arrives. The captain is on his way here, too."

Shit. Lukas glanced behind him. He'd left his portable radio in the car again, a bad habit he'd gotten into recently. He cursed under his breath. The old man would be hot about him not having his radio. Hunter had probably attempted to reach Lukas on the Criminal Investigation frequency.

"Okay. Thanks, officer."

Lukas turned to Adams. "The brass has been on our ass about these murders so I was kind of expecting *something*, but this? This sucks."

"You're damned right it does. I know I wouldn't like having someone looking over my shoulder while I was trying to work." Adams crushed the empty coffee cup in his hand and tossed it in a nearby trash can. "Any idea which detective is coming?"

"If I were a betting man, I would say it's 'Supercop.'" Lukas laughed. "Supercop" was being heralded as an epic crime fighter. The stories were being exaggerated, Lukas knew, but he'd heard of her beating academy records, solving unsolvable cases, extracting confessions from the toughest of men. If half of what he'd heard was true, she was as good as two detectives. And everybody said she was good looking, too.

"Supercop?"

"Yeah, the detective working the murders over in Kingsport. She supposedly has more decorations than a war vet. She just won officer of the year over there."

"Oh, so she's a hot shot." Adams spat on the ground. "Like we can't handle our own cases."

Lukas didn't say anything, but Adams was right. What cop wanted someone looking over his shoulder on one of his cases, especially a cop from another jurisdiction? The only thing that kept him from heading straight for his radio and telling his captain he didn't want any damned help – even if it was from a so-called supercop – was that these murders had been hell on the department. Four local women had been brutally killed in the last three months, two in Kingsport and now two in Johnson City, three of whom were prostitutes. And from what little he'd seen of the latest victim, she would probably take the prostitute tally to four. The two police agencies still hadn't officially linked the murders in Kingsport to those in Johnson City, but the local news agencies had started referring to them as serial murders. They were quickly becoming a public relations nightmare that would have city hall breathing down the department's collective neck.

"Maybe it's not such a bad thing," Lukas said. "Maybe another perspective will shake things loose."

"Is she as good as they say?" Adams asked.

"I don't know. Haven't even met her. But I guess I'm about to."

Lukas picked up the now empty cup from the hood of his cruiser and walked around to the rear door. He reached in and fumbled around in the back seat until he found his radio. Still charged. At least there was that. He looked up and noticed the department Command Center truck pull in among the other vehicles near the outer perimeter. It was followed by an unmarked black Chevrolet Impala and the Forensic Center van.

"Wow, this is really turning into a gala event," Lukas said, turning back to Sergeant Adams. The multipurpose police Command Center vehicle was only rolled out for major crimes or special events. This one qualified as both.

He made his way over to the Command Center. It was positioned away from the news vans and onlookers for security reasons as well as convenience. There would be a media relations officer on board whose sole job was to handle the requests for information from the various news sources. This officer was specially selected and had to be equipped with the gift of gab. His or her job was to give the appearance of cooperating with the media without giving away information that would hamper an investigation or allow a potential suspect, victim, or witness to be compromised. It wasn't a job Lukas envied or would ever want, but he appreciated them nonetheless.

Lukas got one foot on the Command Center stairs before the front door opened and a woman with a long, blonde ponytail and hazel eyes came out fastening a tactical vest proclaiming her a police officer. She was followed closely by his Criminal Investigations Commander, Capt. Martin Hunter. Before Lukas could utter a sound, the Captain's booming voice broke the silence.

"Have you two met?"

"Uh, no, sir." Lukas looked at the woman as she gave him a once-over. He found himself wondering what she thought. He ran a hand through his short, black hair.

"This is Detective Brooke Stevens from the Kingsport Police Department," the captain said. He then lowered his voice and told them to follow him. When they were out of earshot of everyone else, he leaned in toward them and, in as low a voice as he could manage, spoke while looking directly at Lukas.

"Okay, let's clear the air before we go any further. Stevens is the lead detective on the recent homicides over in Kingsport. She has a working knowledge of the scenes, bodies, the whole thing. I just got off the phone with our chief, who just got off the phone with theirs, and he has promised us anything we need, from manpower to money and anything in between. And we are doing the same for them. Miller, if Detective Stevens needs anything, and I mean anything, from a pool boy to a grocery bagger, you better make sure she gets it. Is that understood?"

"Yes, sir."

"Miller, you're the best investigator I have. You get results. That's why you got this gig. Now, I need you two to work together and figure out why some psycho decided to start killing prostitutes on my watch."

Stevens watched and listened, saying nothing. Her face was passive, unreadable. She kept her eyes on the captain, who barely slowed to catch his breath.

"I know this is an unusual situation, Miller. I'm sure it is for Detective Stevens, too. But I want this stopped, pronto. I've got the chief crawling up my butt, and he's got city hall up his. I want the chief out of my butt, and I want city hall out of his. That'll be up to the two of you. Any questions?"

"No, sir," they replied in unison.

"Good. Get to work. And Miller, it'd be nice if you'd keep your radio with you," he said as he turned to leave.

Damn it. Lukas thought he'd gotten by. He nodded at the captain and glanced over at his new "partner."

Detective Stevens started toward the scene. A small smile turned up one side of her full lips. "I think your boss likes me."

"Stevens or Brooke?" Lukas said.

"Beg your pardon?"

"Do you prefer I call you Stevens, Detective Stevens, or Brooke?"

"Brooke is fine."

"Good. Call me Detective Miller."

She shot him a dirty look.

"Kidding. Call me Lukas."

Lukas matched his stride to hers, which wasn't rushed but purposeful. He had to admit, he already had a good feeling about her. He liked her confidence, and they'd been right about her being easy to look at. Maybe the grand experiment would work. They just needed to focus on the case.

He started to take mental notes, sweeping his gaze over the scene before going up to the body. He noticed two uniformed officers standing on the top steps a few yards back from the scene, one of whom Lukas recognized as Officer Slater, a fifteen-year veteran. Slater was holding a clipboard that most likely held the crime scene log. The other officer had that fresh academy smell and looked to be having trouble holding his dinner down. Lukas took the steps two at a time with Brooke now on his heels.

He addressed Slater, "Where are we?"

"EMTs are gone. It's your scene now, detective. No damage done. Scene's good."

Lukas glanced over and pointed to the young officer standing nearest the body whose complexion looked as pale as the pillar he stood beside. Brooke shrugged.

Lukas turned to Slater. "Is he new?"

"Yep, first murder."

"Is he going to be all right?"

"I think so. He's coming around."

"Do you have the crime scene log?" Lukas asked.

"Got it right here."

"Okay." Lukas grinned. "Put us down. List me as Superman, and this is Wonder Woman." He pointed to Brooke.

"I know who you are, Superman, but I'm afraid I don't recognize Wonder Woman."

"Detective Brooke Stevens with the Kingsport PD," she answered.

The officer jotted the names on the log then handed it to Lukas to inspect.

He looked over the names. "So, just the three paramedics, you two, and now us, right?"

"That's it. Paramedics are back sitting on their thumbs in the wagon. Waiting on you two, I guess."

"Good, keep that list running." He handed the log back to the officer.

Brooke broke away from him, going to the opposite side. She appeared to be taking in the scene in its entirety. They both started from the outer edges, gradually making their way to the body of the young woman. Lukas watched the way Brooke approached the task. Even though they came from different departments and had been trained by different people, they both used basically the same approach. They looked for anything leading to or from the scene. Footprints, blood, weapons, property, anything out of place. Many leads had been obtained by picking up clues or evidence on the perimeters of crime scenes. It was too early to know about the supercop stuff, but he liked the way she was handling herself so far.

They met at the body at about the same time. Lukas fully took in the sad, macabre sight for the first time. The body was hanging approximately six inches off the ground. It was positioned directly in front of the main entrance, right beside the library's community board. He glanced at the advertisement for the upcoming book drive and a poster with the dates of a pro-choice rally to be held here later next month. The library was apparently more of a happening place than he realized.

Lukas looked out toward the command and emergency vehicles. A large crowd had gathered because some psychopath had chosen to display his work here. And it was one hell of a display. He shook his head and refocused on the victim. The woman was suspended by a cheap nylon rope that looked like it could have been purchased at any home improvement or big box store. The rope was tied around the victim's neck haphazardly. The knot was a crude one, a granny knot or square knot. Nothing fancy there. Her hands were by her side, not bound in any way. Neither were her feet. This indicated several possibilities to Lukas. The victim was likely either unconscious or dead when the body was placed and there was little to no resistance from the victim when she was hanged. There was a slack of about three inches in the loop around her neck, indicating that the hanging was most likely not the cause of death. He felt sure the autopsy would confirm his suspicions. The crude basic knot? Someone not used to working with their hands maybe, or could he have just been in a hurry. They were all possibilities. He made mental notes that he would later commit to paper and digital files.

Lukas was jostled out of his trance by the scent of faint perfume. Not one that he recognized, but pleasant, not too strong. He leaned in toward the body, thinking it was too expensive to be a working girl's. Nope. Not coming from the body. He glanced behind him and saw Brooke writing in a worn leather pocket size notebook. Must be hers. Her long, blonde ponytail had fallen forward over her shoulder and was now cascading over her right breast.

She caught his stare and stopped writing.

"Something wrong?"

"Uh, no," he said. "I was just wondering why you still used that old academy-issued antique."

"I guess you can say I've got a few old-school habits." She shrugged. "My dad was a cop for decades. I like some of the old school ways."

"I let those guys do the writing." He motioned toward the scene entry point where the Crime Scene Unit technicians were being logged in by the new officer, who had apparently recovered from the shock of his first murder.

The CSU team quickly started setting up equipment. Lukas and Brooke needed to finish and head back to the command center.

Lukas stood and turned toward Brooke. "Guess we better move it along."

She nodded.

Only one last thing to do. The morbid task of examining the wounds of the deceased woman. Lukas catalogued the details in his head. White female, mid-twenties to early-thirties, with short dark hair and green eyes. No ID, no keys or personal belongings of any kind. There was nothing that gave any clues to her identity. The woman wore a pink halter top and a pair of black tights. She wasn't wearing a bra, shoes or socks. There were obvious ligature marks around her neck and stab wounds and cuts to her genital area. Lukas couldn't tell how many wounds there were without removing the tights, but it looked to be several. Blood at the scene was minimal considering the wounds, another indication the hanging was post-mortem.

He noticed Brooke jotting down a note and closing her notebook just as they were joined by the Forensic Death Investigator, Odessa McCabe. McCabe was considered the "go-to" forensic death investigator in Johnson City, and, in some cases, for the surrounding agencies as well. She was working with Lukas on another prostitute who had been murdered two weeks earlier in Johnson City. There had been two in Kingsport, so tonight made a total of four. After a short but thorough look at the body, McCabe offered Lukas her assessment.

"Based on the lividity, state of rigor, and the amount of blood drying, I would say she died between three and four hours ago and was not killed here."

"Look at the marks on her neck under the rope," Lukas said, pointing at the bruises. "Do you think that was from the rope or ante-mortem?"

"I don't believe the bruising was caused by the rope. See the width of the bruise pattern? It's wide and somewhat dim compared to the pressure that would be exerted by a small rope. It was caused by a different device. Could have even been hands for that matter."

Lukas nodded and Brooke flipped her leather notebook open and continued with her notes.

Odessa frowned. "Obviously, I can't give a cause of death yet and won't be able to until the autopsy is complete. And the mutilated genitals? That's your department, Lukas, but this is one sick individual you have on your hands here." She paused and looked over at Brooke. "I'm sorry, I don't think we've met."

"Detective Brooke Stevens. I'm working similar murders over in Kingsport. Just here to consult."

"Odessa McCabe, pleased to meet you." She offered a gloved hand.

"Same."

"Detective Stevens, would you excuse us for a moment please?" Odessa asked politely.

"Sure, I'll just wait over at the Command Post."

When she was sufficiently out of earshot, Odessa continued, "Consultation? Really?"

"Really. Kind of. I mean, I guess we're working together now."

"She's cute."

"This is strictly business." He hesitated, wondering where the conversation was heading. "Like she said, she's lead on the murders over in Kingsport, and somebody up the chain of command decided it would be a good idea to bring her over to look at the scene here to see if they may be related."

"And how are you taking this?"

"I don't know yet. How would you feel if someone came in from another forensics office and was ordered to double-check your work?"

"I wouldn't like it, but I know what kind of press this is getting. And I can see the pressure you're under. We're dealing with a sick, twisted waste of skin. But he's obviously smart, and he's careful. We've worked a bunch of cases together, Lukas. It'll take all of us to solve this one, probably including her. This is the first serial killer we've ever had around here."

Lukas considered her remarks, wondering what direction the investigation would take moving forward. He nodded and walked toward the Command Center without a reply. Lukas found himself hoping they could find the sick bastard before the feds found a reason to get involved. There was exactly one fed he liked in the area, an agent named Danny Smart. The rest of them were arrogant and treated the locals like peons. For now, at least, all the murders were state crimes and fell under state and local jurisdictions. The feds were shut out. He hoped it would stay that way.

CHAPTER TWO

Brooke watched the interaction between Lukas and the forensic woman with curiosity. They thought she couldn't hear them, but she could. What the hell? She wasn't there because she wanted to be. She was just following orders.

"Brooke?" Lukas approached her. His jaw was clenched. "Let's talk inside."

Brooke welcomed the warmth of the Command Center. She'd been freezing her butt off out there, but she sure as heck wasn't about to show it. She steeled herself against a shiver and followed Lukas to a room that contained a dry-erase whiteboard and a small, oval table with comfortable-looking swivel chairs. There were two separate stations that contained computers that she assumed were linked to the same database as those at headquarters. Written on the board were assignments for the various detectives and officers who were helping with the scene, along with a time-line and other victim's names and details about their deaths. Her name was written beside Lukas's. Lukas saw it, and Brooke saw the resignation on his face. She didn't want this to go sour before they even left the crime scene. She fixed a smile on her face and tapped on his shoulder.

"I know you probably don't like this arrangement," she said, "and I don't blame you. This is your deal, your territory, and I'm just here to observe and assist. Honestly, I'm not real comfortable myself. It puts both of us in a difficult position. But it looks like we're stuck with each other."

"Let's just get down to business, how about that?" Lukas said.

"Sure, whatever you say."

Lukas's eyes locked with hers for a moment. He broke off the gaze and turned to the whiteboard. "Let's go over yours first."

Brooke took out her well-worn notebook, flipped a few pages, stopped, and looked at her notes. She ignored her annotations and spat out the facts. "My first victim was found on August twenty-fifth. Third-shift manager found her in a dumpster behind his convenience store in a rough part of town. She was a white female named Cindy Sullivan, twenty-six years old, a well-known prostitute. Left behind a six-year-old daughter and a mother who seemed apathetic toward her daughter's death. According to our records, she had no significant other. She was a local girl, lived about three blocks from where she was found. Cause of death was asphyxiation by mechanical means. No sexual trauma or mutilation. No witnesses or forensic evidence was found."

As Brooke spoke, Lukas was making notes on the whiteboard. She flipped a few pages over and continued.

"The second was found on October fourteenth. A white female named Melanie Salem, twenty-two years old, found on the front lawn of an abortion clinic on the east side of town. Cause of death was multiple stab wounds to the chest, signs of sexual assault, cuts and abrasions to her genital area. She had a four-year-old boy, no other family that we could find. A previous child of hers had died of SIDS. She was also local. No witnesses or leads as of now. Both women had multiple arrests for prostitution and minor drug violations. We don't know if there was any relationship between the two murders other than the victims' occupation, and it appears that the victims were killed somewhere else and moved to the location where they were found." She looked up from her notes as Lukas finished writing. "That's it. I have virtually nothing."

Lukas continued to write as he spoke. "My first victim was found on September twenty-seventh, which was about one month after your first one. Her name was Jamika Bradley, thirty-one, black female, found at the entrance to the Johnson City landfill hanging on a fence. Cause of death was blunt force trauma. She had kids, eight-year-old twins, a boy and a girl. There were no signs of mutilation or sexual trauma. And now this new victim. It's been roughly two weeks since the last one. This crime looks very similar to the others." Lukas looked away from the whiteboard and down at Brooke. "Do you agree?"

Brooke looked at the board. "My first instinct is to agree. Assuming our victim tonight is what we think she is, we have the same general MO. They were all most likely killed somewhere other than where they were found. Four of them in a relatively short amount of time. It all says serial killer, but as far as solving them, I'm not seeing anything that jumps out. That's been the problem from the start. No consistent patterns. I think he's figuring it out as he goes along. Evolving, you might say. Experimenting."

"So, do we agree all of the murders were committed by the same person?" Lukas said.

"Based on the time frame and the fact that all of the victims were hookers, I'd say yes," Brooke said. "If it walks like a duck and talks like a duck…"

"It's a duck, I know."

Brooke looked up at the board, studying the details they had catalogued thus far. "We have one new lead. The rope. This marks the first time the killer has left something at the scene besides the victim."

"True. I'll make sure you get a good photo of it to follow up on in Kingsport. I'll check here in Johnson City as well. Who knows? We've solved murders on less." Lukas looked back to the board and appeared to be studying hieroglyphs. "One thing that jumps out at me are the times. The first was August twenty-fifth, the second was September twenty-seventh, the third October fourteenth, and now October twenty-ninth. One month between the first two, then two weeks. Not as much time between them now. Our killer is accelerating."

"True. But that's not really a pattern by definition," Brooke said. She watched Lukas's eyes flash. He tapped the back of his chair and paced in front of the white board.

"Yes, it is. It doesn't tell us when the next one will be, but it tells us it won't be long. That's why there's so much pressure to end this from the brass." He turned to her. "I'm sure it's bad for you, too."

"You have no clue," she said, thinking of her recent meeting with the administration in Kingsport. That had definitely not gone well. She shrugged. "I guess that's why I'm here."

"What's your instinct say about the murders?"

"I try not to rely on instincts. I follow the leads, read the evidence, and go where it takes me. It's worked well for me so far."

A "gut instinct" wasn't a tool for catching criminals, as far as Brooke was concerned. It was a liability, if anything. Made you second guess the facts. And facts didn't lie. Unlike guts.

"Leads can only take you so far," Lukas said. "For instance, *why* is he killing hookers?"

"It doesn't matter *why*. All that matters is that we follow the evidence that will lead us to him and stop him."

"*Why* will be how we catch him. *Why* is everything."

"We're going to have to agree to disagree," Brooke said.

Lukas's stare startled her a bit. His dark brown eyes seemed to bore into her, giving her an icy feeling.

The door to the room opened and a uniformed officer stuck his head in. "Miller, a witness has been located. They've taken her to headquarters, and she's asking for you."

CHAPTER THREE

He always felt the need for Pam after he killed. Each time, he hoped things would be different, that the latest killing would allow him to be able to become aroused, that his sexual desires would be satisfied. But each time, at least so far, he'd been disappointed. He'd pleased Pam, but he'd had to do so with the aid of a sex toy. He remained flaccid, unable to perform. His sexual failings infuriated him, frustrated him, depressed him. *Next time*, he would think. *Next time.*

In the dark of his room, he considered calling her now. Maybe tonight would be the night. Maybe tonight he would grow hard and explode in ecstasy. Maybe.

First, he needed to get in the mood. He closed his eyes and thought about the whores. The killings started out as experimental, but they'd gradually grown to something more. He didn't fully understand what was happening; he wasn't sure if he ever would. Did his understanding even matter? Probably not. He was going to keep killing regardless.

They say you never forget your first. Well, not exactly the first, but the first one he had actually killed with his bare hands, the first one he had looked in the eye while the light flickered out like a match in a breeze. Her name was Cindy Sullivan, but her friends called her Sully. He had watched her for weeks. He watched her work, or at least that's what she called it. They called themselves working girls, as though they were productive members of society. Just putting in another day, punching the time clock. How ridiculous was that mentality? He thought back to the night he'd decided it was time to do something about her, the night he decided to remove Sully from the gene pool. She did one guy in a car and another in the seedy motel she often used. Two more received blow jobs in the shadows beside the motel.

He would never forget the look on her face when she realized what was about to happen to her: shock mixed with terror. She had completed her sleazy strip tease and stood naked in front of him, waiting for something that was never going to happen. He was new at choking a woman to death, but he found it easier than expected. He'd always had thick, strong forearms and big hands, most likely inherited from the father he never knew. He felt Sully's throat constrict in his hands as she fought for breath, for her very life. He'd never felt anything so visceral, or so satisfying. He felt as though he was in complete control for the first time in his life, and he was. It was powerful, that feeling of taking a life. He knew right then he would have to do it again.

Afterward, he was filled with euphoria, but as time drew on he became worried that he'd made a mistake. He'd taken weeks to plan, but no matter how long or how thoroughly you planned, mistakes could still happen. He watched the news, listened to the scanner, checked the internet and social media sites, read the paper. The more time passed, the more he became convinced he'd gotten away with it. It may not have been the perfect murder, but it was close enough.

Then the need came back. It appeared as a gnawing at the edges of his mind, but over time the gnawing became obsession, and he could think of little else. Before he knew it, he found himself back out there on the street, waiting and watching, stalking them.

He opened his eyes and turned on the Bearcat scanner that sat on the table beside his recliner. He adjusted the volume. There were the usual routine calls typical of a Friday night: domestic disturbances, bar fights, traffic stops, and of course, the big news of the night. The body at the library.

He could visualize the scene. There would be someone in charge issuing orders to a host of detectives. The detectives would be going about their duties, including canvassing the neighborhood. Evidence collection teams would be there, as would forensic people, looking for any clue that would lead them to the person responsible for the crime. The scene would be covered by all three local TV news agencies as well as beat writers from the newspapers. A public hanging in small town, USA, was big news.

One thing that surprised him was the mention of a Detective Stevens coming in from Kingsport. That was odd. According to the papers, she was working the murders there. He wondered if she was being called in to consult. He smiled. He was causing them problems.

After several moments of silent contemplation, he decided it was time. He picked up the phone. After several rings, Pam's sleepy voice answered, "Hello."

"It's me."

"Oh, hey. What time is it?"

"It's going on eleven. I'm sorry to wake you."

"Oh, no. It's okay. Really. I was watching television. I guess I just dozed off. What's up?"

"Do you feel like company?"

"Sure. What you got in mind?"

"I thought maybe we could play."

"Do you think you're up for it?"

His forehead tensed as a flash of anger ran through him.

"I'm up for trying. At least you'll have a good time."

"All right." She chuckled.

"I'll be over in about an hour. Are you hungry?"

"No, I'm good. Thanks, though."

"See you soon."

He packed a bag of clothes and some items that would be needed for the next day's activities. The plan had been in the works for months, and now that the time was near, he felt both relieved and excited.

CHAPTER FOUR

Brooke kept stride with Lukas as they walked up the rear steps of the Johnson City Police Department headquarters just after midnight. She hoped her five-year-old daughter hadn't worried when she didn't call her to say good night. Lately, Sierra had been clingier than usual. The child hadn't yet reached the stage where moms were an embarrassment, thank goodness. Brooke hoped it wasn't something at daycare, like being bullied by a classmate or some other school related issue. It was hard not to worry, but Brooke had tried to teach Sierra to be strong.

Lukas pulled Brooke's attention back to the present. He was waiting. He had opened the rear door that led to the Criminal Investigation unit and was holding it for her. Nice, but not necessary.

Brooke walked through the door and a welcome rush of warmth greeted her. It felt good on her chilled skin. She gazed around. Impressive. The structure was new, state of the art. It even smelled new, as though plastic had just been pulled off everything.

The place was nothing like what she was used to in Kingsport. The coffee was usually as thick as hops, and the chairs were all held together with duct tape.

The inviting smell of freshly-brewed coffee made her start looking around for a Styrofoam cup. But that would have to wait. She was immediately directed down the hall to Lukas's squad room. The room held eight desks. Each had its own cubicle. The names of the detectives were etched on brass plates and displayed on the outside panels. On each desk was a standard computer and monitor, along with various awards, family pictures and coffee cups. Each desktop told at least a small part of its occupant's life story. The room itself was large, bland, practical, serviceable, and efficient.

Lukas walked over to a coat rack in the corner and took off his thin jacket that had the word POLICE embroidered in white across the back. Brooke noticed Lukas's build for the first time. His department-issued polo covered muscles that were well-defined. She looked away quickly. There was no way she was going to let him catch her checking him out.

Lukas came back a short time later with two steaming mugs that had the Johnson City Police Department logo and badge on either side. He set one down in front of her, a gesture she genuinely appreciated. The coffee was as good as it smelled. She sipped slowly, letting the heat warm her from the inside out. Her eyes were drawn to the large TV monitor on the wall adjacent to the entrance that had video feed of four separate interview and interrogation rooms. Three of the rooms were empty. The fourth contained a petite, white female with auburn hair and fair skin seated at a table. In front of her sat a can of Pepsi. She was dressed like a prostitute.

Lukas walked over and adjusted the volume on the monitor just as a uniformed officer walked into the room.

"Detective Miller?"

"Yes?"

"We were asked to round up any witnesses we could find, and I located her about three blocks from the library," he said, pointing toward the monitor. "I asked her to come down to headquarters. I thought she might have some information on our victim since there aren't that many hookers in town. I mean, it's a pretty small circle, right? But the thing is, when I asked her if she had any contraband or drugs on her, she pulled out a small bag of weed. I'll have a charge on her when you're done, but I wanted to let you have a run at her first in case she gets hinky when I tell her about the charge."

"Okay, let me talk to her first, and we'll see where we go from there."

"You want me to start the arrest report?"

"No, hold off until I see what she has to say."

"Okay."

Lukas turned back to Brooke. "Be right back."

"Want me in there?" She started to move.

"I think she'll be more likely to talk to me. I know her." He pointed to the monitor. "You can see it all here anyway."

Lukas walked out with the uniformed officer. Brooke turned her attention to the monitor and saw Lukas enter the interrogation room. She was surprised when the girl jumped up and hugged him.

The audio feed came through clearly.

"Lukas, I'm so glad to see you!"

"Hey, Razzy. How have you been?"

"Oh, you know, getting by." The woman fiddled with one of her many zippers and put a hand on Lukas's shoulder in a familiar gesture. "Lukas, I did exactly like you told me. When that cop asked me if I had drugs, I just told him the truth. I already told him I'd come down to the station with him. He didn't have to handcuff me. I ain't never been a problem, have I?"

"No, but he has rules he has to follow. Don't be mad at him, okay?"

"Is he going to charge me for the dope? I told the truth." More agitated flipping with her zipper.

Lukas motioned for the woman to sit and pulled out the chair across from her.

"We'll talk about that later. Right now, I need you to know there's been another murder, and I want to ask you about Jamika again. I know we discussed it before, but I wanted to ask you again if you've heard anyone talking. Have you heard about anyone seeing anything suspicious or out of the ordinary?"

The girl seemed to be thinking. Brooke was startled by a buzzing sound on the table and looked down instinctively. She saw Lukas's phone light up as a call came in from someone named Gabriele. Brooke returned her attention to the monitor. The girl seemed in deep thought. Her hands stopped fiddling with the zipper, and a mournful look came over her face.

"I heard some of the girls talking earlier tonight, and they said that something happened at the library. They said they thought it may be another one of us."

She was becoming upset. "Was it, Lukas? One of the girls?"

"We don't know yet, but maybe. That's why I need your help. That's why it's important to think about anything you may have heard or seen."

"The girls don't talk about it. They're all scared to death."

Brooke thought about the irony of her comment. *Scared to death. They better be.*

"I need you to think hard, Razzy," Lukas said.

"I do remember someone – and I don't remember who – was talking about a red car that has been seen creeping around. Nobody knows the dude, so they stay away from him."

"Do they know anything about him? Race, what he looks like, anything?"

"If they did, they didn't say. Lukas, you have to promise me you'll stop this guy." She began to cry softly. Her hands were trembling. "If you don't, it looks like he's gonna kill us all."

Lukas reached out and touched her hand.

"I will, Razzy," he said. "I promise."

Lukas removed his hand from Razzy's. He walked out of the interrogation room and back to the squad room.

"Really?" he said to Brooke. "A red car? That's all we have after four homicides? A red car?" Lukas started pacing. His hands went to his temples.

"It's more than we had an hour ago," Brooke said calmly.

Lukas looked like he was about to respond when Captain Hunter came into the room.

Hunter nodded to them both. "I watched the interview, and I'll get the information out to everyone about the red car. We'll charge her for the drugs and let her sit in jail for a while. That'll give her some time to think things over. Maybe she'll change her mind about what she's seen or heard."

"She won't change her mind, Captain," Lukas said.

"Really? How can you be sure?"

"She doesn't know anything else. She would have told me. And I don't want her charged."

"Why not?"

"She's a good informant. I've solved cases based on her information in the past, and right now, we need all the help we can get. Besides, it was just a little weed."

"Captain, I know I really don't have standing here, but for what it's worth, I agree with Lukas." Brooke noticed a surprised look on Lukas's face.

"Glad to see you two are already on a first-name basis," Captain Hunter said. "Okay, fine, we won't charge her, but let's try not to stray too far from the rules." Hunter turned on his heel and stalked out of squad room toward his office.

Lukas nodded at Brooke. "Thanks for the backup."

"No problem. I just happen to think you're right. That's all."

"I hope so. I'll need to take her home. Want to ride along?"

"Sure."

The three left the station and rode in silence for the most part. Lukas engaged in some small talk which seemed to lighten the somber mood a bit. He swung in to a local burger joint and bought food for Razzy and her son, Timmy.

When they arrived at the rundown apartment complex that Razzy called home, Lukas gave Razzy the food and squeezed her hand. "Tell the little man I said hello."

"I will. Thanks for the food. And remember, Lukas, that freebie is a standing offer."

She laughed as she got out of the car and winked at Brooke. Lukas smiled, nodded, and drove off as soon as the apartment door closed.

On the way back to the station, Brooke was the one to break the silence. "Captain Hunter mentioned you were in special operations in the military. Which branch?"

"Air Force, pararescue. I served for six years."

"I saw a documentary on them on TV a month or so ago. That looks like tough training."

"It was. You have to like water to get through it. How about you? Any military?"

"Nope. I went to college, majored in criminal justice, and here I am doing what I've always wanted to do. But no matter how many classes you go through, or how many mocked up scenes you work, you're never really prepared for cases like this, are you?

"I guess not."

"Well, that's where we are right now." The conversation was interrupted by the buzzing of Lukas's cell phone.

"I'm sorry, Gabby," Lukas said. "I got caught up in a case. I know. Look, I'll call you back as soon as I can. Okay. Well, I'll call you in the morning then."

Lukas hit the end button on the cell phone as they pulled into the station. He was clearly irritated, and it was still in his voice as he turned to Brooke. "I guess we stay in touch with each other with updates on the cases, right?"

"Sure." She handed Lukas her card with her contact information and took his in exchange. "I'll be in touch if anything breaks on my end."

Brooke got out of the car and watched Lukas drive off. She could tell the man was tired. The murders were starting to wear on him. The two she was working had certainly worn her down. She thought about the red car Razzy had mentioned. It wasn't much of a lead, but she would get the information out to her people anyway.

She'd gotten a good look at how Miller's squad was handling the murders and wasn't surprised to see it was much the same as hers. Brooke knew there was something she'd missed, something that would break the case, but she was unsure what to do or where to go next. She'd never had a case like this and it was apparent she would need to raise her game to get this maniac stopped. This was the most pressure she'd experienced in her brief law enforcement career. And it didn't help that she was a woman in a profession dominated by men. She felt as though she had to prove herself continuously.

She'd been under the microscope from day one. Her father, John Stevens, had been a highly-decorated and successful police officer and detective who had retired with over thirty-five years of service. She was a chip off the old block. She and her father both expected her to follow in his footsteps. So far, she'd excelled at the job. She solved some tough cases, earned some nice awards. She'd heard the nickname "supercop" that the guys were tossing around. She hated it, but she hated this case even more. It was slowly chipping away at her confidence, and it could very quickly undermine the respect she'd worked so hard to earn.

Her thoughts turned to her daughter. Brooke hoped these murders would be solved soon, because she hated spending so much time away from her little girl. Her ex-husband was keeping Sierra this weekend, so at least she didn't have to worry about shuffling her around with all the extra hours she'd be working. It was hard being a single mom under the best of circumstances, let alone while being a police detective chasing a serial killer.

She realized how tense she'd been as soon as she pulled into her driveway. The rural area between Kingsport and Johnson City where she lived was the ideal location to raise a kid and to get away from everything. Just knowing she was home allowed her to relax a little. She loved the place and the area. And she'd enjoyed bringing life back to the old 1950s farmhouse.

Home. It looked so beautiful and welcoming in the moonlight.

By the time she undressed and showered, the bone-weariness had turned into a few nagging aches, but she wasn't sleepy. That was a problem. She knew she had a long day ahead of her tomorrow with the investigation and the Citizen's Police Academy class she was scheduled to teach. It was the chief's pet project, and not even a public relations nightmare like the case they were working got in its way. The CPA trumped everything, serial killers included. She'd already been reminded by her captain multiple times that she was expected to be there and to be punctual.

She needed to sleep. As she lay in bed and watched the numbers change on her digital alarm clock, Lukas popped into her mind. He was pretty much what she had expected from the things she'd heard. He seemed somewhat arrogant and self-centered, but he also seemed smart and resourceful. She'd heard other female officers talk about how hot he was. They were right, but it didn't matter. She wasn't about to get involved with a colleague, especially one who was already in a relationship.

Brooke fluffed her pillow, rolled onto her back, took several deep, slow breaths, and felt her mind and body begin to relax. There would be plenty of time for worry and tension tomorrow. She felt herself sliding toward the abyss, and eventually slipped into unconsciousness.

CHAPTER FIVE

After he'd dropped Brooke off, Lukas immediately went back to the scene. The news crews were gone, as were most of the onlookers now that the body had been removed. Nothing thinned out a crowd like a departing hearse or ambulance. Some of his squad detectives were still milling around. Lukas spotted his longtime friend and colleague, Rafe Carrizales, standing under the awning of the command post.

"Hey. Anything new?"

"Nothing yet. Some of the guys are just filtering in now, though, so who knows? Who was your witness?"

"She was a working girl that happened to be out when we did the canvass. Kimberly Raznovich. Do you remember her?"

"Hooker, right? Pretty, could have gone in a different direction?"

"That's her."

Razzy was poor, but she was pretty and smart and she could have led a different life if not for the car wreck halfway through her senior year in high school that put her in the hospital with a fractured spine. The doctors prescribed opiates, and she became addicted. Neither she nor her mother knew how to manage her addiction, and once she got out of the hospital, she was on her own. The doctors would no longer prescribe the pain medication, but they wouldn't help her get into a program to kick the addiction, either. She wound up stealing to support her habit, then she wound up stripping, and finally she wound up hooking. When she became pregnant with her son, her mother turned her back on Razzy, and now she was alone in the world, doing her best to get by one day at a time.

"What'd she have to say?"

"Nothing much. She said that some of the girls had mentioned seeing a red car snooping around lately, but they didn't have any information about the driver's race and no description. Nothing. Hell, it may have been a woman driving for all we know."

"How did it go with the detective from Kingsport? What was her name?"

"Brooke Stevens. It went fine, I guess. We're still feeling each other out. She seems as frustrated as I am. Is Captain Hunter still here?"

"I think he's gone. He's hotter than a three-peckered billy goat about these murders."

"I know. He's made that abundantly clear."

"Anything you need, you let me know," Carrizales said. "I know what it's like on your end. Well, not quite to this degree, but I feel your pain."

"Appreciate it, man."

Lukas ambled away from the command post and got lost in the night. He thought about the crimes in both cities. There had to be something he was missing.

Nobody was this good. Somewhere, he or she or they had made a mistake. He was almost positive it wasn't a woman doing the killing. Women very rarely did serial killings, especially when the victims were women. But women were certainly doing the dying.

The fact that the victims were prostitutes had kept the general public from going nuts, at least for now. But the press coverage was growing, and with each murder the pressure was becoming more palpable. If this continued without an arrest, it wouldn't be long before the cases were taken out of Lukas's hands, despite his reputation as an excellent detective and Brooke's reputation as a supercop. Someone up the chain would eventually force the issue. Politicians would become involved, and as always, the shit would flow downhill, right onto Lukas's and Brooke's heads. It probably wouldn't end their careers, but it would derail them. And it could take years to undo the damage.

Lukas couldn't let that happen. He'd just have to work harder than everyone else, dig deeper, and stay longer. He liked going back to the scene once everything had quieted down and the news hounds had gone back to the safety of their offices and homes. He could think better, often connecting dots that were overlooked because of the excitement of the moment.

He surveyed the scene. Why hookers? And in two different cities. A black woman and three white women had been killed, so race didn't jump out as a motivating factor. What about the times? It was clear that the killer was accelerating or escalating. There didn't seem to be any significance in the locations where the bodies were found. Manner of death was inconsistent. The condition of the bodies, the mutilations, and the sexual assaults also tended to confirm his suspicion that the killer was escalating. He was enjoying it now.

Lukas's thoughts turned to Gabriele. Another problem. Just what he needed. She was clearly upset with him for not calling to inform her that he wouldn't be able to make their date. He'd just flat-out forgotten with all that had gone on. He'd learned that Gabriele was quick to anger. He'd have to make his oversight up to her once this nightmare was over.

Lukas returned to the station and switched off his computer. He tidied up his desk before leaving. Tomorrow he would start completing the case notes on the new victim's murder and comparing them to those from the others now that he had Brooke's notes.

When he finally made it home it was just after three in the morning. He had a feeling he wouldn't be sleeping well.

CHAPTER SIX

He was right. The night's events wouldn't let him rest. His own mind was his worst enemy, as always seemed to be the case.

He slept for maybe two hours, awoke early, showered, shaved, and dressed in a pair of khaki pants and a black polo shirt with the Johnson City Police Department badge stitched into the left side at chest level. He ate a quick breakfast of eggs and bacon, strapped on his Sig Sauer Legion 229 semi-automatic pistol chambered in 9mm, and clipped his badge on his belt. He picked up his keys on the way out the door and headed for the library.

On his way, he put in a call to Gabriele. It rang once and went to voicemail, so he left a message telling her again that he was sorry and giving her a brief synopsis of the new murder. Maybe that would appease her.

He was relieved to find the library was open because he had feared it might be closed due to the murder the previous night. He strolled quickly up the concourse towards the front entrance until he was cut off by a news reporter named Sarah Anderson.

Lukas and Anderson didn't get along, and it was more than the normal friction in a cop-reporter relationship. Lukas didn't doubt that Anderson felt jilted. She'd made it clear that she was interested in him during a law enforcement and media cooperative banquet that was put on by the Chief of Police last summer, but Lukas hadn't reciprocated. She was a semi-attractive redhead, but he flat refused to get involved with a reporter. Anderson was new to the area, and she may have just been trying to make a contact inside the department to further her career. It didn't matter to Lukas. He didn't want anything to do with her.

She stepped directly into his path and planted herself and her microphone under his nose. "I don't suppose you'd be willing to talk about the murder we had here last night, would you? Rumor has it you're the lead detective on the case."

"You know how rumors are, Sarah, especially since you specialize in them." He sidestepped her, and she hurried to get in front of him again.

"Don't be an ass, Miller. I'm just trying to do my job."

"Me, too, and part of my job is directing you to our public relations officer. I don't comment on ongoing investigations. You know that."

Lukas pushed on past, leaving her scowling after him, and entered the library. He quickly found the manager at the front desk and asked to see the previous night's security video. Lukas was taken to a control room in the rear of the building where the cameras were operated. The manager, with Lukas's help, found the footage from the times Lukas requested. The images were relatively clear, but there was a problem with the front camera. It only covered a partial view of the front part of the concourse.

The manager returned to the floor and left him alone in the room. Lukas watched the footage for thirty minutes or so before he found something of interest. At 9:05 p.m., the camera on the west side of the building caught a brief flash that looked like the headlights of a car. Then the lights went off.

Lukas kept watching. Something told him this was the guy who staged the scene. Three minutes later, a hooded figure came into view on the front camera for a brief second. He was carrying something over his shoulder and disappeared in the general direction the body was found. At 9:15 p.m., the same figure was running back toward the left side of the building. Seconds later, headlights appeared and then disappeared. Because of the distance from the camera to the mysterious figure, there was no way to make an identification. The only thing he could determine was that it appeared to be a man of average height and weight. The man's clothing was likewise indistinct. He was wearing a hooded sweatshirt pulled low over his forehead, and he appeared to be wearing jeans. Not much to go on, but maybe the department's computer geeks could clean it up to reveal more details. They were experts at working with digital files. Lukas found the library manager and had him burn the footage to a DVD as evidence before he left for headquarters.

On the drive back, he made a quick call to Odessa McCabe.

She answered with a tired hello.

"Hey, it's Lukas."

"Don't you ever sleep?" she said.

"Not so much lately. What have you found?"

"I don't have an identity. I'm waiting on you for that. But strangulation was the cause of death, just as we thought. The rope was post-mortem like we thought, too. The wounds in the genital area were post-mortem and cr▪▪ and I think, but can't be sure, she was raped with something. We found small splinters of wood in her vagina, but the stab wounds were so severe it's hard to make a definitive call on exactly what happened. Whoever did this is one angry, psychotic individual. I guess you've already figured that out, but if this is one guy, he's growing more desperate. It's taking more to satisfy his lust and his anger. He's torturing them now. I've shared files with the ME's office in Kingsport, and we both feel the murders are connected. We think it's the work of a single killer based on the facts that all the victims were prostitutes, the timeframe and the MO. Is that what you're seeing?"

"We've gone over all four murders, and the evidence leads us to believe it is. The times between the murders are lessening, and the wound patterns are becoming more disturbing. I mean, if this were New York or Chicago, I might buy a multiple-person theory, or at least give it some more consideration. But here in Johnson City, nothing else adds up. Anyway, thanks for putting a rush on this, Odessa. I need to get her identified as soon as possible."

"Good luck."

"Thanks. Bye." Lukas ended the call just as he arrived back at headquarters.

He parked his Crown Victoria in the back lot and walked the short distance into the rear of the building that led directly to the detective's squad room. It was

Saturday, and the room was deserted. He put on a half-pot of coffee, sat down at his desk, and began making entries on the case notes log and looking through the crime scene photos and evidence receipts. It was much the same as the others. Nothing. Next, he pulled mug-shots from known prostitutes and began comparing them with the victim. After an hour, he found her. Mary Tenner. He shot Brooke a quick text: *"Identified the vic, going to notify next of kin. Let you know how it goes."* He wrote down the last known address, picked up the mug-shot, and left the station.

As Lukas pulled up to the address he had written down, he noticed the house was in disrepair. The shutters seemed to be hanging on by sheer willpower, and the screen door was torn in several places. He walked up the chipped and cracked concrete steps to a partially rotted front porch and knocked on the door. He could hear what sounded like a small dog barking and then the voices of young children. He saw a dirty, ripped curtain being pulled back before a frail, elderly woman cautiously opened the door. Lukas could see the worry in the woman's eyes.

"Mrs. Tenner?"

"No, I'm Mildred Connors. What's wrong, sir?"

"Mrs. Connors, I'm Detective Miller from the police department. Is this your daughter?" He handed her the picture.

"Yes, that's Mary." Her eyes began to water. She knew.

He cleared his throat. This part of the job was never easy. "I'm afraid I have some bad news," he said, but his voice was drowned out as the woman began crying loudly. She stood in the doorway, her frail body shaking as she continued to sob.

Lukas heard tiny voices in the background. "What's wong, gwanny?"

He reached out for the woman and she fell into his arms. He hugged her, knowing it offered little comfort.

"We heard about a woman on the news, and I prayed it wasn't her," Mrs. Connors said between sobs. "I told her to stay here. I begged her to. What am I supposed to do with these little ones?"

By now, the two children had joined in the wailing, making the scene even more tragic.

"We'll see that you get some help, Mrs. Connors. I'll have some people come over later today and discuss some of the programs we have available. Are these two young ones her children?"

"Yes, her twins. Just turned three." The woman's tears started up again.

"I'm so sorry."

"Do you know what happened to her? How it happened?"

Lukas didn't have the heart to tell her all he knew, and she didn't need to know anyway. "We don't know anything definite at this point, but we're doing all we can to find out exactly what happened. I know this may not be the best time, but if I could ask you a few questions, it may help with the investigation."

"I'll tell you what I know."

Lukas took out his note pad and pen. "When did you see her last?"

"Let's see. I think it was about 6:30 last night. She hadn't been out in a few days after hearing about that other girl. I tried to stop her."

"Did she know the other victim?"

"She did, but I'm not sure how close they were. I guess you could say they were competitors."

"What about the men she saw? Did you know any of them?"

"No. I didn't approve of what she did. I mean, it made ends meet and all, but I'd tried to get her out of that life for a long time. She was very secretive about who she worked with."

"Did she carry much money with her?"

"Mary didn't have much money to carry."

"Did she say where she was going or who she was meeting when she left last night?"

"Like I said, she didn't discuss it with me. She just told me to watch the kids because she was going out for a while. Then she left."

"Okay, Ms. Connors. If you think of anything that may help, or if there is anything you need, give me a call at this number." He handed her his card.

"Thank you. I don't know what I'm going to do." The hand holding his card trembled. "I don't know…"

"We'll do everything we can to help you. Someone will be in touch soon."

He hated to leave, but the woman turned, clutching the children to her, and shut the door. He'd send someone over from the Department of Human Services immediately.

Lukas walked back to his Crown Victoria, clenching his teeth. The empathy he felt for the woman and the two small children had quickly turned to scorn for whomever was responsible for the killings. It was one thing when drug dealers or gang members shot each other to pieces. That was a risk they took. It was part of the game they played. But when kids started being orphaned because young women were being slaughtered, no matter what their occupation, things ramped up a notch. He had to put a stop to these murders. There was no failing, no letting up.

Back at the station, he phoned the police chaplain and victim coordinator and relayed the information about the death notification and the address, along with the condition of the house and the fact that the woman had the victim's children. They would reach out to Human Services, and the well-intentioned but inefficient and top-heavy bureaucracy would attempt to help.

Lukas drove to the big box home improvement stores and mom and pop hardware stores to see if he could match the rope that was found outside the library. He'd taken several photos of it to use for comparison. Color, material, gauge, and how it was put together were all things he was looking for. He stood in the aisle of Gentry's Hardware looking at a possible match. The color was the same, as was the size, but the material looked to be different. There was no telling how old the rope was that the killer used, which could account for the difference in appearance.

He found the manager and asked him about the rope while showing him the photographs he had taken. He was told that they had only recently started carrying that particular type of rope, and his records showed the only sale had been to a local Boy Scout troop. They'd bought 25 feet of it. Lukas made notes and left the store.

When Lukas arrived back at headquarters, he got all four murder files out. The two he was working and the two in Kingsport. Poring over them seemed his best option right now. There had to be something. He felt it. Something was here among this pile of nothing: a code, a sign, a message, *something*.

He dived in, starting with the manner of death. Strangulation, blunt force trauma, stabbing. There was no consistency. He'd been taught that most serial killers stuck to a common method once it proved effective. This maniac was breaking the rules.

Killing the women no longer seemed to be enough. He'd moved on to torture. And hopefully, that meant he'd make a mistake sooner or later. Lukas couldn't accept that, however. A mistake would be great, but at what price? Another dead woman? He continued scanning the files.

Where were the bodies found? The first was in a dumpster, the second at the city landfill. Maybe that was a sign. They're trash, garbage? But the third was at an abortion clinic, the fourth at the library. No pattern there.

He retrieved the photos from the two crime scenes Brooke was working. It was the first time he'd had the chance to look at them. They were excellent. He wasn't sure if Brooke had taken them or if they'd been taken by the crime scene unit from Kingsport. Still, nothing jumped out and screamed, *"Here! I'm what you're looking for!"* Next, he laid them out side-by-side and started looking at them out of order. Again, nothing.

He was gathering the pictures when his phone buzzed. He looked at the screen. It was Gabriele. He hit the accept button.

"Hey."

"Hi, I'm on break. I got your message."

"I'm sorry about last night. I couldn't get away."

"Couldn't or wouldn't?"

"Come on, Gabby. That's not fair."

"And neither is standing me up without even a phone call or a text."

"I'm sorry. You're right. I should have called. But there was nothing I could do." A long, awkward pause ensued.

She sighed. "I saw you on the news. Sorry to hear you caught another murder."

Lukas wasn't really listening. He was looking at the photographs of the latest crime scene.

"I'll call you back," he said suddenly. He didn't wait for her goodbye; he ended the call and picked up the photo that caught his eye. The photograph didn't draw his attention because of the victim. He'd looked at those so many times he knew them by heart. The importance was what was behind it. It was the pro-choice rally poster. He hurriedly looked at Stevens's case file on the second murder in Kingsport. The body was found at an abortion clinic. He sat back, thinking. The third body was found at an abortion clinic and the fourth was in plain view of a pro-choice rally advertisement. Was he against abortion? Had his victims obtained abortions? Was that why he was killing them? Did they need to check out employees at the abortion clinic? They'd be the ones who would know of women who'd had abortions.

He placed a quick call to Brooke. Maybe he should bounce it off her to see what she thought. The call went to voicemail, so he left a message for her to call him. He tidied up the files and left for home and some much-needed rest.

CHAPTER SEVEN

Brooke walked slowly behind the cadets as she slipped on her department-issued ear protection and adjusted her shooting glasses. She watched the cadets for safety issues and made corrections to any serious defects she noticed in their form.

Some had pretty good form, others required attention. Through her hearing protection, she heard the muffled commands of the range master. "Ready on the left! Ready on the right! The line is ready! Fire!"

A steady stream of staccato shots began as the targets turned to face the cadets. The "cadets" were members of the Citizen's Police Academy, a program where community members were selected to attend and receive a small taste of what police work was like.

After the firearms qualification was over, the cadets returned to the classroom where Brooke gave an hour-long block of instruction on basic crime scene investigation and evidence collection techniques. Following her presentation, she held a question and answer session. A woman in the back of the room whose nameplate identified her as Molly Richards was the first to raise her hand.

"Yes, Molly."

"I hear a lot in the news about computer forensics. Does the KPD have a team that specializes in this area?"

"All of our detectives have a certain amount of training. To be honest, it's kind of new to us here. The FBI has been doing it for a few years, and they've been willing to help us with any cases that require specialized equipment. But as the technology grows, there will be an increased need, so programs are being designed for additional training."

A man on Brooke's right raised his hand. "I have a question. Have you ever had a serious case where there was little to no evidence or leads? And if so, how did you handle it?"

A good question, Brooke thought to herself. *Especially right now.* "Yes, I have, Paul. How did I handle it? You just follow every lead, talk to every possible witness. Sometimes something breaks, sometimes it doesn't. But you never give up. You keep digging. Perseverance is the key when there isn't much evidence."

Another hand went up. "Yes, Linda."

"What are the toughest cases for you to work?"

"For most cops, I'd say it's crimes against children. And I think it's worse if you actually have children of your own." Several heads nodded in agreement. "Okay, looks like we're out of time for tonight. We'll see you guys back next week. You're dismissed."

Brooke packed her files and computer, walked outside, sat down on the bench, and listened as the crickets began their lonely night song. They'd be stopping soon, after the first hard frost. The nights were growing chillier.

She loaded her car and checked her phone. She'd missed two phone calls. The one from her mom was followed by a text about dinner and trick-or-treating with Sierra. The other was from Lukas Miller. She called him back on the drive home. The phone rang twice before a tired, sleepy-sounding Lukas picked up. She listened as he gave her his theory about the abortion angle.

"I think it's something we definitely need to follow up on," he said.

There was a slight pause. She heard him inhale and exhale slowly. Finally, he said, "It could be that in his own sick way, he's trying to tell a story with the bodies."

"Okay, let's say you're right. What are you proposing?"

"I'm not sure. I think we need to go over the files again, maybe even visit the scenes. Do some interviews at the abortion clinic. I was also thinking about making another run at the families. And I have a friend at the FBI office downtown with profiling experience. We could talk to him to see if he has any advice."

"What do you want me to do?"

"You take the families."

"I'll get on it ASAP. How did it go with the last victim's notification?" she asked, changing the topic.

"It was bad. She had two small children, twins, who will more than likely be raised by their grandmother now. I interviewed her briefly. She didn't have much to offer. She didn't know much about her daughter's working habits."

Brooke shook her head. She'd told the class earlier that crimes against children were the hardest to work, but crimes where children were collateral damage were almost as tough. Brooke, like other cops, felt deep sympathy for innocent children who were left orphaned by senseless violence.

"Oh," she said. "I don't mean to change the subject again, but I meant to tell you I have a meeting with my chief Monday morning. We can get together after that if you want."

"Sure thing. Just give me a call when you're done."

"Will do. Good night."

Brooke drove the rest of the way home on autopilot. She barely remembered the trip. She switched the lights down to dim as she made her way up the gravel driveway. She noticed the front porch light was off.

"That's odd," she said out loud, "I thought I turned that on. Probably burned out again." She parked her black, unmarked Impala in the driveway on the right side of the house. A quick glance at her phone showed it was just after eight. Sierra should be smack in the middle of her trick-or-treat routine and was most likely wearing her grandparents out. It was decent of her ex-husband to share Sierra on this holiday, especially since it was his weekend to have her, but Brooke suspected he probably had a date and a party to go to. Alex, as much as she hated to admit it because it meant she'd made a mistake when she married him, was a jerk. Brooke sighed, unlocked the door and braced herself for the frenzied greeting she was about to get. Judging by the barking, she'd been missed.

Gus, their two-year-old miniature Schnauzer, went into a tailspin around her legs. She bent down and scooped his wriggling body into her arms. "Hey buddy, have you kept a good watch on the house?"

Brooke poured herself a glass of tea, took a long drink, and headed to the living room. She kicked off her shoes, placed the glass of tea on a coaster, and turned on the TV. Cartoons were on from the last time the TV was used, so she turned to a news channel. A report about a huge burglary ring that had been busted in Dallas reminded her of the outside light that was mysteriously off. She forced herself from the comfy chair and headed to the front door. She flipped the switch, and the light came on.

She cringed. She was going to have to be more mindful. She'd let her mind wander too much lately. She needed to relax. And she knew just the thing.

She changed into her orange University of Tennessee sweats and retrieved a cigarette and lighter she had hidden in a kitchen drawer. She walked out the French doors to the covered porch. Smoking was a habit she had picked up while she was in the police academy. She rationalized that an occasional smoke wouldn't kill her. Besides, she stayed active and was in great physical condition. Not that she'd admit to anyone that she smoked. She went to great lengths to keep her little vice a secret. She kept the cigarettes hidden, only smoked outside when nobody was around, and she kept an artificial flower pot on the back porch where she placed her butts. She emptied it every other day or so. The pot looked authentic, but it had a removable top and housed a secret compartment. It was designed as a safe – it had a key and everything – but she just used it for hiding cigarette butts. She'd thought of everything.

She could count on one hand the people that knew about her dirty little secret. She took a long drag and closed her eyes as the nicotine started to relax her. Her mom seemed to have a suspicion, although Brooke didn't know how. Mothers seemed to have a way of knowing things they shouldn't. She was now grateful for the intuition, since she was a mom herself. Her mother disapproved, of course, even though she knew why Brooke might light up occasionally. She only smoked to calm her nerves or to relax. And after sex, of course. But that hadn't happened in a long, long time.

She told herself to think about something besides the murders. *"How about how good things are? I have Sierra and my parents. I love my job. I love the house."* The furnishings were all hers, her taste, her style. She had an eye for interior design, and everything coordinated perfectly, right down to the curtain rods.

She finished her smoke and reached down for the pot. She removed the top, opened the lid, and noticed that the butts had piled up during the week. There were five in there. She stepped off the porch and emptied the butts into a burn barrel about 50 feet from the house. She burned trash that she didn't recycle every few days, and the butts went up in smoke.

"Can't be too careful," she mumbled to herself as she walked back to the house.

The doorbell rang just as she finished. Close call. She went to the door and peered through the peep hole and saw her little angel all dressed up in her Cinderella costume. She opened the door and heard an adorable, "Trick or treat."

Sierra jumped into her outstretched arms, and Brooke hugged her so tightly she could feel the cheap costume crumble.

"Hi, Mommy. You smell funny. Like smoke."

"I just came from the firing range, baby."

"Are we going to carve a pumpkin?"

"We sure are."

"Let's do the mummy this year. I already picked him out."

Brooke looked out at the waiting car and waved to her mom and dad. They'd picked Sierra up from Alex's place and taken her trick-or-treating. "Wave bye to Grandma and Grandpa."

Her dad must have been driving. The horn honked, and the headlights blinked before they drove off. She wanted to talk to her dad. She wanted to run these cases by him and get his thoughts. But for now, there was a pumpkin to be carved. A big one.

Not long after, Brooke heard the snap of the screen door and looked up to see her best friend, Haley, dressed in far too classy a manner for pulling out pumpkin guts. Brooke glanced at her watch. "Right on time, as usual."

"What do you think?" She spun around, and Brooke realized Haley's outfit was actually Halloween themed. Her glittery sweater had silver spider webs, and her pants sported a stylish swirling script of *Boo* over and over. Leave it to Haley to turn cheesy into *haute couture*.

"Sexy," Brooke said. "Elvira's got nothing on you, girl."

"Well, how about we turn on some scary movies to get the mood right?"

"Uh, I don't think that's such a good idea."

"Please," Sierra said. "I won't be scared or have bad dreams, promise. Please."

"Well, maybe. But I get to choose which one we'll watch."

***

All three of them ended up working on the mummy carving. The pattern Sierra chose was difficult to carve, as usual. But they laughed and half-watched the movie Brooke had picked out – Tim Burton's *Nightmare Before Christmas* – and had a grand time. Sierra fell asleep half-way through the movie, leaving Brooke and Haley to finish the carving.

Brooke spent what was left of Halloween filling Haley in on the latest concerning the murders and other recent personal events, including her new partner. Haley was clearly infatuated with him, even though she'd only seen him on the news twice.

"He's hot," Haley said. "Smoking hot."

"I don't date men I work with," Brooke said. "Besides, he has a girlfriend."

"Have you seen her?"

"No."

"What's her name?"

"Gabriele."

"Probably some exotic Latin siren," Haley said.

"I don't care."

The conversation eventually wound down as they cleaned up, and Haley left.

Brooke sat on the sofa after Haley was gone, brushing her hair and petting Gus at the same time. She allowed her mind to wander. It wasn't long before her mind returned to the murders. Did Lukas have a point about the abortion angle? He could be right. Or it could just be random coincidence. Either way, it was something they needed to investigate further.

They were in a reactive state with the investigation, a fact she didn't like. Waiting for another body was the same as doing nothing, letting the bad guy have the upper hand. And he did. The killer had the initiative. They had to devise a plan to force him to make a mistake, get him out in the open. Lukas had more experience in that area than she did, but he seemed to be stymied as well. He was trying to work it out on his own, she knew. She'd heard it in his voice on the phone.

And what about that prostitute he seemed to be so close to, almost too close? Razzy? Surely, he hadn't crossed the line. Miller probably had a lot of women in his life, which was to be expected with his playboy good looks and the way he carried himself. For her, there was a difference between cocky and confident, and she wasn't quite sure where he fell in that regard. Maybe he thought he could charm anyone.

Enough thinking. Monday would come soon enough, and she had a meeting scheduled with the chief. She didn't know what he wanted, but she was sure it would be a busy day no matter what. She just hoped another body didn't drop between now and then.

CHAPTER EIGHT

The man was off today, and he had a lot of work to do. He wolfed down his breakfast and dressed quickly. Next, a call to make sure the second-hand store was going to be open since it was Sunday. They confirmed they would be open between one and five.

A few hours later, he was sitting in his car in the lot of Rerun Antiques thinking about things he could use. He would have to plan carefully.

Something inside him that he had managed to keep suppressed for years had finally made its way to the surface, and now that events had begun to unfold, he needed to be methodical. So far, everything had gone according to plan. But he couldn't afford to get sloppy now.

He looked at his watch. The store should be open. He walked the short distance to the front door. The bell overhead jingled cheerfully, and a man who looked to be in his mid-50s called out a welcome. The man looked as old as the interior of the store, and just as messy. The place was a wreck. It needed repairs in several places.

"Can I help you?" the man asked.

"Thanks, I'm just looking."

"Okay, sing out if you need anything. I own the place, so I know where everything is."

He nodded. He didn't know exactly what he was looking for. He needed a prop of some kind to allay suspicion. There were several possibilities, but each had complications associated with them. Finally, he spotted something that might be perfect. He walked over and stood in front of what appeared to be surveying equipment.

"None of it works," the proprietor said as he walked up.

"Excuse me?"

"The pieces you're looking at. They don't work."

"I may know somebody who can fix them. How much?"

"Considering the condition, I'll let you have all of it for fifty dollars plus tax."

"Sold."

He carried the equipment to the register, took the money from his wallet, and handed it to the owner.

"Thanks. Come back now, ya hear?" The owner was clearly happy with his end of the deal, and he waved and smiled. The man nodded politely, picked up the equipment, and walked out of the store. There was still much to do.

He drove the green sedan down the gravel road on the outskirts of Kingsport. Keeping his eyes on the road as much as possible, he occasionally looked at the houses off to the side. He'd found the address a week earlier on the internet and had been in the area briefly a couple of times. He made a left turn onto Jankins Loop and found a spot where he could see the house without being too conspicuous. The overgrown fence rows around the farm land and fields helped conceal him. He pulled the car over and parked.

He reached over to open the glove box and took out the small pair of camouflaged binoculars. Holding them to his eyes, he turned the focusing knob on top and brought the building sharply into view. Curtains covered the windows, obscuring any view of the house's interior.

He got out of the car, removed the equipment and placed it on the hood of the car. The house was directly north of the tree line where the cameras were to be placed. Walking down the road and back, he attempted to imitate the surveyors he had seen along the roads. Once he had a clear picture of where the cameras were to be placed, he eased them from the bag lying in the back seat of the sedan and secured them, making sure they were pointed at the rear and sides of the house.

He checked the cameras one last time, then packed up his props and left the area the way he had come in, completely undetected. *Mission accomplished*, he thought to himself.

He loaded the equipment, got into his car, and headed back to the main road toward the city. He began having flashbacks. He didn't know what triggered them, but they were vivid. He thought of nights alone in his bedroom, listening into the morning as his mother had sex with yet another man. He could hear the sounds the drunk men made – the disgusting grunts and moans – as they pawed at his mother.

But most of all, he remembered the night she tried to kill him. He'd been taking a bath after having played until dark at a park a few blocks from the run-down rental house he shared with her. He was 12 years old, and it was late summer. School was about to start back. He heard her come in through the kitchen, and the next thing he knew the bathroom door opened. The lock didn't work. He could smell cigarette smoke and alcohol on her as soon as she staggered in and knew she'd been at her favorite bar, a dive called The Silver Saddle. She took two steps into the bathroom and slipped on some water that had sloshed out of the tub onto the cheap, linoleum floor. She banged her right shoulder into the wall and wound up face down on her belly.

"Are you all right?" he said. He didn't call her Momma or Mom or Mother. He didn't call her by name. He didn't call her anything. When he wanted her attention, he just said, "Hey!"

"You little bastard," she hissed. "I've had about all I can take…"

She came off of the floor and lunged at him. Her hands went around his neck and she pushed his head under the water. He flailed and splashed and squirmed and finally, probably because she was so drunk, managed to get himself free. He scrambled out of the tub and out the bathroom door into the kitchen, gasping for air. A knife was on the counter by the sink. He picked it up and walked back to the bathroom. By that time, she was sitting on the toilet relieving herself, her jeans and panties around her ankles. She looked up and said, "Go ahead, boy. You better get me while you can, because next time, I won't let you get away."

He gripped the knife tighter and stepped into the bathroom.

"They'll send you to an adult prison," she said. "The men there will make a woman out of you in a week. You'll die in jail, and then you'll go straight to hell."

He'd backed away, knowing that one day he'd get another chance, a better chance. He'd kill her and do it without being caught. And then the relentless squeaking would be gone. The constant squeaking of bedsprings. He was forced to listen to that damned squeaking night after night, hour after hour. His knuckles turned white as his grip tightened on the steering wheel. Sweat ran down his forehead, and his breathing became labored.

Occasionally, he would hear his mother getting roughed up. She had come into his room in the morning many times with a shiner or swollen lips. He didn't care. At some level, he wished one of them would kill her. At another, he wanted to do it himself.

She was a drunk. When she wasn't screwing some john, she was wasted. As he grew older, he became more and more embarrassed. He had very few friends during his childhood and having anyone over to his house was out of the question. He never knew when his mom would tie one on. People had dropped by a couple of times, but he'd hidden to save himself the embarrassment of them seeing his mom passed out drunk, half-naked, slobbering on the couch.

A horn sounded behind him. He looked up and realized the light was green. How long had he been sitting there? *"Damn it! Keep it together!"* He eased the car into motion, joining the flow of traffic. The driver who'd blown his horn came speeding past with his middle finger extended. A nice, friendly gesture on a Sunday. He returned it in kind.

It didn't take long for the thoughts of his mother to return. He'd had no real childhood, and he hated his mother for that. She'd finally done him a favor and given him the opportunity to do away with her when he was 16 years old. She should never have traded sex for that gun. Her "funeral" was a joke. They didn't go to church and had no money, so a few of the other whores she hung around with and a couple of the men she'd banged threw a little party in her back yard before he was removed from the home by social services. The funeral was the same as her life. A sham and a waste of time.

He spent the last two years of adolescence being raised by his aunt, who didn't really want him but took him in, he supposed, because she felt she had to. She was a decent woman, unlike her sister, but she had little time for him and made that abundantly clear on a regular basis. Something in him drove him to finish high school, though, and a guidance counselor at school helped him apply for government grants so he could go to college. He worked part-time jobs and managed to graduate in four years. He found a profession that would allow him to help others, and he was good at it. But he'd always known the rage that smoldered within him would find its way to the surface one day and boil over like a volcano.

He smiled as he parked his car in his assigned space. His plans to make the world a better place had evolved over the years. Now he was cleaning up a couple of cities, one dead hooker at a time.

CHAPTER NINE

Brooke was in Chief Tanner McConnell's office at precisely eight on Monday morning. The office was a mixture of old and new. Several pictures of officers and detectives that appeared to have been taken in the 1940s adorned the walls. Chief McConnell sat behind a giant oak desk that looked slightly out of place in the smallish room. A bookshelf behind him had various police souvenirs he had picked up from different agencies during his thirty-some-odd years of police work, along with the obligatory model car fashioned after the cars being driven by Kingsport officers today.

"Please, sit," he said, indicating a chair with a sweep of his arm. "Thanks for coming in, Brooke. I just want to talk about Friday night to see how things went."

"You mean sending me to Johnson City?"

"Exactly. How did it go?"

"As well as could be expected, I guess," Brooke said. "I think the murders are connected, and a working agreement between the two departments can only help."

"Great. We were hoping that would be the case, and by we, I mean Chief Armstrong and myself," he said. "I know this type of arrangement is somewhat out of the ordinary, but we think it will help us catch this killer faster. Where are we exactly?"

"We have a few small leads, but so far this guy hasn't made any serious mistakes."

"That's what I was afraid of."

He paused a moment and trained his gaze on her for several beats before continuing.

"I'm catching some pretty serious heat, Brooke. We have to get this maniac stopped. I know you're a good detective, and you have a bright future here with the department. But you need to know there's been talk from City Hall of asking the District Attorney to bring in the TBI. If they come in, they'll take over and shut you out. I've got the powers that be calmed down for now. In fact, this experiment with you and their detective over in Johnson City has bought us some more time. But we need to get something going. Got it?"

"Got it."

"Keep me posted and make sure they treat you good over there." He stood up, indicating the meeting was over.

Brooke got to her feet and nodded. "I will, and thanks for your confidence."

Brooke walked out of his office feeling a slight twinge of nausea. If the cases were turned over to an outside agency such as the TBI, it would mean only one thing – she wasn't good enough. And she hated the thought of not being good enough.

Worse, it could also lend credence to all the people who said she was just riding her daddy's coattails. She'd heard it all. The barbs were cruel and varied, like the one she heard about how it's fitting that her initials were "B.S."

since her career was, too. There were those who insinu-ated that her looks had helped her advance, not her brain or hard work. And then there were the inevitable, vicious rumors about how she had gained success by spreading her legs for the right men. Those rumors infuriated her. Not once had she even come close to sleeping with a supe-rior. That was absolutely taboo. It had been hammered into her from the start by her dad. She had never, and would never, become involved in a romantic affair with anyone in her department. But it seemed no matter how hard she worked, her male contemporaries refused to acknowledge that she was good at what she did. She let out a sigh and told herself to stop thinking negatively. To hell with those guys. She couldn't control what they thought.

She walked through the station, eventually ending up in her squad room, which seemed particularly busy this morning. Of course it was busy. Women were dying. The files on her desk commanded her attention. She snatched them up and headed for the rear door of the station and the outside world where she could have some privacy. She walked briskly to her car, tossed the files into the front passenger seat, and drove out of the lot.

Her mind replayed the chief's warning that the case might be taken from her like a broken record. Suddenly, she remembered Lukas asking her to call him after the meeting. Her call was answered on the second ring.

"Hey Brooke, how'd it go?"

"Not terrible, not great."

"What gives?"

"There's been some talk of handing these cases over to the TBI. And from the sound of it, I assume they're talking about your cases, too. Apparently, bringing you and me together was an effort to keep the wolves at bay. Both chiefs were in on it. They're calling it an experiment, but what they're really doing is buying time to keep the TBI out."

"And where do you think we stand now?'

"We'd better get some results."

"I checked on the rope lead, but it didn't go anywhere. I found a possible match at a local hardware store. If it's the same rope, and that's a very big if, the only record of it being sold was to a Boy Scout troop. I'll get the names of the troop leaders and see if anything pops."

"What's the theory, a dad of one of the members?"

"It's thin, but I'm going to check it anyway."

"It could have been bought over here. I'll check on it now."

"Okay. I've been thinking about our next move. We need to get out on the street. At night, when they're out, if they haven't all gone underground. Sometimes, the best way to wash a dog is to get in the tub with it. What do you say?"

"I'm up for anything. I'm tired of sitting on my hands waiting. What time and where?"

"If he sticks to alternating cities, Kingsport is next. Let's start there, and if we strike out, we move over to Johnson City. Let's do it without backup. I don't want a bunch of cops on the street. I don't want a lot of radio chatter. He might have a scanner. Let's just get out there and see how it feels. Who knows what might happen?"

"What time do you want to start?" Brooke said.

"I was thinking probably six tonight."

"Okay. That'll give me time to check out the rope lead and get some other things done. Can you text me a couple of photos of the rope?"

"Sure. Is there anything you need help with?"

"No, but if it turns into anything, I'll be sure to shout."

Brooke disconnected the call and turned her thoughts to Lukas's idea about the abortion poster. She called a nurse she knew at the Sullivan County health clinic and gave her the names of her murder victims and, just to be thorough, the two from Johnson City. She wanted to know if there was any connection between any of them. Maybe a connection, however tenuous, could provide a link as to how they were being targeted. The nurse told Brooke it would be later in the day before she could pull the files.

Brooke swung through a fast food joint for a coffee hoping to change her gloomy disposition. She remembered the rope. While she waited for her coffee, she checked to see if Lukas had sent the photographs. He had.

She visited several hardware and home improvement stores, but she came up empty. They either didn't have that particular type of rope or had no way to track it. She decided on an early lunch and while she ate in the parking lot she flipped through the murder files. Could this be a turf war between pimps? In a city this size? It didn't seem likely considering the murders from the two cities fit the same general MO. And pimps didn't usually migrate from city to city. But it was worth shaking a few trees to see if anything fell out.

She placed a call to the vice detectives and came up with the name and address of Alvin Nelasco, a well-known pimp in Kingsport. According to them, her second victim had worked for him. Brooke had heard Nelasco's name but had never met him. She finished her meal, started the car and decided today would be a good day to make his acquaintance.

The address she'd been given by vice turned out to be an apartment on Stonegate Road. She knocked on the door and was surprised when Nelasco opened the door almost immediately. He was a short man of Hispanic descent. His arms and neck were covered in tattoos. His head was shaved, and a black goatee effectively finished off the menacing look he was obviously trying to convey. Brooke held up her badge.

"Can I talk to you for a minute?"

"Am I under arrest?"

"Nope. Friendly chat."

"And why would I do that? Every time I talk to five-oh, I wind up in jail. But *you* are one fine *mamacita*. I might talk to you if you promise to search me."

"In your dreams, Alvin." Brooke took out a picture of Melanie Salem. "You know her, right?"

He looked at the picture for a few seconds then back at Brooke suspiciously. "You know I do or you wouldn't be here. I haven't seen her in months, though."

"Did you know she's dead? Murdered."

"I may have heard something like that."

"Where did you hear it?"

"Just word on the street."

"If you know more than you're telling me and I find out later that you withheld information in an ongoing murder investigation, it won't go well for you."

"I don't know anything about her murder, and I don't remember where I heard it."

Brooke looked at the man closely, trying to read him. She held up a photo of the first victim, Cindy Sullivan. "What about this girl?"

"I've seen her around. She goes by Sullie, I think. She never worked for me, though."

"Who did she work for?"

"She was a free-ranger. She didn't work for nobody."

"So, you know she was murdered, too?"

"I don't live in a cave. Why are you here? I don't know anything about them murders."

"I was thinking maybe you and another pimp might have a beef and these girls got in the middle. Or maybe Melanie Salem held back some money or was turning tricks on the side and you got pissed off."

"You don't think that, or I would've already had the pleasure of you running those fine young hands over me."

Brooke continued to read him. He was calm. He had no history of beating on his girls. She didn't think he had anything to do with the murders.

"So how about helping me out. These murders can't be good for business. Who do you think killed them? Have you heard anything that might help me? It'd get you a lot of love going forward if you can help us out."

He stepped away from the door and into the apartment, lighting a cigarette as he moved. Brooke followed him inside.

"I got no clue who it is," Nelasco said. "All I've heard is that some nut job is out there killing girls. I heard two got whacked over in JC, too. All the girls are scared out of their minds, and I don't blame them. They're only doing business with the johns they know well. And you're right, business is down. You guys need to get off your asses and catch this dude."

"What about Draxton Little?" According to vice, Little was Nelasco's chief rival.

"He's a *puta*, a little bitch. But no way he's killing these girls. He isn't crazy, and besides, he wouldn't have the *cojones*."

"Have any of your girls mentioned a red car driving around during business hours?"

He crushed his cigarette into an ashtray. "No, why?"

"It's just something we're looking at. Have they mentioned anyone overly suspicious?"

"Not to me."

Brooke fished out a card and handed it to him. "I want you to text me the numbers of your girls. Start with the most active ones."

He took the card. "They won't talk to you."

"They'd better. Or your parole officer and I will be here for a surprise visit."

"And just when I thought we were connecting."

"We'll connect if I don't get those numbers."

"How about a little police brutality before you go?"

Brooke turned to leave. "You wouldn't like it."

"I might."

"Trust me."

Brooke glanced at her phone as she climbed into her car and noticed she'd missed a call while she was talking to Nelasco. There was a voicemail. It turned out to be the nurse from the health clinic. She said her records didn't show any connection between the women Brooke had asked about. The women from Johnson City had never been treated in Sullivan County. There was nothing out of the ordinary in the Kingsport women's records, other than the fact that Melanie Salem had an abortion two years ago. There was no record of where the procedure had been performed, but Brooke had a pretty good idea.

When she returned to her desk at the station she looked up the number for The Cooper Center for Reproductive Health. She hoped she could do this without a subpoena and was pleasantly surprised when a nurse supervisor named Lindsay McIntire answered the phone. She knew Lindsay from when Lindsay worked in the ER. Brooke got just what she needed. Melanie Salem had in fact had an abortion at the Cooper Center. It was still too early to tell for sure, but maybe Lukas was onto something with the abortion angle.

Brooke looked at her watch. The afternoon had flown by. It was time to get ready for the sting.

***

When they finally met at an abandoned factory just outside of Kingsport, Brooke's nerves were buzzing. She felt like a live wire. She noticed Lukas seemed to have that same vibe going. Brooke told Lukas about checking on the rope, the abortion clinic lead, and her interview with Nelasco.

"You should check in Johnson City to see if either of those victims had an abortion," Brooke said. If so, we keep working the angle until we find something that might lead us to the killer."

"But only one of your victims had an abortion, right?"

"Right."

"Sounds like a rabbit hole."

"Shouldn't you check anyway?"

Lukas nodded. "Yeah. I'll check. How about the pimp? You think he's telling the truth?"

"I do. He's worried about his cash flow. He wants us to find the guy. Are you ready to do this?

"Sure," Lukas said.

The area Brooke chose for the surveillance was lively. It was in the old part of Kingsport known locally as Five Points – or The Train District – although there weren't many trains operating these days.

There were the usual nocturnal creatures out, and Brooke and Lukas sat and watched, hoping for any sign, any clue. A red car cruising the area would be a nice start, but after three hours and no sign of anything unusual, they decided to call it a night.

Brooke and Lukas were on their way back to Lukas's car when Lukas's phone buzzed in his jacket pocket. He hit the speaker button and said, "Hey, Rafe. What's up?"

"We need you back over here ASAP. We have another body."

"Shit. We're on our way. Text me the address."

He turned to Brooke, and she could feel the stress level rising.

"I don't believe it," Lukas said. "The son of a bitch got another one."

PART II

CHAPTER TEN

Lukas felt a rush of adrenaline as he headed back to Johnson City with Brooke right behind him. His foot was heavy on the gas. The car's lights were flashing, the siren blaring, and he laid on the air horn when he came to an intersection. Less than fifteen minutes after the call, he and Brooke arrived at the address Rafe had texted to him. He skidded to a stop just behind the department command post and emerged while it was still rocking. He looked back just as Brooke got out of her car. The address turned out to be an upper middle-class neighborhood, something Lukas didn't expect.

All the usual equipment was already on the scene, and all the players were present. He and Brooke walked through the throng of people. The impact this latest body was having didn't quite hit him until he realized they were in the mayor's driveway. *The mayor's driveway? What the hell?*

Lukas sensed something else different about the scene, but he couldn't quite figure it out. The other detectives stood around talking in hushed tones. Even Captain Hunter – who was boisterous in almost every situation – seemed subdued as Lukas made his way toward the body. It had been covered by a white sheet that was now soaked in blood.

Lukas pulled the sheet back and felt his knees buckle. Blood rushed from his head. He knelt as a wave of nausea overtook him and he found himself staring into the lifeless eyes of Kimberly Renee "Razzy" Raznovich.

A deep, gaping, bloody wound drew his eyes to Razzy's tiny neck. She was completely naked. Lukas tried to regain his composure, but he was struggling. He felt a touch on his shoulder and realized it was Brooke. He replaced the sheet, gathered himself, stood up and looked around. The world seemed to have changed. Everything was moving in slow motion. He glanced at Brooke, but her face didn't really register. He walked slowly toward Captain Hunter, who was standing near one of the ambulances talking with one of his squad mates. Hunter's voice cut through the fog in Lukas's mind like a razor.

"Miller are you going to be able to do this?"

"Yeah. I just need a minute."

Brooke touched Lukas's arm again. "Let's take a walk."

Brooke walked Lukas over to her car, holding his arm as though he might pass out. She opened the door and helped Lukas get situated. Just as she was shutting the door, Lukas heard Captain Hunter call Brooke's name. Lukas looked up and saw him motioning for her. "Be right back," she said. Lukas left the door closed. He didn't want to hear what Hunter had to say.

Lukas tried to gather himself. He knew he had to focus, to put his emotions aside and concentrate. He opened the door and walked up to Brooke and Captain Hunter.

"Okay Captain, where are we with the scene?" he said.

"I was just telling Brooke that we have suits doing a canvass and CSU is standing by. Miller are you sure you're okay?"

"I'm fine. If anyone turns up anything on the canvass have them report directly to me."

"Will do."

"Brooke are you ready to go over the body?"

"Ready."

"Let's get Odessa," he said. He signaled for McCabe who was standing near the forensic van.

The three approached the body. Lukas carefully removed the sheet and allowed Odessa her first look at the body. Razzy's head was almost completely severed. Blood had run down from the wound onto her breasts. It was difficult to tell if she had any wounds on her chest, but it appeared her right nipple had been torn off. "What would you estimate as time of death?" Lukas asked.

Odessa picked up Razzy's left arm with a gloved hand. "No rigor, very little lividity. I'd say two to four hours."

"It looks like she's been sexually assaulted," Brooke said. "Brutally."

"Does anybody know how she got here?" Odessa asked.

"They're working on it now. Looks like we went to the wrong city."

"There isn't much else we can learn here," Lukas said. "Let's get CSU in to photograph the scene. Make sure they do blood swabs on the ground near the body just in case it's not all hers. Brooke and I will talk to the mayor. When do you think they'll do the autopsy?"

"We'll put a rush on it. I'd say tomorrow morning, afternoon at the latest."

"Okay. Let's go, Brooke."

They walked up the short sidewalk and were met by Mayor Todd Pennington, who invited them in. Lukas had met the mayor a couple of times but didn't know him well.

"Mayor, I'm Detective Miller and this is Detective Stevens from the Kingsport Police Department. I know you're probably terribly upset and I'm sorry to bother you, but we'd like to ask you a few questions if you don't mind."

"Sure. I have some questions of my own," the mayor said.

"Can you tell us what's gone on here the last hour or so?"

"My wife got home a little after five after picking Jason up from band practice. She came in and started getting supper ready. You know, just normal, everyday things. I was held up at work, so I guess I got home about six-thirty. We ate dinner, put the dishes in the dishwasher, and we watched television for an hour or so. The dogs started barking, and I got up and went to the window, but I didn't see anything and didn't think anything else about it. About forty-five minutes later, my wife took the dogs out and saw something in the driveway. That's when she found her. Glenda was pretty shaken up. So, I went outside to investigate and saw her lying there. I placed the sheet over her. I couldn't leave her out there naked."

"Do you know her?"

"I don't think so. I had trouble looking at her."

"Mayor has anyone threatened you lately?" Brooke asked.

"I'm always getting complaints, but not necessarily threats. Nothing out of the ordinary has happened."

Lukas pointed to the front of the house. "I noticed cameras out there. Do you have them recording?"

The mayor looked down at his feet. "We had a power outage a month or so ago and we never reset the system. We've been meaning to, we just haven't done it yet. It's such a quiet neighborhood. Detective, what do you think this is about? I can't believe this young woman was left in my driveway by accident."

"I know this has to be disconcerting for you and your family. Rest assured, we're on it."

"It doesn't look that way to me," the mayor said. "How many women is this? Five now between here and Kingsport?"

Lukas felt his face flush, but he held his tongue.

"Thanks for your help, Mayor Pennington." He handed the mayor his card. "If you think of anything else, please give me a call."

"I'll be talking to your superiors," the mayor said. "It doesn't appear you have what it takes to handle this."

"I'm doing the best I can, sir. Have a nice evening."

Back in the driveway, Brooke was the first to speak, "Well, that went well."

"Screw him," Lukas said. "And what is it with people not having their expensive surveillance systems working? Why bother if you're not going to use them?"

"Where do we go from here?"

"We go backward and try to find out where she's been tonight. That reminds me. We need to make sure Timmy is okay."

"Who's Timmy?"

"Her son."

Brooke produced her keys. "I'll drive."

On the drive to the apartment complex where Razzy lived, Lukas could tell Brooke had something on her mind. He caught her glancing at him several times.

"You might as well say what's on your mind."

"I was just wondering if you wanted to talk about it," Brooke said.

"I'm fine, really."

"How did you meet her?"

"She was my first vice arrest. The sad part is, she was really a good kid. Just made some bad choices."

"And her son?"

"He tried out for baseball and nobody wanted him because of his mom. I didn't think that was fair, so I put him on my team. He's turned out to be a good little player."

A few minutes later, Brooke pulled her unmarked to the curb in front of Razzy and Timmy's apartment building. Nothing seemed abnormal. The streets were empty around the rundown three-story complex. They got out and walked across the street and climbed to the third floor where Razzy and Timmy lived and knocked on the door. No answer.

"You think he's in there? Maybe been told not to answer the door?"

"I'm not sure. Let's try the neighbors." Lukas knocked on the door across the hall. The woman who answered was a short, plump lady who appeared to be in her late forties. "Hi, I'm Detective Miller from the police department. The woman who lives in 322, do you know if--"

"Timmy? Yes, he's staying here with me, but he's asleep. Has she got herself arrested again?"

"We're investigating a crime, ma'am. What's your name?"

"Oh, I'm sorry. I'm Tammy Blake."

"Ms. Blake, could you watch him just for tonight? We'll have someone pick him up from school tomorrow. Would that be okay with you?"

"I guess so. This sounds serious."

"Did Ms. Raznovich tell you where she was going tonight?

"She doesn't really need to. I know which way is up, detective."

"Was it unusual for her to ask you to keep Timmy?"

"Not at all. I do it all the time."

"And did she mention meeting anyone in particular?"

"No, but she didn't talk much about her work, if you want to call it that."

"Thank you, Ms. Blake. We'll be in touch."

As they made their way out, Lukas said, "At least I know he's okay."

"I was thinking about our next move," Brooke said. What are the chances she hit a convenience store just after she left? Worth a shot?"

"There's a store just around the corner. Let's check it out."

Lukas showed the clerk a photograph of Razzy, and he confirmed that she had been in earlier in the evening around 7:00 p.m.

"Do you know her?" Lukas asked.

"Sure," the clerk said. "Her name's Razzy. She comes in a lot."

"Any chance she mentioned where she was going?"

"She said she was going to work, which meant she was going to have sex with somebody," the clerk said. "She's a working girl."

"Yeah, we know," Lukas said. "Can we take a look at your surveillance video?"

The clerk led Lukas and Brooke to an office at the back of the store. He showed them the system and went back to his duties. Lukas cued it to the approximate time Razzy would have been in the store. After a few minutes they found footage of her walking in. She bought a pack of cigarettes and left on foot.

"Hey, wait. Back that up to where she leaves the store," Brooke said.

Lukas moved the cursor to the rewind button on the screen and ran it back to where she was standing at the register, then hit play again. After she paid and left a white male walked up behind her. He was wearing a heavy, brown coat, jeans and construction boots. He also had on a black baseball cap that was pulled down over his eyes.

"Does he look suspicious to you?" Brooke asked.

"Not sure. Let's cue it back to when he comes in." Lukas ran the video back until the frame came into view.

It was just after Razzy came in. He kept his head down and appeared to be avoiding the camera.

"I wonder if he's doing that on purpose," Lukas said.

"What about a car? Maybe we can get a shot of that," Brooke said.

Lukas let the video run until the man left. He appeared to remain wary of cameras. He left the store just after Razzy and walked around the corner of the building. Lights could be seen a short time later as a car left the side parking lot.

"Damn. He parked out of view."

"Hold on." Lukas cycled through all the available cameras, but she was right. He had parked just outside of camera coverage. "Let's ask the clerk if he recognizes him."

Brooke went to get the clerk while Lukas placed the digital surveillance file on a thumb-drive for evidence. The clerk didn't recognize the man but mentioned that he seemed preoccupied with something. He pulled up the transaction and made a copy of the receipt for them. The man bought a pack of nuts and a soft drink with cash.

"What do you think? Is he involved?" Brooke said.

"Not enough information to go on. It looks suspicious, but in this neighborhood, suspicious is the norm."

"Okay. What now? Back to the scene?"

"Yep."

Brooke drove Lukas back to the mayor's house. Captain Hunter was still there, and CSU was just finishing up. Lukas and Brooke learned that several neighbors had been interviewed, but nobody had seen or heard anything out of the ordinary, and apparently the mayor's neighbors didn't have any cameras. Lukas ran his fingers through his hair and leaned up against his cruiser. "Damn it. So, someone dumps a dead body in the driveway of the mayor of Johnson City and nobody sees anything? You would think *somebody* would have seen *something*. Are we dealing with a ghost?"

"Maybe the autopsy will give us some evidence."

"Maybe. So far, they haven't been very helpful. By the way, what did Captain Hunter say to you earlier? When I was in the car?"

"Oh, we have a meeting with him and your chief tomorrow morning at 8:00 a.m."

"Great. Just what we need."

Brooke was staring out the window of the car. Finally, she turned her head toward Lukas."Can you think of anything else we can do tonight?"

"No. I have a feeling we'll need a little sleep before the meeting anyway. I just keep thinking if I'd put her in jail the night they found her with that dope, she'd still be alive."

"It's not your fault Lukas. Don't even let yourself go there. I'll see you in the morning."

CHAPTER ELEVEN

Lukas suffered through one of the most restless nights he could remember. Gabriele came over and did what she could to help ease his anxiety, but he would have probably been better off alone. He barely even knew she was there.

When he and Brooke stepped hesitantly into Chief Armstrong's office a few minutes before the appointed time, he was wired up, ready for anything. They were told to sit in the waiting room, which felt like an interrogation primer to Lukas. He could hear a spirited conversation coming from within the chief's office, but he couldn't make out what was being said. Whatever it was sounded heated. A few minutes later, the secretary's phone buzzed, and she ushered them in. Chief Armstrong and Captain Hunter were waiting.

They took seats, and Chief Armstrong began without any pleasantries.

"Captain Hunter has filled me in on last night, and to say I'm shocked would be one of the biggest understatements of all time. This one won't be easy to outrun. My initial concern as the police chief is public safety. Then we have the reputation and integrity of the department to consider."

He fixed his gaze on Lukas.

"What about leads? Progress?"

"We have forensic evidence that's being processed, but it takes time. We have a description of a suspect vehicle. The new murder last night may turn up some additional leads as well."

"So, you're not really making any progress, are you?"

Neither Lukas nor Brooke said a word.

"We need more people," Brooke said. "We need more boots on the ground."

"Done. I'll talk it over with Chief McConnell, and we'll get a plain-clothes task force together that will be at your disposal. Use them as you see fit. You'll have anything you need from this point forward. But understand this – I need to see some results. Otherwise, heads will start to roll, and I don't think I need to explain to either of you which direction shit flows. I want written daily updates on the progress of the investigation from you, Captain Hunter. Normally, I'd just ask for a briefing, but at this point, I want it in writing."

"Yes, sir."

"Get out of here. Go catch this psychopath." Chief Armstrong dismissed them with a jerk of his head.

After the meeting, Lukas and Brooke headed to the medical examiner's office to sit in on Razzy's autopsy. Lukas knew it would be tough. He was about to hit the call button to announce their arrival to the ME's receptionist when Brooke's hand stopped him. She gave his arm a slight squeeze.

"You don't have to do this, you know," Brooke said. "I can handle it. Why don't you go canvass the neighborhood again?"

"I have to do this. It's not something I'd expect anyone to understand. And after this, I need to talk to Timmy. I doubt he's been told yet, and I'd rather he hears it from me than from a stranger."

"Okay, but I'll pick up the slack if you need to step away."

"I know. Thanks."

He hit the call button, and they were immediately admitted to the building. Odessa McCabe met them in the front lobby. She led them into Dr. Benjamin Franks's office. They all sat down for a short briefing before the grisly work began.

"Thanks for letting us sit in today, Doc," Lukas said.

"Always glad to have you, Lukas, you know that. And your partner is?"

"Detective Brooke Stevens from Kingsport."

The doctor shook Brooke's hand.

"I've completed a preliminary examination of Miss Raznovich. The forensics and toxicology will take some time, of course. There's one glaring difference from the other killings. This woman was brutally sodomized."

Lukas tensed.

"Semen was found in the anal canal. It's the first body fluid we've found on one of the victims. Now, assuming the recovered semen is from the killer, we may have a solid lead. But, considering her profession…" His voice trailed off.

"The mutilation and violence. What do you think they mean?" Lukas asked.

"I'm not a psychiatrist, but it seems pretty obvious that he's finding it harder and harder to get a thrill. I've worked in Miami, Dallas and Boston, and I've seen serial killer cases. I don't remember one going so far off the rails this quickly."

"What's the earliest we can expect the results back on the semen?" Lukas said, leaning forward.

"We put an emergency rush on it, so, two, maybe three days." He looked at each of them. "Okay, are we ready to go do this?"

"Let's go," Lukas said, standing up. His jaw tightened involuntarily. He braced himself, trying to prepare for what he knew would be gruesome.

Lukas had been present during autopsies before, and they never really got any easier. It was even harder when you knew the person the doctor was dissecting. The ME went through a precise routine, measuring and weighing organs, taking notes of wounds and disease, recording his findings. It took him an hour-and-a-half to finish. Lukas and Brooke learned that Odessa's assessment of the time of death had been on point. Dr. Franks said Razzy had been dead between two and three hours when she was found. The cause of death, to nobody's surprise, was due to blood loss from the cut to Razzy's neck. According to the doctor, the killer used an extremely sharp, edged weapon, most likely a knife.

She had serious bruises on all her limbs and several on her torso. She'd been sexually assaulted with a wooden instrument, maybe a broomstick or an old baseball bat.

Dr. Franks removed splinters of wood from her vagina and anus. There was severe tearing in both areas. The one thing that gave Lukas some comfort was that Razzy also had a severe skull fracture. She may very well have been unconscious during the worst of the attack. The big finding, though, was the semen.

Maybe the killer had finally lost control, Lukas thought. Maybe they finally had the break they'd been waiting for.

CHAPTER TWELVE

The air had turned cooler when Brooke walked out of the medical examiner's office with Lukas beside her. It felt good on her skin after being in the claustrophobic and stuffy confines of the autopsy room. She'd driven from the station, and they sat in her car for a short time, silent, with Brooke waiting for Lukas to speak. Finally, when it became apparent he wasn't going to, she said, "Are you okay?"

"It wasn't as bad as I thought it would be. I think maybe I'm starting to compartmentalize things, become numb. Maybe that happens when you see someone you know and care for brutalized the way Razzy was."

"It's a defense mechanism," Brooke said. "Part of the job."

"And now it's about to get worse. I have to go tell Timmy."

"Where is he now?"

"There's a teacher at his school who's a temporary foster care provider. He's staying with her until the Department of Children's Services can make more permanent arrangements. I reached out to DCS this morning since we haven't been able to find any family. Razzy was all he had."

"Are you sure you're up to telling him?"

"No, but I have to."

Several more seconds of silence followed. Brooke hated to press, but he was so closed off. She knew she'd want a friend with her if she were in his place. She glanced at him.

"Do you want to do it alone? Or could you use some backup?"

"I think I definitely need some backup. Would you mind?"

"Not at all. Are you ready?"

"Let's go."

***

Lukas directed Brooke to a house in a middle-class neighborhood located in the central part of town. The lawn was perfectly manicured, and the landscaping was beautiful, even in November. Lukas could feel Brooke's eyes on him as he took a deep breath and let it out slowly. He looked at the piece of paper the address was written on and matched it to the house.

"Let's do this," he said.

"Do you want me to wait in the car?"

"No, come with me."

Lukas picked up a bag from a sporting goods store that he'd brought with him from the station. He and Brooke walked up the long sidewalk toward the front porch, but before they could ring the doorbell, the door opened and a pleasant looking female who appeared to be in her forties came out to greet them.

"Hello," she said. "May I help you?"

"I'm Detective Lukas Miller, and this is Detective Brooke Stevens. We're here to talk to Timmy."

Before the lady could reply, Lukas heard footsteps. The voice of a young boy cried out, "Coach! Hey! What's up?"

Timmy looked exactly like his mother, except he had blond hair where his mother's was auburn. He was a little undersized for ten years old, but Lukas had seen him compete with boys much bigger because of his athleticism.

"Wait a minute, Coach. I'll be right back," he said. He disappeared back into the house.

Mrs. Clay waited until Timmy was out of earshot and told them that he seemed to be doing well, but that he kept asking when his mother would be out of the hospital. Timmy returned less than a minute later holding a baseball and two gloves. "I want to show you how much harder I can throw, Coach."

"I brought you a new glove," Lukas said, pulling one out of the bag he'd carried from the car.

"Wow, cool. Thanks, Coach."

"Okay, my man. Let's go out in the yard so you can show me what you've got."

"I'll be pitching for you next year," Timmy said, racing ahead of them onto the front lawn. Lukas jogged out after Timmy.

The next few minutes were filled with baseball talk and with Lukas praising Timmy for the hard work he'd obviously put in. *They obviously care for each other*, Brooke thought to herself. The crisp air was filled with the steady sounds of the ball smacking leather. After several throws, Lukas asked Timmy to come over to the steps and sit with him. Brooke stood in front of them a few feet away and listened.

"Timmy, remember when I started coaching you, how I told you sometimes we have to be strong and tough? Like the time you got hit by that fastball?"

The boy grimaced. "Sure, that hurt."

"I know it did. And sometimes, baseball is like life. Sometimes in life we have to be strong and tough. I need to talk to you about something, and I'm going to need you be strong, okay?"

"Sure, Coach, I will."

"It's about your mom, Timmy."

"Yeah, she's in the hospital right now. That's why I'm staying with Mrs. Clay."

"Timmy, your mom *was* in the hospital. But now she's gone to Heaven."

Timmy searched Lukas's face. "You mean she's dead?" Brooke felt tears well up in her eyes. The boy was barely able to hold it together. His face went pale, and he was shaking.

"I'm so sorry, Timmy, she's gone." Timmy lunged at Lukas, throwing his arms around his neck. He began to sob uncontrollably. Brooke could see Lukas was struggling to maintain his composure, too. Lukas held the boy, comforting him.

The crying eventually stopped, but Timmy remained in Lukas's arms, trembling, staring into nothing. He finally raised his head, looked at Lukas, and said, "I need to be strong, right Coach?"

"It's okay to be sad, but yes, you'll have to be strong. You'll get to see her again. We'll all join her one day. Your mom just left us earlier than we would have liked. But I know she would want you to be strong, just like she was. I'll help get you through this. We'll get through it together."

"Will you still come visit me and take me to practice and the games like you did before?"

"Of course I will. That's what friends do, right?"

"Right."

"Here's a card with all my phone numbers on it. If you need anything, all you need to do is call. Okay?"

"Okay."

"Tell you what. I'm really busy right now, but hopefully this weekend I'll have some free time. How about we go down to the field and work on that fastball of yours some more? How does that sound?"

"Yeah," he said, wiping tears from his face.

"Good. Now let's get you inside so Mrs. Clay won't worry about you."

Timmy nodded. He was halfway back up the stairs before turning. "Oh, and thanks again for the new glove."

"You're welcome, bud."

Mrs. Clay had returned and opened the door. Brooke saw that her eyes were red, but she was holding it together for the sake of the boy. She ushered Timmy into the house and clutched the gloves and ball Lukas handed her.

"It's going to be hard on the little guy," she said to Lukas and Brooke. "I'm not sure where we go from here."

"I know," Lukas said. "If there's anything at all you need, call me." Lukas handed her his card. "Timmy already has all these numbers, but I want you to feel free to get in touch, too. Any time. Anything. I mean it."

"I will. And thank you both."

When they reached the car, Lukas spoke first.

"That was one of the hardest things I've ever done in my life." "You did fine, Lukas. You did great."

Lukas nodded slightly and retreated into silence for most of the drive back to the station.

Before they got back downtown, Brooke looked at her watch. "I need to get back over to Kingsport and talk to some of the hookers. I'd like to make contact with that other pimp, Draxton Little, but I'm not sure he'll talk to me."

"I'm going to go back to the scene at the mayor's house to do another canvass. They didn't turn up much last night. I feel like I have to keep at it."

"Okay, I'll catch up with you later. I'll let you know what the chief's got lined up on the task force."

"Thanks for going with me," Lukas said. "Thanks for being there when I needed somebody I could trust."

"So, you trust me now?" she said.

"Isn't that what partners are supposed to do?" he said.

Brooke nodded and smiled. She was pleased to see Lukas offer a warm smile of his own. "It is," she said. "Trust is the most important thing."

CHAPTER THIRTEEN

ukas arrived at the mayor's house, got out of his car, and looked around. The scene had long since been cleared. The only remnant was the yellow police line tape, fluttering in the faint breeze. He'd decided he would start with a sweep of the area. It wasn't that he didn't trust his fellow detectives or crime scene techs. They were all competent. But another pass through the neighborhood couldn't hurt. It was, after all, customary to re-examine the scene in most murder cases.

After three failed attempts at contacting the neighbors close to the mayor's home, he knocked on a door a couple of houses down from where the body was found and was surprised when an elderly lady opened the door.

"Good afternoon, ma'am. I'm Detective Lukas Miller from the police department, and I was wondering if I could have a few minutes of your time concerning the events that took place last night here in the neighborhood."

"Glad to meet you," she said. "I'm Edith Owens. You must be talking about that young lady who was found in the mayor's driveway." She chuckled. "I bet that put a little hitch in the giddyap of the ol' high and mighty."

Lukas looked at her curiously. What a strange thing to say.

She must have realized how she sounded, because her face flushed. "I'm sorry. I don't mean any disrespect to the young lady who was killed. Please forgive me."

Lukas let it go. So, she didn't like the mayor. Big deal.

"No problem," Lukas said. "Did you see or hear anything out of the ordinary?"

"I was going to call your detective division after I watched the news this morning. I just haven't gotten around to it yet. Look at me being rude. Please come in, young man. It's a little warmer in here." She turned and walked into the den. "I was outside last night looking for a lens that fell out of my glasses yesterday evening when I got home from the grocery store. I looked for it when it fell out, but I couldn't find it in the sunlight, so I thought if I went out in the dark with a flashlight, I might get a reflection and find it. So, there I was, squatted down out there with the light to the ground behind the hedge, looking for the lens when I heard a car pull up. I looked over the hedge and saw a man get out of the driver's side of the car and walk back toward the trunk. He opened the trunk, picked up something and threw it over his shoulder. Then he walked up the street, but I didn't see where he went because I went back to looking for the lens.

"But he walked toward the mayor's house?"

"He did."

"Did you get a look at the car?"

"I saw it, but I didn't pay much attention to it."

"Do you know what color it was?"

"I couldn't tell for sure. Maybe red? I've been on the city about replacing that street light out there – some kids broke it out – but so far, they haven't seen fit to fix it. If old high-and-mighty had called, it would have been working before he got off the phone with them. Anyway, I think the car was red, but I'm not sure."

"Make or model?"

She shook her head. "It wasn't a compact car, but it wasn't like a Cadillac, either. Mid-sized I guess."

"What about the man? What did he look like?"

"He was a black man, middle-aged, but I didn't pay that much attention."

"Are you sure about that? That he was black?"

"Absolutely. One hundred percent."

"How?"

"Because as he came around to the trunk where the package was, a car came up the street, and he looked directly into the headlights. There's no doubt in my mind about him being a black man. I thought he was just dropping something off to one of the neighbors. It didn't seem suspicious at the time. That's why I didn't pay much attention."

"Did anyone, police or otherwise, talk to you last night?"

"Someone knocked on the door and rang the bell, but I didn't answer. I stayed in with the lights off. I'm a widow, and I don't open the door after dark. That's why I was going to call today."

"What did the package he was carrying look like?"

The woman closed her eyes as she thought, "It looked like a rolled-up rug."

"Have you talked to any of the other neighbors about this?"

"No, I got up this morning, turned on the news, and saw what they were reporting. That's when I realized what had happened. By then everyone was gone to work."

Lukas handed her his card. "Thank you, Ms. Owens. If you think of anything else, please give me a call."

"I will."

Lukas left Ms. Owens and stood on the sidewalk looking at the area where she said the car was parked. She seemed like a credible witness. He walked up the sidewalk to the mayor's house and knocked on the door. A woman Lukas recognized as the mayor's wife, a pretty woman in her mid-thirties, answered the door wearing a dark blue dress. She had her keys and purse in her hands.

"I'm Detective Miller, Mrs. Pennington, and I'm working the homicides that have occurred recently. Would you mind if I looked around the outside of the house?"

"No, absolutely not. Be my guest. I was about to leave. Will that be a problem?"

"No, I won't be long."

"Take all the time you need."

Lukas looked around the front yard and driveway but, as he expected, found nothing. The killer had left nothing but Razzy's body at the scene.

He left feeling a bit more optimistic than before. A black man driving what might be a red car. He phoned Brooke to tell her about the new lead. The call went to voice mail, so he left a short message with the details and called Odessa McCabe to see if the results were in on the semen. They weren't, of course. There was nothing left to do but take care of paperwork.

Thirty minutes later, he sat at his desk and entered his notes on the autopsy, the death notification to Timmy, and the new canvass. He again looked over the notes taken last night by the various detectives who were on the scene to make sure he hadn't missed anything. Barking dogs, a car door shutting. Those were the highlights of the previous night's canvass. No witnesses other than Ms. Owens.

An African-American male as a serial killer? Lukas knew there'd been dozens of them in America. For some reason, they didn't get the same publicity as John Gacy and Ted Bundy and Jeffrey Dahmer, but there had been several. Carl Eugene Watts, AKA the Sunday Morning Slasher, was suspected of killing more than a hundred white women before he was captured, so it wasn't as though black serial killers were an anomaly. Lukas needed to follow the leads, and this lead was the best he had thus far. Still, he couldn't shake a nagging feeling that two plus two was coming up five. He couldn't say exactly why, but he just didn't think this killer was black.

Lukas picked up the phone and dialed the number of an old friend.

"What gives, Lukas?"

"Hey Danny, are you still working domestic terrorism?"

"Of course. Seventeen years since nine-eleven, and most of our people are still focusing on domestic terrorism. Can you give me something to do to get me out of here?"

Lukas was speaking to Assistant Special Agent In Charge Danny Smart, who worked out of the Johnson City FBI field office. Smart had done some work with the FBI's Behavioral Science Unit at Quantico but was now an ASAIC in Johnson City. Lukas knew there must have been a bump in the road somewhere in Smart's career for him to wind up in the heart of Appalachia, but he'd never asked, and Smart had never offered. They were old friends, having met originally in Afghanistan, where Smart was an FBI liaison and Lukas was a para-rescueman. Lukas had been amazed to learn that Smart had landed in the Johnson City office several years later. Small world, indeed.

"I might be able to give you an interesting distraction," Lukas said.

"Something to do with the murders I've been reading about? How many now? Five?"

"Yes and yes, if you count the two in Kingsport."

"How do you like the woman?"

"She's okay, man. She's sharp."

"Unusual for them to put the two of you together."

"Desperate times call for desperate measures. Listen, speaking of desperate times, I was wondering if you'd work me up a quick profile."

"Come on, Lukas. I'd need a lot of information. Everything you have. And we'd have to make it official, which would mean the bureau would wind up in the middle of your case. Do you want that?"

"No. I want a favor from an old friend."

"So, you want this on the down low."

"I want it underground."

"What's in it for me?"

"How about a steak dinner at the Peerless?"

"Sold. I'm a sucker for a T-bone."

"I'll swing by, say four-ish? What do you need?"

"Just bring me all you can."

"You got it."

Lukas breathed a sigh of relief. Smart might not be able to help, but then again, he might come up with something that would break the case.

Smart had tried to get Lukas to apply to the FBI back when they met, but at the time, Lukas wanted a career as a pararescueman. He loved everything about the job. All of that ended with a bar fight in Anchorage, Alaska, thirty days after Lukas's older brother, Ben, who was a member of the Marine's Special Operations Command and whom Lukas idolized, died when the helicopter he was riding in crashed into the Gulf of Mexico near Homestead Air Reserve Base, Florida, during a training exercise. Funny how the world works, Lukas thought. You serve your country in a combat zone, fight the enemy, then end up being run out of the service because a drunk starts a fight in a bar and gets his ass whipped. Lukas had also had a bit too much to drink. He didn't start the fight, but he'd certainly ended it. Unfortunately for Lukas, the fight also ended his career in the Air Force.

Despite having been decorated and having an impeccable record up to that point, his commanding officers did not take kindly to one of their enlisted men putting an American civilian – even a drunk American civilian – in the hospital for three weeks. At least he didn't get a bad conduct or a dishonorable discharge. Either one would have been disastrous. They simply told him he was leaving and gave him an honorable discharge. There was no mention of the fight in any of his separation papers. His commanding officer thanked Lukas for his service and unceremoniously sent him on his way.

Lukas made electronic copies of everything in his file, downloaded them onto a jump drive, and arrived at the FBI office more than fifteen minutes early for the meeting with Danny Smart. He was antsy. Smart looked him over with a critical eye. "You look like shit."

"I feel it, too. Be nice to have a cushy FBI gig."

"You could have," Danny reminded him. "Still could."

"Hell, I won't even have a career with the JCPD if I can't put this thing to bed. I need you to rush this and do me a solid."

Lukas took several minutes going over the details with Smart.

"What's your instinct tell you?" Danny said.

"I don't know. My instincts are usually pretty solid, but I'm up in the air on this case. That's why I'm here. One thing I have is that I think he's trying to tell some kind of story by the way he's disposing of and display-ing the bodies. I can't tell you exactly what the story is, though. And the latest murder really has me stumped."

"Different?"

"More violent for one thing. And the body was placed in the mayor's driveway."

"Yeah, I heard," Danny said, shaking his head. "That's a little over the top."

"That's not all," Lukas said. "I had a personal connection with the victim."

"And the plot thickens. What kind of a connection?"

"I arrested her once, she provided information to me from time to time, and her son is on my baseball team."

"Interesting. I need to look at your file."

"The other thing is that we have a witness who saw a black man pull a rug out of the trunk of a car near where our latest body was found, but I just don't feel this guy being black. Can't explain that, either. I just don't make him for a black guy."

"All right," Smart said. "I'll look the file over and see if anything jumps out."

Lukas's phone buzzed, and he looked at the screen. It was a short text from Brooke asking for a call back when he had time. He stuck the phone into his pocket and looked back at Danny.

"I'll get something out to you as soon as I can," Danny said.

"I hate to be pushy, but..." Lukas hoped he didn't come off as too overbearing.

"I'm sure the brass is up your ass. I get it. Don't worry."

"Thanks, man. We can use all the help we can get. Even if it's from a Fed."

Danny gave him a friendly smile. "You can get out of my office now."

CHAPTER FOURTEEN

Lukas was at his desk before eight the next morning, checking the tip lines to see if any information had come in overnight. There was no mention of the murders. There were, however, several complaints about speeders and loud parties. Morons. He looked at the field interview reports submitted by beat cops to see if there was any information that might reveal a lead, but there was nothing there, either.

He turned away from the computer and noticed a message he'd missed on a pink sticky note. A woman identifying herself as Claire Andrews had called. She was the mother of his first victim, Jamika Bradley. He had talked to her briefly the night Jamika was murdered. The note said that she had found something that may be of some use. He picked up his desk phone and called the number Claire Andrews had left. She said that she stumbled across something that might be worth a look. He told her he'd be there within the hour. He grabbed his keys and headed for the door just as his phone buzzed. Brooke. She said they were a little light on females for the sting they were planning and encouraged him to get as many female officers as possible. He told her he hoped to hear something more on his end about the task force later that night.

Twenty minutes later, Lukas arrived at Claire Andrews's home. There were crooked numbers on the faded column that was barely holding up the roof that hung over the porch. He knocked on the door, remembering that the doorbell didn't work. After two rounds of knocks, the door opened, and a middle-aged, black lady wearing a housecoat that looked as old as she was opened the door.

"It's good to see you again, Detective Miller," she said as she waved him into the house.

He stepped into a tidy living room with modest furnishings. Pictures hung on the walls, neatly arranged. They reflected Jamika's life, from infancy to high school. Lukas remembered how surprised he'd been at how orderly the house was, given its outside appearance.

"It's hard to believe that's my Jamika," the woman said from behind Lukas. "I did my best for her, but once she got on the drugs, she just went downhill. Can I get you something to drink, officer?"

"No thank you, ma'am," he said. "I appreciate you contacting us. Your message said you found something?"

"I don't know how much this will help, but…" Her voice faded as she stepped into an adjoining room. She emerged a short time later holding a small worn notebook with flowers on the cover.

"I was looking through her things after she was, you know, gone, and I found this. I flipped to the end and noticed the last entry was on the day she was killed." She pointed to the entry.

"*Meeting RO.*"

"Do you have any idea what this means, or who 'RO' is?"

"I stayed out of her business. The less I knew, the better."

"Can I keep this?"

"Be my guest. I was going to throw it out anyway. Like I said, I don't know how much it will help, if it helps at all."

"Thanks, Mrs. Andrews, and I'm sorry for your loss."

"When you find the man who killed my girl, will you call me?"

"I will."

Lukas went back to the station and logged the notebook into the case file as evidence. He checked his messages. There was a message from Captain Hunter detailing the names of the detectives he had allocated for the hooker sting. He picked up his cell phone and dialed Brooke.

"Hey Lukas. How'd the lead go?"

"Do the letters 'R.O.' mean anything to you? They appear to be initials."

"Not that I can think of. What's the context?"

Lukas told her about the meeting with the victim's mother and the diary entry.

"Could it be a new pimp?" Brooke said after a pause.

"Anything's possible. Hold on one second." He unlocked his computer screen and searched the database for persons known to be pimps in the area. "Nobody with those initials shows up here."

Lukas could hear key strokes on Brooke's end. "Same here."

"Ah, it may be nothing. But I'll look through my case files and see if there's any mention of anyone with those initials."

"I'll do the same," Brooke said.

"Thanks. Oh, I almost forgot. I got four people for the sting. Two women."

"So that's seven total, three women. We need one more girl. Any chance you have any probies that could help us out over there?"

Lukas silently ticked off the number of probationary officers that hadn't been on the street long enough to develop a police identity. "Might be a couple in the department we could use."

"You know what?" Brooke said. "On second thought, never mind. I'll do it."

"You'll do what?"

"I'll do the sting."

"You mean you'll be a hooker? I mean, you know what I mean."

"Sure, and you can be my pimp."

Lukas laughed. "When do you want to do it?"

"We'll need some time to get things lined up. How about Friday night?"

Lukas took a quick look at his calendar to make sure there were no conflicts. "Friday's good for me."

"Friday night, then. Have your people meet us at headquarters in Kingsport, and we'll finalize the assignments."

"I'll get the word out. Talk to you later."

Lukas hung up feeling a little more hopeful. He sat in front of the computer thinking about the initials. Or was it an acronym? It could be anything. Another very small lead. But many small leads often led to a break. Eventually. Maybe Friday would bring their killer out of the darkness and put them on the offensive for a change.

CHAPTER FIFTEEN

Lukas showered and dressed in jeans, a plain, navy-blue hooded sweatshirt over a tactical shirt, and his favorite pair of Merrells. He checked the magazines on his Sig Sauer and Glock 42 back-up, stuffed his badge and handcuffs into his black go-bag, and grabbed his Kevlar vest and keys on the way out.

The late afternoon Friday traffic would be bad, so he decided against a direct route. Instead, he took State Route 36. It was a little longer drive than using the interstate, but it would take less time on a Friday at rush hour. Lukas drove with the window down, allowing the fresh air to circulate through the car and invigorate him. This time of year always brought back fond memories of playing football in high school. Those cool October and November nights seemed so far away, but he still enjoyed thinking back.

Lukas's mind turned to the present, which was far more tumultuous than those Friday nights so long ago. He was excited about tonight. He actually had a few butterflies in his stomach. He walked into the conference room at police headquarters in Kingsport right at 6:00 p.m. All the task force members were there milling around getting to know one another. The women who would be the stars of the show were dressed in gaudy hooker outfits. A table at the rear of the room contained equipment that would be used during the sting.

Lukas looked at the clock on the wall and wondered where Brooke was. He slid his cell phone out of his pocket to call her when a sudden hush came over the room. It was as if everyone hit their mute button at the same time. Lukas looked up from the phone and saw stunned looks on all the faces, especially the men's. He turned and realized Brooke was standing in the doorway talking on her cell phone. She was wearing a black leather mini-skirt with black, fishnet hose, four-inch stiletto heels, and a red, skimpy mohair sweater with a neckline that plunged nearly to the middle of her chest, revealing a hot pink bra and ample cleavage. Her hair was loosely curled and seductively pulled back and tied with a pink bow. She had applied her make-up and lipstick thick and heavy. Hooker heavy.

She put away the phone and looked disapprovingly at her admirers.

"Let's get started," Brooke said.

But her co-workers were not letting her get by that easily. The catcalls started. The other women didn't participate in the jokes, and Lukas thought he noticed genuine jealousy on their faces. He understood why. When the room quieted down enough, Brooke and Lukas took center stage for the briefing. Lukas noticed that nobody was looking at him.

"First, I want to thank everyone for volunteering to help us," Brooke said. "Hopefully, we won't have to do this for very long, and you guys can get back to your regular duties."

"Uh, excuse me ma'am, but how much do you charge?"

An officer who looked like a homeless man, obviously a vice cop, had yelled the question from the back of the room. Laughter ensued. Brooke's eyes met Lukas's, and he thought he saw a flash of embarrassment. She recovered and continued.

"Remember why we're here," she said. "We'll be working a couple of hotels on Stone Drive that are known for prostitution. We're looking for a red car – unknown make or model – that may be occupied by a black male. I know it isn't much. Just be vigilant and report anything suspicious, no matter how small or insignificant it may seem. This is primarily a recon assignment, but if we develop any leads, we'll follow them. Ladies make sure you stay in close contact with your handlers. They're your lifeline out there. And handlers, stay close enough to be able to act quickly should the situation demand it. We'll be working off tactical channel two. Ladies make sure you get your wires and have your handlers assist you with them. Grab your radios on your way out. Most importantly? Stay safe out there."

After everyone filed out, Lukas took a wire from the table and began helping fit it to Brooke's outfit. The job brought Lukas into close proximity to some parts of her body that made him feel a bit uneasy. Brooke didn't seem to notice, though, and she certainly didn't seem to mind. As he was finalizing the job and attempting to attach the microphone to the underside of her bra, Lukas heard a low whistle followed by, "Lucky dog."

Lukas looked up at Brooke. "Ignore them," she said, smiling. "You'd think they'd never seen a hooker before."

He smiled back. "Not one that looks like you."

"Was that a compliment?"

"I believe it was."

"Thank you, Detective Miller."

"You're welcome."

As soon as they were finished, everyone headed out, much more somber than they had been at the precinct. The seriousness of the task at hand seemed to settle heavily over the whole crew. It was go time.

Lukas drove to Stone Drive while Brooke navigated. She directed him to a corner of the parking lot of a hotel frequently worked by the prostitutes in her city. The place was a dump, and many of the security lights weren't working. But there was enough light for a potential john to cruise through and notice her. Brooke got out of the car and walked away. Lukas made sure the wire was working and completed a communications check. Then he called her cell phone and adjusted the microphone to increase voice clarity.

"I need you to pick a code word or phrase," Lukas said.

"Let's make it 'big boy,'" she said seductively.

"Got it. If anything goes wrong, or if you feel you've been compromised or are in danger in any way, say those two words. I'll be there in a flash. And remember, once we're off the cell phone, I can hear you, but you can't hear me. We can text, though. So, keep your phone handy."

"I got it. I'm not a rookie, you know."

"You mean you've been a hooker before?"

"No, wise ass. I've done stings before."

"Roger that. I just want to make sure we're on the same page. Remember, any problems at all, you say the words."

"Got it."

"All right. Go live. I'm listening."

Lukas sat in the car, watched from across the lot, and listened to the wire. He could hear her clothing brushing against the microphone and the steady click, click of the heels as she walked. When she stood still, he could hear the night sounds. Sometimes she would talk to herself, momentarily forgetting she was wired. She would comment to Lukas to disregard this or that. If she found a potential customer, she would describe the car and the situation and Lukas would jot down notes. The whole session was being recorded, but notes often came in handy since it sometimes took days to get the recordings transcribed.

Lukas also kept an ear to the radio to see if the other teams were having any luck. The first hour was slow. After a short bathroom break, Brooke was back out on the lot. Lukas heard some chatter about a red Ford Mustang, but one of the other teams called it maroon. It could be the same car based on the loose description.

Well into the second hour, word must have gotten out that at least some of the girls were back in action, because the radio chatter picked up considerably. Brooke's parking lot remained relatively quiet. Lukas wondered to himself if maybe Brooke looked a little too good. She damned sure didn't look like a crack whore or a meth addict. She might be scaring off their killer, who had to be smart enough to realize that if something seemed too good to be true, it probably was. His thoughts were interrupted by Brooke's voice over the wire.

"I've got a red Ford Mustang. It's been around once, and I think it'll be back."

Lukas refrained from texting her. A couple of minutes later, she spoke again: "He's coming back around, slower this time. I'm going to ease out a little farther and see if I can get a look at him."

Before Lukas could text, he heard Brooke on the wire.

"I spooked him. Damn it."

Lukas could hear the frustration in her voice. Another two minutes passed. "Wait," Brooke said. "He's creeping back around. What's up with this guy?"

Lukas texted, "*B patient stay where u r. He is testing u.*"

"Okay, standing by. He's parking now. About fifty yards out."

"*STAY PUT.*"

"Okay, I'll just walk around a little," she said, and Lukas heard the stilettos again. "He's moving again, headed this way."

The faint sound of a car engine emerged in the distance on the wire.

"Hey there, sweetie." It was Brooke's voice. "Looking to party?"

The tenor in her voice had changed. She was talking to the john. Lukas could see them. He saw the car door open and a man begin to climb out. He heard a voice that was indiscernible.

"Oh, really?" Brooke said. "Well, let's see what we can do, honey. What'd you have in mind?"

"I'll tell you what you can do," the man's voice said.

"What's that, sexy?"

"As a matter of fact, I'll *show* you what you're gonna do." The voice was forceful, and Lukas tensed.

"Excuse me?" Brooke answered. She didn't sound as confident as before.

"How about you do this?"

Lukas heard fabric rustle and hesitated. She hadn't said the code words, and he didn't want to blow the operation. But a moment later, he knew Brooke was in trouble.

"Get your hands off me! Stop."

Lukas started the car and slammed it into drive. He could see them struggling. The man had Brooke bent over the hood of his car and was standing behind and almost on top of her. Her top had been partially torn off, and her left breast was exposed and being groped by the assailant. His right arm was across the back of her neck, and her face was being pushed into the hood of the car.

Lukas screeched to a halt, jumped out of the car and hit the man with a flying shoulder check, knocking him off Brooke and flat on his back. The man writhed on the ground, clearly out of breath and incapacitated. Lukas turned his attention to Brooke, who'd also been knocked to the ground. She had a dazed look on her face as he helped her to her feet.

She was a mess. She didn't seem to realize that her breast was exposed or that a small stream of blood was running down her chest. The pink ribbon that had been used to bind her hair was hanging haphazardly at the back of her head. The look on her face suddenly changed to embarrassed fury as she noticed the condition of her sweater and bra. She covered herself as Lukas reached for a handkerchief in his pocket and handed it to Brooke to help her stop the bleeding.

"You okay?"

She nodded, not speaking. Lukas took his sweatshirt off and helped Brooke put it on. As the shirt cleared her face, her eyes widened. She pushed Lukas to the side.

"Look out!"

A flash in his peripheral vision had him throwing up his arm in reflex. But he couldn't escape the blow. A searing pain hit his right arm at the shoulder. He spun quickly and hit the man with a left cross, knocking him out cold. The knife fell straight down, and Lukas thought he heard some teeth rattle on the pavement near his feet when the man hit the pavement for the second time.

Almost as soon as the man was on the ground, Brooke, who had regained some of her composure, had her handcuffs out. She slapped the cuffs on the unconscious man.

Lukas staggered and clutched at his shoulder. A burning pain radiated from the site of the wound down his arm and into his right hand. He felt as though his whole arm was on fire. His time as a pararescueman had taught him the process of tending to all manner of wounds, and he knew the first step was assessment. He found his balance and rolled up his tactical shirt. The wound was deep and bleeding badly. The first order of business was to get the bleeding stopped.

Brooke had finished with the assailant and was now standing next to Lukas. He let her inspect it.

"It's pretty deep," she said. She took the handkerchief he had given her earlier out from under her shirt and placed it directly on the wound. "There. Hold that."

Lukas applied pressure. Brooke gave him a gentle pat, kicked off her stiletto heels, and pointed toward the handcuffed assailant. "Watch him."

She ran quickly to Lukas's car. He could hear her summoning the other officers. Two of them arrived within minutes.

Time seemed to thicken and slow down for Lukas. The effort of applying pressure to his shoulder was wearing on him. He was losing blood quickly. Brooke helped him into the car. Lukas heard a voice ask what had happened, and Brooke told him to hold the scene and she would explain later.

She got behind the wheel and started weaving through traffic at break-neck speed, and time suddenly revved right back up for Lukas.

"Keep pressure on that wound," Brooke said.

They zigged and zagged between cars with the lights flashing and the siren and horn blaring. The woman could drive, Lukas had to admit. Five minutes later, they pulled up to the emergency entrance at Kingsport Memorial Hospital.

Lukas tried to open the car door, but a rush of dizziness overwhelmed him. He knew the loss of blood was taking its toll. Brooke helped him to the entrance and announced in a loud voice that she had a wounded officer. The effect was immediate. Several nurses assisted

Lukas to a stretcher and rolled him into a trauma room. The world was starting to swirl. Lukas opened his eyes wide attempting to maintain consciousness.

The last thing he saw was Brooke standing in the corner of the room biting her fingernails nervously.

CHAPTER SIXTEEN

Lukas awoke to bright lights and a leathery-faced doctor who looked and smelled like he didn't follow the American Medical Association's advice about smoking cigarettes.

"How are you feeling, detective?" the doctor said.

"I've felt better. How bad is it?"

"We stitched it up and got some blood in you. No arteries or bones were damaged, just muscle. You'll be out of service for a few days, and it'll hurt like hell." He checked something on the chart and looked up. "You'll be sore, too, and you'll need to keep the wound clean and change the dressing often. But, all in all, I'd say you were lucky. It could have been a lot worse."

"How's the other detective who came in with me?"

"She's fine. A small cut on her chest, some bruises and abrasions, but otherwise fine. You'll both be discharged as soon as the paperwork is done."

He dropped the clipboard into the bin at the foot of the bed and left.

Lukas laid his head back on the pillow. He'd barely closed his eyes before the scraping metal sound of someone sliding the curtained petition brought him to attention. He looked over and saw Brooke standing there watching him. She was wearing blue scrubs and slippers.

"How are you feeling, cowboy?"

"Oh, you know. Just another day on the range."

"They said 18 stitches."

"Did you watch?"

"No, they were working on me." The conversation was interrupted by the sound of Captain Hunter arguing with a nurse outside the curtained room. He won the disagreement and stormed into the room.

"Well, aren't you two a sight?" His gaze encompassed them both, and he narrowed his eyes. "What the hell happened out there?"

"The guy got a little out of hand, and we dealt with it," Lukas said.

"A little?"

Lukas didn't attempt to answer. The question was rhetorical. The captain was working up to a scolding.

"We have one officer battered and bruised," he said, pointing at Brooke, "and one with a severe stab wound. And the perp has a broken jaw and four missing teeth. You call that getting a little out of hand?"

"The guy got off easy. What's his story?"

"We've had him in the box since he woke up. He's not our killer."

"Are we sure?" Brooke broke in.

"Relatively. He gave us permission to search his residence, which turned out to be a hotel room. He's here on business. He's only been here since this morning. We double-checked with his employer."

"Maybe our killer is a traveling salesman," Lukas said.

"No criminal record," the captain said. "Wife and two kids in South Bend, Indiana."

"He went after Brooke hard and he stabbed me. He may not have a record, but he's definitely violent."

"We'll take a close look at him, but I don't think he's our man," Captain Hunter said.

Brooke's shoulders slumped.

The captain took a few steps forward and rested his hand on the edge of Lukas's bed. His tone softened.

"But he's facing charges of sexual assault, attempted murder, and two counts of aggravated assault on a police officer. So at least you took a violent sexual predator off the street. He might not be a serial killer, but you both did a good job. Lukas, take a few days, but get back as soon as you can. Brooke, your chief will be down soon to check on you."

He nodded at each of them and left. The room was much quieter in his wake. Brooke smiled.

"I thought he'd be more upset. Feel like taking a walk?"

"Not really, but why not? Where to?"

"Follow me." She led him out of the trauma rooms and turned left down the hall to the rear exit of the emergency rooms. They walked out of the building into a small courtyard and over to a wooden picnic table. Brooke sat down while Lukas stood for a minute and took in the cool night air. Looking back at Brooke, he noticed she was in the process of lighting a cigarette. Her gaze caught his.

"If you tell anyone about this, I'll kill you."

"What? That you're a closet smoker?"

"Exactly. If you value your life, you'll keep it to yourself."

She took a long drag, exhaled, and held up the cigarette. "It's not something I do often, but after the night we've had, I need one. There are only a handful of people who know about my dirty little secret. So, if it gets out, it'll be your ass."

"Your dirty little secret is safe with me. Don't worry." Lukas sat down beside Brooke, breathed deeply, and immediately regretted it. The doctor was right. He was going to be sore.

Brooke absentmindedly flicked ashes from the cigarette.

"Thank you, Lukas. You saved me from a serious situation tonight. Maybe saved my life. I let him get too close to me. I didn't think he'd… I messed up. If –"

"Hey, don't say another word. That's what partners do, right? We have each other's backs."

She smiled and took another drag. "Yes. Yes, we do."

"Speaking of thanks, you saved my ass, too," Lukas said. "If you hadn't pushed me, that knife would have caught me at the base of the neck."

"Don't say another word," she said. "That's what partners do, right? We have each other's backs."

He slid closer to her, put his good arm around her, and pulled her closer.

She didn't resist.

CHAPTER SEVENTEEN

Midway through the following afternoon, Brooke sat at her desk and concentrated on the reports from the previous night. She finished the suspect resistance report and moved on to entering the case notes. She checked the case files looking for any mention of the initials R.O. but found nothing of interest. She turned her attention to the red vehicle lead. She pulled the video from the convenience store where her first victim was found and cued it back to the approximate time the body would have been dumped, but she didn't find anything.

Leaning back in her chair, she stretched, feeling her stiff, sore muscles resist. The movement pulled at her chest, and a sharp pain made her catch her breath. She knew she was lucky. Aside from the cut on her chest and her bruised head, she felt fine. The soreness would dissipate. Her mental state, however, was a bit shakier.

She felt responsible for the whole mess. She should have realized the danger and used the code words that she and Lukas had agreed upon. But it all happened so fast. What could she have done differently? She could have recognized the danger more quickly. Had she done so, nobody would have been injured, except for maybe the perp. At least she'd recovered enough to help Lukas. She'd saved him from a more serious injury. She was sure of that.

She thought of sitting at the picnic table outside the emergency room. Lukas was badly injured, yet he was the one offering comfort. He didn't patronize her. He didn't blame her for anything. He was just there for her, and that was what she'd needed more than anything at that moment.

She turned her attention back to the report, which would require the records from last night. She had to go back to the hospital. She sighed, grabbed her coat, keys, and purse, and headed for the exit.

The drive to Kingsport Memorial was a short one. She waited in the lobby of the records department while a middle-aged clerk who looked like she would rather be anywhere but there made copies of the medical records and incident reports. She sent a quick one-line text to Lukas: *Checking on you.*

Getting the records took less time than she had thought, and she found herself back at the station within the hour. Brooke made her way through the squad room. For a Saturday, it was busy. A couple of uniforms were wandering around, as was her longtime friend and partner, Sam Browning.

Sam was near the end of his career, and it had been a productive one. He'd been good to Brooke. When the others made fun of her or doubted her, Sam stood by her. He'd taught her a lot about being a detective, and she was grateful. She'd miss him when he retired, but that didn't seem imminent. Nobody, including Sam, knew when he would hang it up.

Brooke tapped his shoulder. "Hey, Sam, did you get a call out?"

"Hey there, kid. No, I'm just going over some training material for a class I'm teaching next week. I heard you had quite a night last night. Are you okay?"

"A little sore and stiff, but I'm fine."

"You did good, young lady. Don't doubt it."

"I don't know. I feel like I should have done something different."

"That's normal. Every time we do something that doesn't end exactly like we think it should, we second guess ourselves. If you go home at the end of the shift to your little girl, that's a win. If you collar a bad guy in the process, that's a bonus, and that's what you did. You also may have saved that Miller guy's ass from what I heard."

"Well, he saved mine first."

"How's he doing?"

"Fine, I think. I've tried to call, but he isn't answering."

"He's probably sleeping. Can't blame him. I'll bet he'll be hungry when he wakes up."

Brooke looked at Sam. He was grinning mischievously.

"Don't go there, Sam. He's got a girlfriend."

"I didn't say you should ask him to marry you."

"I don't want to cause trouble."

"Does the girlfriend work? I'm just saying he may need a friend. He's your temporary partner until I get you back full-time. You should at least check on him."

"Maybe so. But I've got to pick Sierra up from my parents. I haven't seen much of her lately. I miss her."

"Okay, girl. I've got to run. Do you need anything?"

"I'm good. Thanks, Sam."

Brooke put the records in the case file book and looked over the reports from the other officers from the previous night. Overall, the operation was a bust as far as the murders were concerned. Sure, they got a predator off the streets, but the goal had been to get a lead on the murders, and that hadn't happened.

She looked at her phone again. No word from Lukas. She thought over what Sam had said.

What the hell. An hour later she pulled into the driveway of Lukas's house. It was a little after 6:00 p.m. She checked her makeup and hair in the mirror before walking the short distance to the door with a steaming hot pizza in one hand and a six pack of beer in the other. What cop could resist that? Lukas answered the door shirtless, wearing only a pair of blue sweat pants with a "U.S. Air Force" logo in white down the right leg.

"Oh, hey, Brooke." His face registered surprise.

"Hi, I thought you might be hungry. Can I come in? This pizza is burning my hand." She pushed through the door to find a surface for the hot pizza.

"Uh, sure."

Brooke set the pizza down and shook her singed hand. She wiped it on her jeans and turned to see a woman dressed in purple scrubs walk out of the kitchen. The woman was holding a fresh gauze bandage. They locked gazes, and the woman's dark brown eyes flashed. She swept her long, dark hair over her shoulder and stared at Lukas.

At first Brooke thought the voluptuous woman was a home nurse ordered by the department to assist Lukas with the wound dressing. But the temperature change in the room indicated otherwise. Brooke stood there with a six pack of beer in her right hand and looked back and forth between Lukas and the woman. *Shit. How do I get out of this gracefully?*

"Lukas?" The woman shifted her stance. "Who's this?"

"Oh, I'm sorry. Gabriele, this is Brooke. Brooke, Gabriele." Brooke realized she was still holding the beer. She set it down on the cluttered coffee table and walked over to shake Gabriele's hand.

"It's a pleasure to meet you. I'm sorry to intrude. I didn't mean to... I mean, I didn't know... I just thought I'd swing by and make sure he was still alive. Again, I'm sorry."

Brooke turned and started toward the door. "I'll talk to you later, Lukas."

"Nonsense." Gabriele flashed a smile that Brooke knew was fake. "I was just about to change his dressing, but I'm running late and since you're here, maybe you can do it?"

"Sure," Brooke said.

"I need to get back to the ER. Besides, I'm sure you two have a lot to discuss." She walked up to Lukas and gave him a quick kiss on the lips. "Call me later."

"Okay," he replied, his face betraying his discomfort. When the door closed behind Gabriele, there was a moment of silence. Brooke felt like she wanted to become one with the paint on the wall. She couldn't believe she was standing in Lukas's living room, having just chased his girlfriend off. And him shirtless no less.

Lukas walked over to the gauze and picked it up.

"Care to help?" He held up the bandage. "The one-armed man can't quite do this for himself."

"Lukas, I'm so sorry. I don't know if I've ever been so embarrassed. But I called, and you didn't answer. I was worried. I guess I know why you didn't answer now."

"Phone was dead. Forgot to charge it last night. It's charging now."

Brooke picked up the dressing as Lukas sat down in a kitchen chair. She started removing the old bandage from the wound.

"Sorry I invaded your Saturday like this," Brooke said. "I should have waited until I talked to you on the phone."

"It's okay. Actually, I *am* hungry, so your timing's good. And we need to discuss the case. Ouch." He winced as she tore the tape off the wound. "You better hand me one of those," he said, pointing to the beer on the coffee table. Brooke handed him a beer.

"Hurts that bad, huh?"

"Only when I breathe."

She lifted the gauze. "I've seen worse, you sissy."

"And I've had worse."

"When?"

"In Afghanistan."

"Care to elaborate?"

"No. Want to see the scars?"

"No."

Brooke finished dressing the wound and stepped back. "There. All done."

"Thanks, Florence Nightingale," Lukas said. "Let me grab a shirt real quick, and we'll take that pie out on the deck."

As Lukas walked away, Brooke noticed something that looked like an angel and some writing she couldn't discern on the seat of his sweats. It wasn't exactly how she pictured him dressing. She picked up the pizza, grabbed a beer, and walked outside to the deck.

The view was beautiful, much like the view at her house. A line of pine trees bordered his property, and her seat afforded a perfect view of the mountains. The sound of the screen door shutting announced Lukas's arrival.

"I'm starved," he said. "I see you got extra cheese. Something else we have in common."

"It's nice here."

"I like it. Quiet. Peaceful. Kinda away from everything, but not too far."

They talked a bit and devoured most of the pizza, lounging on the deck until the cool night air forced them inside. Brooke sat down on the sofa as Lukas went for another round of beers. Returning, he handed her one and sat down in the recliner.

"She's mad, isn't she?" Brooke said.

"No, she's fine," Lukas said, but he didn't sound convincing. "She understands work is work. Don't worry about it. So, what did we learn last night?"

"First, I need to ask you a question. And I don't want you think I was looking at your ass. But what does the symbol and writing on the back of your sweats mean?"

Lukas smiled. "It says, 'That others may live,' and it's an angel holding the world." He stood up and turned around, giving her a perfect view of the symbol and what it covered. "See?"

Yeah, she saw, and she liked. "So much for not looking at your ass."

Lukas laughed and sat back down.

"What's that from?" Brooke said.

"It's the pararescue motto."

"What exactly is pararescue, anyway?"

"It's a unit that was originally formed to rescue pilots who had been shot down or crashed. We were trained to conduct search and rescue operations in all kinds of environments, all kinds of terrain. Pararescue has evolved over the years and several of the units are now part of the military's Special Operations Group. The guys are basically combat medics. They go into hot combat zones and pick up Rangers, SEALs, Green Berets, Delta operators, anyone that needs to have wounded soldiers evacuated. They even help with civilians in some extreme cases. Their primary mission is to save lives, not take them, but they're capable of doing both."

"So, you've been in combat?"

"I have, and I don't mean any offense at all, but I'd rather not discuss it."

"No offense taken. Are you sure you don't wear those sweats just to get women to look at your butt?"

"My butt gets looked at plenty without them."

"Nice to know you think so much of your butt. So how about we get back to last night? I still have a lot to learn. The guy just came at me, and I didn't react quickly enough. It all happened so fast. It was a blur."

"That's what the code words are for. That's why we went over them."

"I guess I wanted to get this thing right so bad, to get some kind of a lead, I let it go too far. And in the process, I learned a hard lesson and almost got you killed."

"At least it was a lesson we both walked away from."

"Who knows?" Brooke said. "Maybe we altered our killer's plans last night and saved a life. Maybe he was out there, and he knows we're upping the pressure. Maybe he'll make a mistake."

Lukas swallowed the remainder of his beer and sat the empty bottle on the table. "I feel like we're making progress but at too slow a pace. The leads we have aren't getting us any closer to solving it."

"Oh, that reminds me. I checked on the red car and the R.O. lead, but I didn't find anything."

"What about the patterns? Can you think of anything there?

Brooke leaned back on the couch and rubbed her temples. "I think the abortion clinic and poster are too obvious to dismiss. I'm not sure about the others."

"The locations could just be places of opportunity or convenience," Lukas said.

"They could be. But with all the evidence that's building up, I'm beginning to doubt it."

"Have we ruled out the pimp war theory?"

"I think so," Brooke said. "It just doesn't fit. First, there's no connection between the pimps here and in Kingsport. And when I interviewed Nelasco, he seemed genuinely afraid. If he knew anything, I think he would have spilled it."

"And the rope lead?"

"It's a long shot."

Brooke's cell phone pinged. It was a text from her mom wondering where she was.

"Damn, it's later than I thought," she said. "I need to pick up Sierra."

Lukas stood and walked her to the door. "Are you good to drive?"

"I've had two beers. Of course I'm okay to drive." She turned to face him as she stepped out on the porch. "Before I go, I wanted to thank you for last night."

"For what?" He looked genuinely confused.

"For just being there for me."

"Oh. No problem. And thank you."

"For?"

"Changing my bandage. And noticing my butt."

CHAPTER EIGHTEEN

The man marveled at the clarity of the cameras. The placement was pretty damned good, too, considering he was an amateur. The cameras were advertised as having a range out to forty meters. He estimated his cameras were at about the fifty range, but they were still remarkably clear. They served his purpose well. He could see what he needed to see.

He sat in the spare bedroom of the apartment where he had his computer set up. The video feed came through his computer monitor. He cycled over and over between the cameras.

"Where are you tonight?" he whispered to himself. The clock on the wall over the computer showed it was after eight. "You're out late, young lady. Where are you?"

He felt the anger rising like lava from a long-dormant volcano. He wondered where she could be. After last night, he would have thought she would be at home spending time with her little girl. That's where she should be, not out carousing like a trollop.

He got up from the computer desk and walked to the living room. He turned up the volume on the scanner. Maybe she was still working. Did he miss something? He doubted it. He walked to the refrigerator and pulled out a bottle of water.

As he stood in the kitchen drinking, he could tell the images on the computer screen were changing from the reflections on the wall in the dark room where the computer was located. He hurried to the room to check the monitors.

He watched as the two figures disappeared out of sight toward the front of the house. A moment later, he saw lights switch on in a steady pattern throughout the house. He'd done some closer reconnaissance of the house, so he knew the layout. First, a light in the living room, then the dining room, followed by the little girl's room, and finally the master bedroom. He inched closer to the screen as if it would improve his view.

Shortly after the lights were switched on, they were extinguished in the same order. He could see shadows through the blinds. From what he could discern, the TV in the living room had been switched on. He let the footage run for a few more minutes just to make sure there was nothing else he could learn. Satisfied, he turned off the monitor, ending the night's surveillance. He ambled over to his well-worn recliner and adjusted the volume on the scanner. He listened to the calls go out as the various cars were dispatched and wondered what must be going through the minds of Brooke Stevens and Lukas Miller.

Who would find the next body? That must be a worrisome thought for them. He was still ahead. He was winning. He had no doubt he would win in the end. The thought gave him a deep sense of satisfaction.

He had carefully orchestrated everything. They'd tried to stop him, but nothing had worked. He almost felt sorry for them.

"I believe it's time," he whispered. He closed his eyes and sat listening to the scanner for a few more moments. It was quiet. He nodded his head in the darkness. The quiet wouldn't last for long.

CHAPTER NINETEEN

Three days after Lukas was stabbed, he was back on the job. He'd worked the case as much as possible from home by running down leads by phone and conferring with other agencies about serial killers targeting prostitutes. He checked and rechecked his case files, especially those concerning Razzy, to see if he could make any plausible connections. He spent hours poring over the files and had re-organized the murder book, going over the pictures again and again. The caveat to being back in the office was that he wasn't allowed to get out except for mundane paperwork details, but he was not going to let what little momentum they had stagnate. He was seated at his desk going over the reports from Friday night's sting when his cell phone rang. It was Danny Smart.

"Hey, Danny, what's up?"

"Not a whole lot with me, but word on the street is you've had an interesting few days. Do you care to confirm or deny?"

"There's no way the truth could possibly compare to what's been going around, and I'd hate to spoil your fun."

Smart chuckled. "Seriously, how are you?"

"I'm good. A little sore, but every day it's a little better. Got any good news for me?"

"I need to return your jump drive and I'll be happy to share what I think. Unofficially, of course. Can you swing by?"

"Sure. Be there in an hour."

Lukas was anxious, so he arrived at the FBI field office early. Smart met him at the rear entrance to the building.

"Let's do this out here." He pointed at his car, which was parked close by. Smart handed over the jump drive as they climbed in.

"So?" Lukas said.

"I read the case notes and looked over the photos, read the bios of the victims, the whole deal. Now, before we go any further, remember, this is off the books. It's in no way official or binding. And, as with all profiles, it's only accurate to a degree, and—"

"I know, I know. Hell, Danny, I'm not asking you to sign a prenup. Just tell me what you think."

"For starters, a black male doesn't fit the profile."

"Okay. Who does?"

"I believe you're looking for a white male, mid-thirties, give or take five, above-average intelligence, has a steady job he likes and is good at. Probably not married. He obviously doesn't care much for women, or at least prostitutes."

"Are we looking at a lone wolf killer?"

"I think so. He might have some help, it isn't unheard of, but this is probably the work of one man. The increased violence and mutilation to the bodies show an escalating psychological disorder."

"What about patterns?"

"Not much there, really, other than the vics are all prostitutes along with one other thing I'll get to in a minute. This guy had some serious problems in his childhood or early adolescence. My guess is his mother was a hooker. And a lot of these serial killers survived attempts on their lives by one or both parents. That anger turns to rage, the rage smolders over time, and eventually it boils over, and they act out. This guy is escalating, which tells me his psyche is deteriorating at an accelerated rate. The body at the mayor's house was a grandiose gesture. He thinks he's smarter than you guys, and he's toying with you. That was pure contempt for law enforcement. That was a sign that he thinks he's invincible."

"Which means he'll make a mistake soon. He's becoming overconfident."

"Maybe, but there's something else you missed that might play into catching him."

Lukas thought about the patterns he'd examined, all the evidence he'd gone over and over and over.

"What did we miss?" Lukas said.

"All of the victims had children."

Lukas leaned back. Children? What could that mean? He reached into his pocket and started rubbing the jump drive between his fingers as though the information contained within it would magically reveal some answer. But what Smart was saying was true. All of the victims had children, and he and Brooke hadn't made the connection. It was right there.

"What's it mean?"

"I'm not sure, but there's one thing I'm sure about. He isn't through. I don't know when or where he'll strike next, or how, but he won't quit. He can't. He's on a high right now. He's enjoying this."

"Maybe he's enjoying it too much," Lukas said. "Maybe enough to get careless."

"I hope so," Danny said, "but I hope you don't have to wait until he kills again to find out."

Lukas shook his head and let out a long breath. "Mama said there'd be days like this. Thanks, Danny. I won't say a word to anyone."

The drive back to the station gave Lukas more time to think. He dialed Brooke's number, and she answered almost immediately.

"How's the arm?"

"Better. I talked to Danny Smart."

"Is he done with the profile?"

"I don't want to go into it over the phone. Can you meet me somewhere?"

"Sure. I'm hungry. How about *Lucky*'s in thirty?"

"I'll be there."

CHAPTER TWENTY

B rooke listened quietly as Lukas went over Danny Smart's assessment. When he was finished, she sat there with a blank look on her face. She was disappointed they had both missed the child connection, but at least it was something that might be considered another lead. It wasn't much of a lead – sort of a cryptic lead – but it was information they hadn't recognized previously, so it was something new.

"I can't believe we missed that," she said. "Damn, it seems like for the past week every time I turn around I'm feeling like I've made a rookie mistake. You know what? We need to turn the tables on this guy. It's high time someone else started feeling stupid."

"Calm down, tiger," Lukas said. "I know how you feel. I felt the same way when Danny dropped that little tidbit on me."

Brooke was silent for a long minute. Then she said, "Okay, looking on the bright side, we have a new lead. Where does that leave us?"

"Nowhere," Lukas said. "Square One."

"I love your optimism."

"Just being realistic. We're no closer to him than we were on day one. So, he kills hookers who have children. His mother may have been a prostitute. She may have tried to kill him. So, what? None of that identifies him. None of it really helps us."

"It's been over a week since Razzy," Brooke said. "The next one will happen soon. He knows he has us on edge, and Agent Smart is right. The killer is on some kind of high, like he's going through a manic phase. We need to get back out on the street. I'll talk to my people and see if we can get an operation going for tonight. Are you in?"

Lukas glanced at his right arm and slowly back to Brooke with an incredulous look.

"Shit. I forgot. You can help me in the ops center. That's not against the rules, right?"

"They won't let me near an operation right now. Captain Hunter made it clear – no action. If I get another injury, it had better be a paper cut or a coffee burn. That's the deal I had to make to get back to my desk. Besides, I've got something I really need to take care of tonight. It's important."

He noticed that they both had only eaten half of their meals. Their appetites disappeared when Agent Smart's findings made their way to the forefront of the conversation. Lukas pushed his chair away from the metal table.

"Will you be working as a handler?" Lukas said.

"I'll be overseeing the whole thing. We're short-handed even with you. Without you, we're like a three-man basketball team. I think we'll work your turf this time, though. Any advice?"

"Not really. Our guys know the area well, so they should be able to bring you up to speed." Lukas glanced at his watch. "I've got to run. Be careful. Call me if anything breaks."

"I will."

Brooke left Johnson City and drove back to Kingsport to the Cooper Center to follow up on the abortion angle. She didn't put much stock in the theory that the killings had anything to do with abortion, but she felt an obligation to look under every rock. She wound up wasting two hours, then went to the station to put the final touches on planning the operation for that night. It was to be much like the one they'd conducted in Kingsport. They'd get out on the street, among the hookers and johns and pimps, and see if anything broke loose.

***

In the meantime, Lukas spent the afternoon cleaning up Gabriele's place, not that it needed much cleaning. He bought flowers and two bottles of pinot noir, which was Gabriele's favorite. An hour before she was scheduled to get off work, he left and drove ten minutes to their favorite Italian restaurant and picked up two orders of shrimp scampi, some garlic bread, and some pasta that he'd already ordered. He set the dining room table, lit candles. By the time Gabriele arrived, the food was hot, plated, and ready to eat.

She walked in the door, and Lukas picked her up and kissed her gently.

"I've missed you," he said. "We have some catching up to do."

She squeezed him, and he winced.

"Sorry," Gabriele said. "The shoulder?"

"It's okay. It's getting better every day. Are you hungry?"

"I'm starved."

"Good. Let's eat."

They sat at the table and ate the food and drank wine. Lukas steered the conversation toward her work, her friends, her family, anything but the murders. When they were finished, Lukas cleared the table, loaded the dishwasher and straightened the kitchen while Gabriele took a shower. She came back out and came in the kitchen to help him.

"Go in the living room and take a load off," Lukas said. "I'll be with you in a minute."

"Are you telling me I need to preserve my energy?" she said.

"You could take it that way, yeah."

He finished in the kitchen, tossed the dish cloth he'd been using in the washing machine, and walked into the living room. Gabriele was sitting patiently on the couch, listening to music. Lukas picked her up gently. She submitted, putting her arms around his neck, her mouth gently brushing his cheek. He carried her down the hall and into the bedroom. Just as he laid her on the bed, his phone rang.

Damn.

He'd meant to leave it in his car. He took the phone out and glanced at the screen. It was Odessa McCabe. He hit the decline button, switched the phone to vibrate, and placed it on the nightstand. He turned back to Gabriele, hoping the mood hadn't been spoiled.

Before he was able to get into bed, the phone buzzed. It was the loudest and most obnoxious cell phone buzz he'd ever heard in his life, and it seemed to go on forever. Things were quickly going to hell in a handbasket.

The phone pinged. A text.

"Lukas, you may as well take care of that," Gabriele said. He could tell from the tone of her voice that the evening was already ruined. He walked into the kitchen and called Odessa.

"It's about time. Where have you been?"

"I was a little busy." He glanced back at Gabriele. She'd gotten out of bed and was now sitting on the couch with her knees pulled up to her chest, staring at the TV with a blank look on her face.

"You'll have to tell whoever she is that it'll have to wait. We got a DNA hit on the semen we recovered from the last victim. Captain Hunter is mobilizing the tactical team and the CSU."

"On my way." Lukas knew Gabriele would be madder than hell, but this could be the break they'd been waiting for. She'd just have to understand.

"Gabby, I—"

"I know."

Lukas walked over to where Gabriele was sitting and kissed her on the head. "I'm so sorry. I really do have to go."

She scowled. "Of course you do. You always do."

Lukas picked his keys up off the kitchen counter and walked out without saying goodbye. He wasn't sure if their relationship would survive this one.

CHAPTER TWENTY-ONE

Brooke was trying to find a way around the line of cars that was holding her up on the way into Johnson City. Her phone chirped. It was Lukas.

"Hey, I've been talking to Captain Hunter and we have a name," Brooke said. "I'm on my way in. I'll swing by and pick you up."

"I'm not at home. I'm leaving Gabriele's now. What's the story?"

"The suspect's name is Rodney Odell. He's a black male who's had multiple collars for solicitation and drugs. From the initial appearance, he seems good for it. He owns a red Cavalier, the initials match Jamika's journal, and the sperm they found in Razzy matches his DNA. They've mobilized the tactical team, and they're working up a threat assessment now."

"What's your feeling?"

"It seems right. I'd say it might be worth getting our hopes up."

"Doesn't fit the profile from Danny," Lukas said.

Brooke laughed. "Yeah, well, profiles have never been wrong, have they?"

"Point taken. I'm on my way in. Is there anything you need?"

"I just need this to be over with, and at least now there could be a light at the end of the tunnel. One last thing. Captain Hunter asked me to give the briefing before everybody goes out to get this guy. He said it's because you've been laid up. Any problem with it?"

"None. See you in a few."

Brooke arrived at the department about the same time as Lukas. She could feel the buzz in the rooms she walked past. They were alive with activity. Different units were having discussions about the upcoming bust. She overheard someone she didn't recognize announce that the briefing would take place in the conference room at 8:00 p.m. She looked at her watch. Fifteen minutes.

The conference room was big enough for one department's people, but since both departments were there, it was crowded, almost claustrophobic. Captain Hunter signaled Brooke and Lukas to take two seats he'd saved at the front of the room.

"Okay, people, we've got a lot to go over," Captain Hunter shouted over the din, "and it's way too crowded to be in here any longer than we have to. Everyone here is aware of the murders we've had over the last two months in Kingsport and Johnson City. The forensic people learned earlier today that the semen that was found in our latest victim, Kimberly Renee Raznovich, matches the DNA profile of a black male here in Johnson City. His name is Rodney Odell, and his last known address is 118 Madison Avenue." A mugshot of Odell, who looked to be in his mid-thirties, appeared on the screen. "At this time, I'm going to ask Detective Stevens to fill you in on the details."

Brooke walked to the computer. A slide presentation had been prepared with the details about the murders. She began running through the slides as she talked.

"During the course of the investigation, we received information that a black male was seen carrying a rug near Mayor Pennington's driveway, which is where the last body was dumped not long before being discovered. We've also received a couple of tips that indicated a red car may have been near one or more of the areas where victims were abducted. Another witness provided the diary of one of our victims. The last entry said she was going to meet 'RO,' which could be Rodney Odell. Rodney Odell has a red Chevrolet Cavalier registered to him. He has a history with prostitutes, and he's a known drug user – or has been in the past according to vice. When you add the fact that his sperm was inside our last victim, he could very well be our guy. What we find in his home and car will be crucial. Captain, do we have a search warrant?"

"We will momentarily."

"Obviously, we consider this man armed and extremely dangerous. The tactical team will have full control of the scene until the suspect is apprehended. Once that happens, the suits will move in. Questions? All right, I'll turn it back over to you, Captain."

Captain Hunter took center stage only long enough to introduce the special ops commander: "I'll now turn the briefing over to Captain Thomason."

A short, bald man decked out in full tactical gear walked up to the computer. He hit a few keys, and the images on the screen changed to what appeared to be real time footage of the house they were about to hit. It looked as though cameras had been placed some distance away from the house, covering all sides. Brooke hadn't seen this done before, but she immediately realized that this tactic would make planning much more effective. The captain gave a short synopsis on the target and structure and listed concerns about tactical disadvantages and safety issues. The house was a single-story, wooden building with more bare wood showing than paint. There appeared to be a large oak tree in the front yard. The only thing Brooke saw that would raise her alarm were the two large dog houses at the rear of the house. She didn't see any dogs, however.

After Captain Thomason had completed the threat assessment, he turned the briefing back over to Captain Hunter, who walked to the center of the room. "I don't need to tell you what's at stake here. Stay focused and sharp. Let's get this guy. Any questions?"

"Is there any reason to believe there may be booby traps or explosives?" Brooke didn't recognize the man, but from his attire he was clearly with the bomb squad.

"We have no information to suggest that it's a possibility. You guys are here as a precautionary measure. Anyone else? Okay, we'll stage at the elementary school parking lot a block from the house. Let's go."

The room emptied quickly. Captain Hunter motioned for Brooke and Lukas to stay.

"I know you two have worked hard on this case. You were put in a bad situation when we asked you to work together. But you didn't cry or bitch. You handled it like real professionals. And for that you are to be commended. Miller, how's the arm?"

"It's fine, captain."

"When we get this scumbag, I want you both to have a run at him. Together, just like it's been up to this point." He gave them both an approving nod. "Let's go. This is what we've been working for."

Brooke and Lukas exchanged nods and walked out of the conference room behind Captain Hunter. They took Brooke's car and followed the entourage of ten vehicles. Once they got to the staging area, Brooke watched as the tactical team disappeared into the night like wraiths. They followed not far behind, and Brooke soon noticed there were no lights on in the house, which was odd at this time of night. Was he there? The car mentioned in the briefing was parked in the driveway. After about five minutes, she heard a commotion as the assault on the house began. The wraiths were now in full go-mode. She saw bright lights and loud pops from the flash bang grenades and could hear excited shouts from the team as they entered the house.

Minutes later, some of the tactical team members filed out, adjusting their gear. From what she could see, no one was moving with any sense of urgency. That was quick. Brooke looked over at Lukas.

"Ready?"

"Always."

They walked across the street and down the block toward the house where the suspect had apparently been detained without incident. The nearer she got to the scene, the more disturbed Brooke became. She sensed that something was wrong before she made it to the house. The lack of urgency, the look on the faces of the officers that had been inside and were now walking back towards the staging area told her all was not well.

Her thoughts were interrupted by Captain Hunter. "Good news and bad news."

"What's wrong?" She sped up, growing more anxious.

"Slow down, Stevens. I'm an old man here."

She slowed and finally stopped. "Sorry, Captain. I'm just in a hurry to get up there and—"

"You can take all the time you need. Odell's dead."

Brooke was stunned. She looked at Lukas, who was standing beside her rubbing his right arm and looking up into the black night sky as if he had just discovered a new constellation.

"Dead? What do you mean?"

"It means that the suspect known as Rodney Odell has assumed room temperature. What the hell kind of question is that?"

"I'm sorry, Captain. I meant to ask how."

"That's your job." He looked at them both. "Keep me posted."

Brooke checked in with the uniform who was keeping the crime scene log while Lukas talked on his cell phone. Walking into the house was an exercise in dexterity. It was difficult to tell whether a small tornado had blown through or someone had ransacked it. There was hardly a place she could set her foot down without stepping on something. And that something could very well be evidence.

They made their way to the bedroom at the direction of the crime scene officer. The bedroom was in much the same condition as the rest of the house, although not quite as cluttered. Odell was lying in the middle of a bed that was situated in the corner of the room. He was on his back with his arms out to his sides in a crucifixion pose. He wore only boxer shorts and a pair of mismatched socks. The head of the bed and one side had been pushed into the corner against the wall. A lamp on a small table near the other side of the bed emitted an eerie red glow. Brooke could make out the shapes of three syringes that were lying on the table beside the lamp. A darkened television sat on a stand in the opposite corner of the room. The walls were bare except for two dirty, wrinkled Jimi Hendrix posters. Brooke looked around for identification and found Rodney Odell's wallet on a dresser on the other side of the room.

"Got ID over here."

"Is it our guy?" Lukas said.

"According to his driver's license, yes." She held the license next to the upturned face on the bed for comparison.

"Odessa is on her way."

"Good."

"How long you think he's been here?" Lukas said as he looked over Brooke's shoulder at the license.

"I'm not sure. But it's fairly cool in here, so decomp would be minimal. I'd guess not more than two days."

Brooke started going through the dresser drawers. She found nothing she wouldn't expect in a single man's home. The clothes looked to have been thrown in the drawers in no particular order. There were two pairs of shoes under the dresser, another pair under the bed. She opened the lower right dresser drawer and found some porn videos.

"Found the nightly entertainment," she said as she held them up.

"Nice. I've seen all of those," Lukas said.

"Are you in any of them?" Brooke put the videos back.

She was looking around the room when she saw Lukas open a drawer in the bedside table, reach in, and pull out a clear vial that had no labels or writing of any kind. He held it up to the light, and she noticed a small amount of liquid in the bottom. Not enough for a dose, just the remnants of some type of drug. It was most likely Rodney's drug of choice and could possibly be what he overdosed on if that's what the cause of death turned out to be. Lukas marked them, so CSU would pick them up. Meanwhile, Brooke turned her attention to a stack of papers that looked like unopened mail. She was interrupted by Lukas.

"Hey. I may have something over here."

Lukas had his head in the closet at the back of the small room. Brooke walked over. Inside the closet were several pieces of women's clothing. There were shoes of different designs and sizes, bras, panties. It looked as though there were enough clothes for several women. And it was a mixed lot. Some of the items appeared to have blood on them.

"Well, well, well," Lukas said. "I'll bet my next pay-check these items belong to our victims. And I'll double down the blood is theirs too."

Lukas carefully picked up a pink bra and stared at something.

"Initials are KRR. This is Razzy's." He showed it to Brooke with a look on his face that was a mixture of sadness and anger. "Is this the norm? For hookers to initial their bras?"

"How should I know? Maybe. I guess when you don't have much, maybe you do."

All the women's clothing items were placed in a pile and marked for CSU to collect.

Brooke noticed Lukas walking out of the room while she was making notes in her notebook. Before she could finish writing, he walked back in with Odessa in tow.

Odessa was the first to speak. "Hey, Brooke, glad to see you again. And glad this nightmare is over. We hope."

"You, too. Yeah, we hope."

Brooke gave a quick rundown of her theory as Lukas and Odessa joined her by the bedside table. "He's clearly a needle doper, most likely street level." She pointed out the syringes for Odessa. "There are no obvious signs of trauma, no signs of a struggle. No suicide note. No way to tell whether he was depressed, other than the fact that he lived in this dump. My guess would be accidental overdose. Lukas?"

"That's where the scene is taking me, but I have some problems with it."

Brooke shrugged. "Like what?" She looked around the room, wondering what Lukas had seen that she hadn't.

"There are several things, actually. But let's not get sidetracked here. Let's finish the scene. We can talk it over after."

Odessa turned and looked at the body. She ran her gloved hand over his skull as if she was massaging it. "No fractures that I can feel. Fairly recent needle marks in the bends of his arms." She reached down and took off his socks and spread the man's toes. "You can barely see some marks between his toes. Not recent, though." Next, she opened his eyes, checking for petechial hemorrhage, which could also show signs of trauma.

Finishing her preliminary, she turned. "I would put the time of death at thirty-six to forty-eight hours based on the state of rigor, body and room temp. And I put the preliminary cause of death as an accidental overdose, pending a toxicology report, of course."

A uniformed officer stuck his head in the room. "Detectives, there's something out here you should see."

Brooke followed the officer with Lukas right behind her. Outside, he stopped next to the suspect's vehicle. The trunk had been opened. Brooke took out her mini MagLite and shined it around in the trunk. In the right corner was a short length of rope. She picked it up and showed it to Lukas. "Does this look familiar?"

"It looks like the rope used at the library. I wonder what other secrets are in here." Lukas bent down and shined his light in the trunk. "It looks like there's blood here on the carpet. Some hair, too."

"We'll need to have it all tested."

"I'll mark it for CSU."

Brooke heard someone approach from the rear. She turned to see Captain Hunter peering into the trunk.

"Are you two done here?"

"For the most part," Lukas answered.

"I'll be in my office. When you get things wrapped up here, I'd like to see you for a debriefing."

"Yes, sir."

Thirty minutes later, Brooke walked into the Johnson City Police Department headquarters along with Lukas. The building was becoming familiar to her. It almost felt like home. Brooke pulled Lukas into a dark, empty conference room as they walked past, shut the door and turned on the lights.

"Okay, you mentioned some things at the crime scene, and said we'd talk about them later. I know we didn't have much time with all that was going on, so let's clear the air now. What did you see that I didn't?"

"The condition of the house for one thing. Absolutely no organization. I mean, his house was a wreck. This guy has been one step ahead of us the whole time. Do you think a guy who lived like that could outsmart us?"

"It's a stretch, I'll admit," Brooke said. "But I've seen stranger things."

"And Odell was a street junkie. He lived from one fix to the next. I have a hard time believing he would have had enough foresight to plan this thing out."

Brooke didn't answer. She was starting to see where Lukas was going, and she didn't like it.

"And then there's Danny's profile," Lukas said.

Brooke leaned against a table and folded her arms across her chest.

"Odell does go against that, but I don't have as much faith in a profile as you do. Sometimes they're just wrong."

"And how did he know who to prey on?" Lukas said. "How did he choose the victims? I don't think it's a coincidence that all of the victims had children."

"I agree," Brooke said. "He either knew them personally or had to have access to records with their personal information, and Odell wouldn't have had that kind of access. But what about the evidence we do have? The evidence at the scene."

"Obviously, we can't ignore it. The victims' clothing, the rope in the trunk matches what we found, the red car, black male, not to mention his sperm. It's all there." Lukas walked around the room running his fingers through his hair. He turned back to Brooke. "We either got lucky, or this is frame job, and an obvious one at that."

"What do we tell the captain?"

Lukas shrugged his shoulders. Brooke knew what was at stake. They were about to meet with Hunter about the case, and he was going to want answers. Did they have the guy or not? A mountain of evidence was at their disposal. It was almost too good to be true.

"Just follow my lead," Lukas said, and he walked out of the room.

They made their way through the detective division to Captain Hunter's office. The door was open, and they were beckoned in and offered seats in front of his large, mahogany desk.

"Thanks for coming in so quickly. It's been quite a night so far. I'm supposed to brief the chief within the hour, so I need to know exactly where we stand. When I brief him, he'll want to know all the details. Nobody knows these cases like you two. So, let's have it. Is this our guy?"

Brooke glanced at Lukas. Their eyes locked, and he began to speak. "Everything we need to make a case against Rodney Odell is there, sir. The victims' clothing, a red car, the rope, the fact that we have a witness who saw a black male carrying a rug near the mayor's house close to the time a body was dumped in his driveway. And the most important piece of evidence is the guy's DNA from Razzy. There are some loose ends that need to be cleared up, of course."

"I don't like loose ends." The captain turned his attention to Brooke.

"What do *you* think?"

"The evidence at the scene points to Rodney Odell as the killer," she said.

"What about Odell's death? Anything suspicious?" the captain said, looking back at Lukas for the answer.

"Nothing other than the fact that it was mighty convenient for our serial killer to wind up dead with a house full of evidence around him. It effectively ends the investigation, because dead men don't talk. Rodney Odell can't tell us a thing."

"I sense you doubt he's our killer. Why?"

"I just have some problems with the convenience of it all. I also have some problems with the condition of the house, the fact that Odell is dead—"

"So, you think somebody's framing him?"

"I don't know, sir. It's possible."

"Anything's possible, Detective."

"Cases as complicated as this are never perfect. Like I said, there are just a few minor things to follow up on. Nothing major."

The captain leaned back in his well-worn leather chair and gave a glare, first at Lukas, then Brooke. "What are the two of you up to?"

Brooke decided to enter the game. She pointed at Lukas. "Like he said, there're just some small things to follow up on."

Hunter sat there looking back and forth between them as though he was measuring them up.

"I'll brief the chief in thirty. Any suggestions?"

"Just that it's still an active investigation. Less is best," Lukas said.

"Damn it, Miller, I'm not feeling very confident. Do we hold a press conference and say we got the guy?"

"Yours and the chief's call, Captain," Lukas said. "That's why they pay you guys the big money."

"Shit," Captain Hunter said. "You're no help. Get out of my office."

Brooke followed Lukas down the hall to the squad room. Several officers and detectives were milling around in jovial moods. The stress caused by the homicides over the past weeks seemed to lift like a morning fog with the discovery of Odell's body and the treasure trove of evidence.

Brooke spent the next two hours helping Lukas sift through the evidence bags that had been collected by the

CSU team. Everything was carefully catalogued and sent to the property and evidence room, where it would be stored before being sent to the lab for testing and comparison. Brooke sat at the table in the center of the squad room and stared at the empty interview rooms on the monitors. Her mind wandered back to the night Lukas interviewed Razzy. It seemed like an eternity ago. She glanced over at Lukas who was entering case notes in the file. He seemed to feel her gaze and turned to look at her.

"What's on your mind?"

"I was just thinking about the night Razzy was in there." Brooke pointed to the empty interview room on the monitor.

"I still have trouble believing she's gone." Lukas lowered his voice so the others in the room couldn't hear.

"I'd really like to believe this is over, but I don't," he said. "I think there's another layer that's even more sinister than what we've been dealing with."

"God help us if Odell isn't the guy," Brooke said. "That would mean someone has now committed six murders, is still out there, and will keep on killing."

CHAPTER TWENTY-TWO

Brooke sat on Sierra's bedroom floor with her rudimentary set of mismatched tools. The Cinderella bed lay half-finished in front of her. She picked up the instructions, looked them over, sighed, and promptly tossed them back on the floor. How was she supposed to turn this mess into the beautiful bed pictured on the box? She wasn't even sure what some of the screws were called. She'd never seen anything like them.

She picked up the phone and dialed her dad's number. It went to voicemail. She'd forgotten that he was with her mom at their cabin this weekend and probably didn't have cell service. She set the phone down and rolled over on her back, massaging her temples.

"Mommy, how long until you get the Cinderella bed done?" Sierra was standing at the door.

"I don't know, sweetie. I'm doing the best I can. We might have to wait until Grandpa gets back home."

"But you promised."

"I know, but I don't think I have the right tools here."

"Then call Daddy. Please."

"Don't worry, I'll work something out." She glanced at the clock on the wall. She had to be at the firing range at 2:00 p.m. for the last session of the Citizen's Police Academy class and the graduation ceremony. She had roughly four hours to fulfill her promise to Sierra and get the bed put together.

"It's okay, Mommy. You can do it later when you have some help." Sierra, who was still at the door, seemed to sense her frustration. She walked into the room and threw her arms around Brooke's neck before she went back to the living room and her Saturday morning cartoons.

Brooke threw her hands up and laid back. She stared up at the ceiling. So much to do, so little time. She sat up and hit Lukas's number.

"Hey, Brooke, what's up?"

"Not much. What are you doing this morning?"

"I couldn't sleep last night. I just got out of bed and am fixing a pot of coffee."

"Oh, I'm sorry. I'll call you later."

"It's no problem. I'm up now. What's on your mind?"

"I've been thinking about Odell, and something is bugging me."

"What's on your mind?"

"Actually, I just lied. I need some help putting together a bed for Sierra. I promised her I'd do it this morning, but it's a lot more complicated than I thought it would be. Are you any good at assembling kid's toys?"

"I don't have any kids, but I'm a man of many talents. Text me your address and I'll be there in less than an hour."

"I don't want to hijack your Saturday."

"Text me the address."

Lukas arrived a short while later, and Sierra opened the door before he could knock.

"Hi."

"Well, hi yourself." Lukas stood there with a cardboard tray in his hand that contained three cups. He looked back and forth between daughter and mother. Brooke could see the look of surprise on Lukas's face. She'd seen the look before. People were often shocked at the resemblance between her and her daughter.

"Sierra, this is Lukas Miller. He's a friend of mommy's. He's a police officer too. Lukas, this is Sierra."

"Hi there." Lukas held out his hand and Sierra took it. "It's nice to meet you."

"Mommy is putting my new Cinderella bed together. But she gets mad. Are you going to help?"

"I sure am. We'll get it together, I promise."

"I wouldn't be so confident, Mr. Goodwrench," Brooke said. "It's a mess."

"Oh, ye of little faith." He handed her the tray. "Hold this. Coffees for you and me and a hot chocolate for Cinderella. My toolbox is in the trunk of my car. Be right back."

When they finished assembling the bed an hour after they began, Sierra was ecstatic. She even gave Lukas a hug, which seemed to surprise him as much as it surprised Brooke. Sierra jumped on the bed and began to play as soon she was given the go ahead.

As Lukas was packing up his tools, Brooke took the opportunity to slip away and prepare a lunch of sandwiches and chips. Lukas came out of Sierra's room and accepted Brooke's invitation to the table.

Brooke served the meal, and as they ate, Sierra jabbered on and on about how much she loved her new bed.

Once they were finished eating, Sierra disappeared back into the bedroom.

"I really appreciate you coming over and helping out. I wish I could stay here and enjoy Sierra and her new bed, but duty calls."

"On a Saturday? After they announced the man they believed to be the serial killer was found dead?"

The two departments had issued a joint press release announcing that the serial killer who had been terrorizing the communities of Kingsport and Johnson City was dead.

"They took the coward's way out," Brooke said. "I don't think either chief or any of the captains believed what they were selling."

"Doing it by press release was the best way," Lukas said. "They didn't have to answer any tough questions and if things go badly later and there's another murder, they can blame each other."

"If there's another murder, I promise the district attorney generals in both of our districts will take the case away from us and give it to the TBI," Brooke said.

"Yeah, well, we've done the best we can."

"Have we? Are you planning to stop looking at the file and following up leads?"

"Not a chance. I'll just have to do it on my own time."

"Same here. Back to what we were talking about, it's the last day of the Citizen's Police Academy, and that means graduation night and dinner."

"And you have to be there?"

"I've told you before. It's the chief's pet project. I have to go."

"At least we got Sierra's bed finished. I enjoyed it. It seemed to mean a lot to her."

"You have no idea. She's not usually so open with new people. She even gave you an unsolicited hug. That's big, believe me." Brooke's phone rang. She looked at the ID. "Excuse me," she said. "Hey, Haley."

"I need a favor."

"You've got it. What can I do?"

"I know I'm supposed to watch Sierra for you, but I was wondering if there's any way you could get your mom or dad to watch her."

"They're out of town, Haley." Brooke looked at Lukas and rolled her eyes.

"You know I wouldn't ask if it wasn't important. But I got a last-minute date."

"Who's the lucky guy?"

"It's the hottie from my apartment complex I've been stalking. I finally got him to notice me. We are, or were, going out to a movie and then later he's taking me to dinner. But I can cancel it. I promised you, after all."

"No, don't do that. I know how long you've been lusting over this guy, and I don't want you to bail because of me."

"But I feel so bad. I mean, I promised."

"Not another word. I'll handle it. Go have fun. Bye."

"Babysitter issues?" Lukas said.

"Yes. Of all the days."

"Who are you going to get?"

"I'll call Alex and get him to watch her. It's not his weekend to keep her, so he'll be pissy. Then I'll have to listen to a lecture about responsibility and career choices."

"So, Alex is your ex?"

"Yeah, Alex Fisher. I changed my name back to Stevens after we divorced."

"I could watch her."

Brooke was surprised, almost shocked.

"Absolutely not. I'm not going to completely ruin your Saturday."

Sierra came running across the room and jumped into Brooke's arms.

"Thanks again for fixing my bed, Mr. Miller."

"It's Lukas, and you're welcome."

"Are you good with bicycles?"

"Sierra, that's enough," Brooke said.

"But you said you'd fix that, too. And since Mr. Lukas has his tools here, why can't he—"

"That's it," Lukas said. "I'm staying. What kind of man would I be if I left Cinderella without a ride?"

Brooke watched the grin cross her daughter's face. "Please, Mommy, please?"

"Lukas, are you sure about this? I really don't want to impose on you any more than I already have."

"I'd be more than happy to stay. I'll fix the bike and keep an eye on the princess. As long as you're comfortable with it."

"Of course, I'm sure you two would do fine." As she spoke, she thought about how Lukas interacted with Timmy the day he delivered the awful news about Timmy's mother. "But what about you? Don't you and Gabriele have plans?"

"She isn't too happy with me right now. I was planning on chilling today. But now it looks like I have a date with Cinderella – if she'll have me, that is."

"Yes," Sierra said. "Cinderella wants you to stay."

"Okay," Brooke said. "It looks like I'm outnumbered. You two win."

Sierra grabbed Lukas's hand. "C'mon, Mr. Lukas. I'll show you my bike."

Brooke watched as Sierra led Lukas through the kitchen and out the French doors to the back yard where the bicycle was. She wandered over to the window and watched the two of them.

Before she left, Brooke gave Lukas a rundown of where Sierra's snacks were located, and then left for the police training facility. The drive was pleasant. The afternoon was cool but not overly so, allowing her to drive with the windows down and the air off. She thought about how nice it was of Lukas to volunteer for babysitting duty on a Saturday, especially with a child he didn't know well. He was becoming a good friend. The problem was, she found herself wanting more.

When Brooke arrived at the range, she looked over the materials for her presentation, which was to be on evidence collection. It took her just over an hour to give her talk. Afterward, while the cadets played with some of the department's favorite police toys, she checked in with Lukas. Sierra seemed to be having a good time, and Brooke clearly heard a football game on the TV in the background.

The last part of the night for Brooke was the graduation ceremony. She assisted the chief in presenting each student with a certificate. Hopefully, the academy had given the cadets a better understanding of what police work was really like. As they filed out, several of the students shook Brooke's hand and thanked her for her time. Some she recognized, some she didn't.

She was packing her files up when the chief approached her. "Brooke, I want to thank you for the commitment you gave to this class. You did a great job, and you did it while handling an incredibly difficult case. It's over isn't it?"

Brooke looked up, surprised by the question.

"I hope so. There are some things that we need to follow up on, though."

"We were between a rock and a hard place with the press release," the chief said. "We were aware of your concerns about the levels in Rodney Odell's tox report and the possibility that he'd been framed. But based on the evidence that was found at the scene, we thought it would be irresponsible not to get something out to the public. We kept things pretty vague. What they choose to write or broadcast is up to them."

Brooke packed up her things and drove home. She walked up the sidewalk to her house, and as she stepped up on the porch, she looked into the living room through the window. Lukas was sitting on the couch with his feet propped up on her coffee table like he had lived there his whole life. He was engrossed in a football game, completely at ease. Sierra was lying on Lukas's lap in her Cinderella Halloween costume. She was sound asleep.

Incredible. Brooke sighed and opened the door, wishing things were different between her and Lukas.

But the time just wasn't right, and she had to accept that it might never be right.

CHAPTER TWENTY-THREE

The following Monday found Lukas staring at the giant homicide book he and Brooke had put together. Before he knew it, he was flipping through the pages. There was something he just couldn't let go of, and from his experience, that usually meant something had been missed. He knew he might be mistaken, but he needed to get whatever was nagging at him out of his mind.

Lukas flipped to the section in the book that contained Rodney Odell's personal information. Odell had three children from two relationships. He perused Odell's priors. Drug charges, solicitation for prostitution, along with three shoplifting and two traffic charges. He also had two arrests for being behind on child support, but nothing violent. Committing a string of vicious murders seemed totally out of character.

Lukas sat back, rhythmically tapping a pen on the top of his desk. Would Odell have lashed out against prostitutes with children *because* they had children? That didn't make sense. Besides, he apparently liked hookers. At least that's what his priors revealed.

Lukas closed the book and looked up at the white, tiled ceiling. The more he thought about Odell, the more his head hurt. He turned on the computer and hammered out a subpoena for Rodney Odell's cell phone records. Maybe they could learn something from those. He printed and saved the digital copy of the subpoena to the case file.

After a quick trip to the coffee pot he returned to the murder book. He found the CSU evidence slips that were taken from Odell's house, and noticed a brief description of the vials that were found at the scene. He turned back to the photos of the crime scene at Odell's and of the vials. The photos showed the two glass vials on the table. Something about them bothered him. He looked closer and realized what it was. They were clean, a stark contrast to the filthy table they sat on and to the rest of the house. The entire place had been filthy.

Lukas checked the evidence log to make sure the vials had been collected. They had. He glanced at his watch. It was 3:05 p.m. If he hurried, he could have enough time to collect the vials from evidence and get them over to Odessa. He jumped up and almost ran to the evidence storage room to sign out the vials.

Twenty minutes later, Lukas wheeled into the parking lot of the forensic lab just as Odessa was walking out. He met her halfway to her car holding the yellow evidence bag. Odessa propped her hand on her plump hip. "I've seen that kind of bag and that look before. Can't possibly be good at this hour."

"I really need a favor."

"The staff have all left for the day. It'll be tomorrow." She took the bag from Lukas and read the writing on the outside. "Lukas, this is from Odell's house. What do you want me to do with it?"

"I just want you to run it for prints."

"All right, but if I do this and it comes back with only Odell's prints, will you please let it go?"

"You have my word."

"I want more than your word. I want you to buy me dinner."

"Deal. But I can't tonight."

"Of course you can't. Okay, I'll take a rain check. Just remember you owe me."

"You're a peach."

'I'll get to it as soon as I can tomorrow. You have fun with whatever it is you're doing tonight. I'll call when I have the results."

Lukas got back into his car. The clock on the dash read 4:35 p.m. He had just enough time to get the subpoena for Odell's phone records signed if he hurried.

CHAPTER TWENTY-FOUR

The next morning, Lukas made three phone calls to Odessa from his desk phone. The first two went to voicemail. She answered the third call.

"Lukas, you only call me like this when you need something."

"Any news on the vial?"

"I told you I'd call you when I had something. Have I ever let you down before?"

"No, I just thought maybe—"

"When I have it, I'll call you."

Lukas closed his eyes and leaned back in his chair. He checked his watch for what felt like the hundredth time. His cell vibrated, and he saw Odessa's name on the ID.

"Odessa, hey, what did you find?"

"There were no fingerprints on the vials. But there is something else. Can you come by the office?"

"I'll be right over." He hung up the phone and headed for his car.

Lukas drove to Odessa's office and soon found himself standing over a microscope looking at the vials.

"See what I mean? They appeared to have been wiped clean, but see the stripe on the sides? It looks like something was there, a label maybe."

"I see it."

"I think these were hospital vials. The question is, where did he get them? A street user with access to hospital vials? The toxicology came back on him a little while ago. They found enough morphine in his system to kill two people, and strangely enough, they found the pain killer dilaudid, too."

"What's that mean to you?" Lukas said.

"I'm not ready to say he was murdered yet, especially in light of the other evidence found at the scene. But users like Odell know how much they can shoot up. They've been doing it for years. Sure, occasionally they'll go heavy on the plunger and sign off, but the amount he had in his system doesn't make sense. And neither does the dilaudid. That's not a drug known for abuse. It's hard to get and would cost a mint on the street. In high doses, it becomes more of a sedative. He had to know he was taking a huge risk with this cocktail."

Lukas was trying to make sense of this new information. What was the stripe on the sides of the vials? "Do you think he overdosed, either accidentally or on purpose, or was he murdered?"

"I don't know, and I'm not going to speculate. Let's figure out what the lines on the vials are. My guess is they're glue from a label that's been peeled off.

"There aren't any fingerprints on the vials," Lukas said. "Which means somebody wiped them."

"Okay, let's say you're right in thinking the scene at Odell's was staged and he was murdered. What are you going to do?"

"I'll find some tangible evidence." He headed for the door.

"Lukas—"

"I'll be in touch. Thanks."

He left without looking back. Outside, he dialed Brooke's number.

"Hey, Lukas."

"Are you busy?"

"I'm scheduled for court this afternoon. What's up?"

"It's about the vials we found at Odell's. Can you swing by the department when you get free?"

"Sure. What about them?"

"Just swing by when you get done."

"I will."

Lukas spent the afternoon researching both the drugs found in Odell's system as well as the vials. Dilaudid was a high potency pain killer, and like Odessa said, it was expensive and hard to come by on the street. She was also right about mixing dilaudid with morphine. Apparently, that was a deadly combination. Brooke texted him to say she was outside just as he was finishing his research.

They headed to Odell's, and Lukas filled Brooke in on what Odessa had said about the vials. They arrived at Odell's just after dark, and after two hours of searching, they found nothing that would support the theory that Odell was murdered, at least nothing that would hold up to the "beyond a reasonable doubt" standard used in criminal cases. Lukas stood in the room where Odell was found, thinking about the vials.

"Hey, Lukas," Brooke said. "It doesn't look like CSU took the trash."

She bent down with gloved hands and delicately started going through the trash can beside the bed. Lukas shook his head and walked over to join her. CSU didn't usually leave trash at a crime scene where a body was found.

"Look at this."

Brooke held up an adhesive strip with a series of numbers and what looked like a bar code. He studied the strip. They could very well have come off the vials that Odessa had examined. Lukas wondered whether they could match them up.

"Here's another one," Lukas said. "It looks the same as that one."

"I wonder if we can track them."

"Not sure, but at least we found something. Let's bag these and get out of here. I have an idea."

When Lukas and Brooke arrived back at the Johnson City headquarters, Lukas used the computer at his desk to research the numbers found on the labels. An hour into the search, he pushed the chair back, turned, and looked at Brooke.

"I didn't find much, but it looks like the labels are from a drug manufacturer. The question is whether they came from a hospital pharmacy or somewhere else." Lukas picked up his cell and dialed a number. "But I think I know someone who could tell us. If... hey Gabby. I need a favor. Are you working tonight?"

"No, I'm off."

"Listen, if I give you some numbers I found on some labels that I think were on drug vials, can you find out if they came from your hospital?"

"I don't know. I've never had to do that. And it's late. I don't know if anyone I trust in the pharmacy is around."

"Would you do me a favor and try? Make a call or two?" There was a pause. He knew she wasn't happy with him right now, but maybe she'd try. "Gabby?"

"I'll call."

"Tonight. Now?"

"Yes, Lukas, tonight."

"Thanks, I'll text you some pics."

Lukas disconnected the call and took photos of the labels with his phone. He texted them to Gabby's number. He looked at Brooke, whose eyebrows were arched.

"What?"

She shrugged.

"What? If you have something to say, you might as well spit it out."

"No, nothing. Really."

"Do you think I shouldn't have asked her to help? Is that what it is?"

"Hey, I'm not getting in the middle of this. I think I've caused enough problems."

"You haven't done anything wrong."

"The only thing that bothers me is that she's a civilian with no connection to the case. You might be asking her to do something that will get her into trouble with the hospital. She might even lose her job if it turns out she's doing something she's not supposed to be doing."

"You might be right. But let's say we go through the normal channels. The hospital finds out we're investigating a crime where a man has been a victim of an overdose due to one of their people smuggling out morphine, maybe dilaudid, and who knows what else. The attorneys go straight into damage control mode. Next thing you know, the records somehow mysteriously disappear. All because big corporate is worried about a lawsuit. And there goes what might be a good lead on five dead women."

A few minutes later, Lukas's phone lit up. Gabriele.

"Hey, what did you find?"

"Donna Blalock is the charge nurse tonight. I talked to her, and she talked to someone in the pharmacy she trusts. The meds came from University Hospital, both vials. They were signed out in the ER on November seventh. The bad news is that there's no way to tell who signed them out. I just have the names of the nurses who were on shift that night."

"You mean there's no control protocol on narcotics?"

"There is, but it should probably be better. Basically, a nurse signs out the meds with a patient's ID number. But once they're dispensed, there really is no control."

"Meaning, if a person was in pain, and the nurse signed out, say, morphine, she could either give it to the patient or put it in her pocket?"

"I suppose so, I mean if the patient didn't complain up the chain that he or she wasn't getting pain meds, and nobody asked. It's not something that's ever even entered my mind."

"Can I have the names of the nurses on duty?"

"I'm not sure I want to be the cause of someone losing their livelihood."

"Gabby, if a nurse is stealing narcotics, they need to be fired, they need to lose their license, and they need to be prosecuted. Can I please have the names?"

She paused. "You're putting me in a tough spot, Lukas."

"I know, and I'm sorry. But it's important. I know this sounds dramatic, but lives may be at stake."

"Okay. Stephanie Remine, April Summerton, Kate Snowden, Paul Dolan, and yours truly."

"We can rule you out, right?"

"Come on, Lukas, really? Please be discreet. For me."

"I promise."

"Listen, I know things have been a little cold lately, but I was wondering whether you might like to go up to Dad's lake house and spend a nice quiet weekend together. Maybe we can, you know, kind of reconnect." She lowered her voice. "What do you think?"

"I could definitely use something like that right about now. And thanks again for doing this for me. I'll call you later. Bye."

Lukas looked over the pad he had written the names on. "So, one of the names on this list smuggled the vials containing morphine and dilaudid out of the ER at University Hospital."

"Which means the vials that were found at Odell's house were most likely sold or given to him by a name on that list," Brooke said.

"Let's start with the names. Gabriele's name is on the list. I promise we can count her out. Three of the others are women and one is a man.

Lukas plugged the names into the criminal database one at a time. In return, he got photographs and criminal and traffic records. He printed each out and laid them on the table in the center of the room.

Brooke pointed to the last picture he'd printed out. "Lukas, I recognize this guy."

"Well, he's a nurse from the ER here in Johnson City. Could that be it?"

"I've only been there once or twice. Not enough to recognize any of the nurses. No, it's from somewhere else." She stood and walked around the room, rubbing her temples.

"Could it be someone you've arrested?"

"No, I don't think that's it." Suddenly, she turned to face Lukas and pointed a finger at him. "The Citizens Police Academy. He was one of the cadets."

"Are you sure it's the same man?"

"Positive!"

"Okay, calm down. Let's see if he's working tonight. I'll call the ER."

Lukas dialed the number from his desk phone and confirmed that Paul Dolan was working. He looked up at Brooke. "We'll swing by there and have a little chat with him."

They drove separately to the ER. The precipitation that had been in the forecast for the last two days was finally making its appearance in the form of spitting snow. Lukas focused on finding someone at the hospital he could trust. He found Donna Blalock at the charge nurse station.

"Hey, Lukas," Donna said. "Gabriele is off tonight."

"I know. Listen, Donna, I kind of need a favor. And I need you to keep this between us, if that's okay with you."

"Sure, what's up?"

"Gabby called you earlier asking about some vial labels?"

"She did. I checked with the pharmacy and confirmed that they were checked out through the ER. She asked me to find out who was on the floor that night, so I did, and I gave her the names. What's this all about?"

"We're just tying up some loose ends on a case. Would you mind walking us through the ER department? We'd like to talk to Paul Dolan if possible."

"Sure, let's go."

There were a few familiar faces in the ER. A couple of them nodded as they walked by. Donna stopped and had a quick conversation with another nurse, then approached Lukas.

"Paul *was* working tonight."

"What do you mean, was?"

"Apparently, he left about fifteen minutes ago. He said he was sick."

Lukas had printed out a copy of Dolan's driver's license photo. He showed it to Donna.

"Is this him?" Lukas said.

"Sure is. Let me see when he checked out. Follow me."

He and Brooke followed her back over to the nurse's station. Lukas noticed a yellow pad lying on the desk with the names Gabby had given him and the date of November seventh along with Gabriele's name and number.

"Donna, did you write this?"

"When Gabby called, I called the pharmacy first, and then wrote down the names and date when I checked the schedule."

"Did anyone else notice this?" he said, pointing to the yellow pad.

A young, blonde-haired nurse Lukas didn't know spoke up. "Um, actually, I was standing here when Paul asked about those names earlier. I didn't know, so I told him to check with Donna."

Lukas grabbed Brooke's arm and darted for the ER door. "Let's go."

"Where?"

"Gabriele's. Shit, Brooke. He's going after her."

CHAPTER TWENTY-FIVE

The spitting snow had become a light but steady fall, turning the grass white and clinging to the trees. The roads were still in decent condition, although Lukas could see the occasional slick spot. Lukas dialed Gabriele's cell and landline numbers, but there was no answer. He hit speed dial for the ER, and Donna answered.

"What does Dolan drive?"

"A green Chevrolet Cruze, I think."

Lukas disconnected. A mailbox or fence post whizzed by as he dialed 911. "This is Detective Lukas Miller, unit number Charlie Oscar Seven. I'm headed to 112 Landau Street on a possible 10-57." Lukas placed an emphasis on the police ten code for an assault. "I'm in a black unmarked Impala. I need all units to converge on that location, code three. Have them BOLO for a green Chevrolet Cruz being operated by a Paul Dolan. He is to be considered armed and dangerous."

The dispatcher responded calmly. "Detective Miller, we will reroute all available units, but be advised most units are tied up on traffic accidents at the moment."

"Just do the best you can. And have all units report descriptions of any vehicles seen in that area. I don't have radio communication, so keep this line open for me, please."

"Ten-four, Detective Miller. From this point forward, I'll be your personal dispatcher on this line."

Lukas directed Brooke to Gabriele's house while talking to the dispatcher. The conditions were getting worse by the minute, but Brooke was doing an excellent job of handling the vehicle at high speeds.

Brooke handed Lukas her cell phone. "Call her again."

He tried Gabriele's home and cell phone again.

"No answer either place. Damn."

"Maybe she's in the shower or something. Think positively."

"Something's wrong. I feel it."

Five minutes later, they pulled up to Gabriele's house, and Lukas informed the dispatcher they were going inside. He placed the phone in his shirt pocket to act as an improvised microphone for the dispatcher on the other end. He found the rear garage door standing open. The house was completely dark. Gabriele's car was still parked in the garage. He drew his Sig Sauer 229 and held it pointed towards the ground. The SIGLITE night sights glowed in the darkness. He signaled to Brooke – who had her Glock 23 drawn – that they would use the button hook clearing strategy. She nodded. Lukas entered the door first moving to the right while keeping his back to the door. Brooke followed immediately, moving left.

They separated and moved slowly and methodically forward, checking every inch of the garage, including the car. Lukas could feel his heart pounding.

Once they cleared the garage, they moved to the kitchen using the same strategy. He kept Brooke in his peripheral vision, moving with her. From the kitchen, they made their way to the living room. Lukas sucked in a deep breath. His gut clenched. At that moment, he knew she'd been taken. The vase that held the flowers Lukas had bought for her was lying shattered on the floor. A chair was turned over in a corner, and the coffee table that was supposed to be in the middle of the living room was pushed up against the couch. Lukas and Brooke cleared the house in less than two minutes and started looking for anything that might give them a lead.

Lukas found a smattering of blood on the kitchen floor near the garage exit and a bloody handprint on the door frame leading to the outside. A wave of hopelessness swept over him. What had he done? First Razzy and now Gabriele. He had to get this maniac stopped. Brooke came over and took his phone from his shirt pocket. Brooke identified herself to the dispatcher and told her that the house had been cleared and that Gabriele should be considered abducted.

Brooke gently handed the phone back to him and took his hand.

"It's not your fault, Lukas."

"I know, damn it, it's *his* fault."

"We'll get her back. At least now we know who he is. Let's stay focused."

The dispatcher called his phone.

"Detective Miller, we have a unit in pursuit of the suspect vehicle. It's currently on Meadows Avenue headed south."

"We're on our way. Have CSU respond to my present location for processing, please. I'll keep the line open."

"Ten-four."

They were out the door and headed for the car before Lukas could finish the conversation. The snow was falling more heavily now and had obliterated any tracks that might have been left by vehicles. Brooke slammed the selector into drive and hit the gas. Traffic was light, but the cars that were out seemed to be struggling. Lukas spoke into the phone.

"What's the current location of the pursuit?"

"They're now heading west on Payton, passing Main."

"We're two blocks away."

Lukas could hear confusion on the dispatcher's radio in the background.

"Detective Miller, the marked unit that was in pursuit has been involved in a 10-45 and is out of service. We've lost contact."

"Shit! Step it up, Brooke." Lukas knew it was now or never. The marked unit had crashed. The direction Dolan was traveling would take him out of the city. If he made it out, Gabriele would be dead by the time they found her.

They topped the hill on Payton and saw the police cruiser that had been following Dolan. It had skidded off the road into an embankment. The red and blue strobes marked the site like a lighthouse beacon. Brooke stepped on the accelerator as Lukas clung onto the door. The vehicle started to skid as they rounded a curve, but Brooke regained control just before the rear tires left the road. Lukas strained his eyes and thought he could see tail lights ahead through the blinding snow.

"There! See the lights?" he said. "That has to be him." He spoke into the phone, "We are continuing pursuit. Currently westbound on Payton, passing Blackman Pike."

"Ten-four."

"Careful, Brooke. There's a sharp turn coming up." He had no more than gotten the words out when he saw it. Sitting on the side of the road, teetering on the edge of a thirty-foot ravine, was the green Chevrolet Cruz.

Brooke hit the brakes, but the snow that had covered the road kept the Impala from stopping. It T-boned Dolan's Cruz on the driver's side. Lukas's head struck the dashboard. He watched helplessly through the windshield as Dolan's car slid out of sight down the steep embankment. The hood of Brooke's Impala had buckled. He could feel their vehicle teetering. He reached for the door handle, but the door was jammed. He looked over at Brooke. She still had a death grip on the steering wheel, but otherwise appeared to be fine. Lukas braced himself and hit the door with his shoulder. Nothing. Again. He felt the car shift and looked back over at Brooke. Her eyes widened as the car slowly shifted and slid over the cliff and into the ravine.

Lukas could see only smoke, falling snow, and trees and rocks as they slid by. He felt like a passenger on a runaway train. At one point the car turned sideways. Lukas felt sure it was about to start rolling, but it suddenly stopped. He heard a hissing sound coming from the engine compartment. The Impala's hood was now pointed skyward. The windshield had spider-webbed. He looked at Brooke, who seemed addled.

"Are you okay?" Lukas said.

"I think so. What the hell just happened?"

"Are you sure you're all right?"

"Yes, go, I'm right behind you."

He climbed out the now shattered passenger window and took stock of the situation. It appeared that Dolan's car had rolled several times based on the damage to the roof and sides. He trudged through the mud and snow toward the Cruz. He retrieved his mini MagLite and lit up the car. He pulled his Sig. Nothing was moving inside.

He stepped closer, shining the light into the driver's side compartment, holding his pistol on the window. He approached from the passenger side, and when he got near enough to see clearly into the interior, he found the car vacant.

He shined his flashlight around the area looking for a body. Nothing. Where were they? Turning his attention back to the car, he noticed the keys were still in the ignition. He retrieved them and moved to the trunk. Placing the key in the lock, he opened the hatch. Gabriele. Thank God. She wasn't moving and appeared to be unconscious. With great trepidation, he shined his light on her to check for possible wounds. There was a deep cut on her forehead, but he didn't see any other obvious injuries. He called out to Brooke as he continued his triage. He found her right wrist and checked her pulse. It was strong. Good.

Brooke made her way to Lukas. "Found your phone. Dispatch is sending an ambulance."

"Thanks. Gabby, hey, can you hear me?" He turned to Brooke. "She's alive. Did you see Dolan?"

"No. Nothing. It all happened so fast. Where could he be?"

The faint wail of sirens sounded in the distance. Gabby was limp and pale. Lukas wanted to take her in his arms, to hold her, but he knew he shouldn't move her. He caressed her hair and face, thankful she was alive. "I'll stay with her. Go up and meet the cavalry." He looked back down at Gabriele. "Stay with me, girl, stay with me."

Within moments, the area was alive with activity. Three ambulances and five cruisers had converged on the scene. The on-duty K-9 unit was searching nearby. Lukas was watching the paramedics attend to Gabriele when Sergeant Adams approached.

"Any news on Dolan?" Lukas said.

"We have a clear track leading away from the scene from up top. He won't be able to outrun the K-9's. We'll have him soon. Apparently, he got out of the car before you guys hit him."

"He probably left the car in that spot purposefully hoping we'd crash into it and give him some time."

"Is he that clever?"

"He has been so far."

"We'll get him."

"Good. Keep me posted."

Lukas couldn't get a clear read on Gabriele's condition, but from the actions of the paramedics, it seemed to be serious. He thought he'd seen everything during his training and the missions he'd undertaken in the Air

Force, but he'd never witnessed anyone being triaged in the trunk of a car. He looked over at Brooke. She, too, was being attended to by medical personnel. She gave him a slight nod and a wave, and signaled for him to go with Gabriele, who was being loaded into an ambulance.

"I'll meet you at the hospital," she said.

Lukas saw Adams walking toward him and talking on his shoulder mic.

"There's been a carjacking two blocks from here. The suspect fits the description of Dolan. He's no longer on foot."

"Damn it."

"Worse news is the car he jacked was a four-wheel drive."

Lukas made eye contact with Brooke. She seemed to know what Sergeant Adams had just told him.

A paramedic yelled across at Lukas that they were about to leave. Grateful for the ride, he hurried over and took a seat in the rear of the ambulance with Gabriele.

Within minutes, Lukas was back in the University Hospital ER. The nurses on staff had likely heard rumors of Dolan's possible involvement in the murders. Gabriele was one of theirs, and she was getting plenty of attention. Lukas helped them get the gurney inside, and then was asked to wait in the lobby. He felt like he needed to be in there with her, but knew he'd just be in the way. The last hour seemed to have happened in minutes.

Lukas looked up and was relieved to see Brooke walk through the door.

"How is she?" Brooke asked as she sat down in the blue plastic chair beside Lukas.

"I don't know. They're checking her out now. Any word on Dolan?"

"I rode over with a patrol unit. They're looking for him, but they haven't found him yet."

The doors to the waiting room opened, and Captain Hunter came lumbering through. His massive frame was covered by a beige trench coat. He looked like a walking cliché.

"Please tell me that I don't have an unmarked at the bottom of that ravine," the captain said.

"No, Captain," Brooke said. "It's mine."

"Are you two all right?"

Lukas detected genuine concern in Hunter's voice.

"We're fine, considering."

"I heard we have a banged-up nurse?"

"We do."

"But one who's alive, thanks to you two."

"I hope she feels the same," Lukas said.

The ER doors opened again, and a doctor came out. Lukas stood as he approached. The lab coat the doctor wore had his name embroidered on the left chest and identified him as Dr. Moseby.

Lukas introduced everyone and held his breath.

"She has a concussion and some pretty bad bruising, but she'll be okay. She's conscious now, but she's drowsy from the meds we've given her. You can see her if you'd like, but only for a few minutes. She needs to rest."

"Thank you."

Lukas shook the man's hand and sent up a quick prayer of thanks. He followed the doctor through the door to the trauma rooms. Each trauma room had two beds separated by a privacy curtain. Dr. Moseby led him to trauma four and told him to keep the visit short. Lukas pulled back the privacy curtain and entered Gabby's section alone.

She looked up at him and then down at her hands, adjusting her IV.

"Hey, girl." He noticed the bruises on her face and arms.

"Hi."

"Gabby, I'm so sorry. So sorry. I never meant for this to happen."

"He kept saying that my boyfriend should have let it go and should have kept his nose out of his business." There was anger in her voice.

"I'm sorry. We'll find him."

"What was he going to do to me, Lukas?"

"It doesn't matter. You're safe now. We'll put a team on your room. He won't be able to get anywhere near you."

"I'm tired. Just really tired."

"I know—"

"I don't think you do."

She obviously didn't want his company or his comfort. "I'll leave you alone now," Lukas said, "but if you need anything from me—"

"I won't."

Lukas stood to leave, but as he got to the door he heard Gabriele say, "Lukas, why did you involve me in this?"

He shook his head slowly. He walked out through the curtain and headed back to the waiting room where Captain Hunter and Brooke still sat.

Hunter fidgeted with the paper cup in his hand. "I figured since you two are without transportation, I'd give you a ride back to headquarters. We have a lot to go over."

"Right," Lukas said. "I'd like to question the staff some while we're here."

Hunter glanced at his watch.

"It won't take long, Captain," Lukas said.

"Sure, take your time." He held up his empty cup. "I need another jolt anyway."

He led Brooke over to the triage station and was granted access to the ER. They walked down the hall to the charge nurse's station. "Hey Donna, I was wondering if we could get some information on Paul Dolan. His file would be great."

Donna looked around before she spoke. "I'm really not authorized to—"

"Donna. It's for Gabby. Please."

Donna looked down and then back at Lukas. "What the hell. If the bosses come after me…"

"We'll cover you. Promise."

She shook her head. "I'll be right back."

Donna walked out of the ER and vanished down a hall that Lukas assumed led to the HR department.

"That's ballsy," Brooke said.

"Let's ask a few questions," he said walking toward the young nurse who had initially alerted him to Dolan's disappearance.

"Hi, I'm Detective Miller, and this is Detective Stevens," Lukas said.

"Thanks for getting Gabby back. I'm Abby Manchester."

"Abby, can you tell us anything about Dolan's personal life? Who his friends were, or what he was into? Anything?"

"Not really. Paul was aloof. He didn't seem to play well with others."

"Meaning?" Brooke asked.

"Occasionally we would all get together and have a drink or a cookout at someone's house, you know, at holidays and special events. Paul never showed up."

"Did he ever talk about his significant other or family members?"

"Not to me."

Lukas looked toward the doors to the lobby then back to Abby. "Who here knew him best?"

She bent over and picked up what appeared to be a schedule. "Let's see… I'd say Donna, his supervisor. Or, maybe Tom Clifford. Yeah, Paul and Tom ate together sometimes. Took breaks at the same time, too."

Lukas noticed Brooke writing in her antique notebook. He handed the young nurse his card. "Thanks Abby. If you think of anything else, please call us."

Lukas and Brooke walked back toward the door Donna had gone through.

"What do you think he intended to do with Gabriele?" Brooke asked.

"I don't even want to think about it."

Lukas heard the door behind him open and saw Donna approach with a manila envelope in her hand. She handed it to Lukas and said, "You didn't get this from me."

"You're a gem. Donna, do you have any idea where Paul would go?"

"Paul stayed to himself. He wasn't the outgoing type. He never spoke about his personal life, and I don't think he has any family. I have no idea where he'd be."

On the way back to headquarters, Lukas and Brooke brought Captain Hunter up to speed on what had occurred over the past couple of days. Hunter told them that the vehicle Dolan had carjacked had been located, but Dolan was in the wind. He agreed to place a security detail on Gabriele.

When they arrived at headquarters, Hunter told them to take a few minutes to get their thoughts together, then they would formulate a game plan. Lukas nodded. He had to catch this bastard. Lukas had no doubt that Dolan would have killed Gabriele. Dolan *was* their killer. He'd murdered and tried to frame Rodney Odell, he'd killed Razzy and the other girls.

Lukas thought about calling Gabriele, just to apologize again and make sure she was okay, but ultimately, he decided against it. She'd made it clear how she felt. The relationship between Gabriele and Lukas was more than likely finished. He leaned against the wall, trying to clear his head, when Brooke walked around the corner.

"Need you two over here." Captain Hunter called them back into the squad room, and the three sat down. "We're going to need warrants drawn up for Dolan's arrest for kidnapping and assault, and we'll need search warrants for his car and home. But you two aren't going to be in on it."

"What?" Lukas stood. "What do you mean? It's our case. I'm not quitting, and you're not taking me off this case." Lukas knew he was overstepping, but he didn't care.

"Calm down, hotshot. I'm not taking you off the case. But you two have been going on this all day, and you're not going to be worth a damn to me tomorrow if you stay here all night writing warrant applications. I'm calling in some more suits to help us. So, go home, both of you. Get some rest and be in here bright and early tomorrow."

Brooke smiled sheepishly. "There's just one small problem, Captain. I don't have a car."

"Yeah, right, I forgot. I'll make arrangements to get you home, and you can have another car issued to you tomorrow. I'll call your chief myself and tell him what's going on."

"I'll take her home," Lukas said.

Hunter looked at them both. "Okay, whatever you want. Do you want me to call your chief, Detective Stevens?"

"I'd appreciate it."

"Fine. Now go, both of you."

They started walking toward Lukas's car when Brooke looked at her watch and said, "Listen, you really don't have to do this. It's been a long day, and you'll have to make a trip back over here after you take me home. It's already late."

"I'm not taking you home. You're staying at my place."

"No, I couldn't do that."

"Yes, you can. Where's Sierra?"

"My mother's staying with her tonight. When this started to break, I didn't know if or when I'd make it home so I called her and asked her to spend the night."

"Then just come on over."

"I'll need clothes, everything. It'd be too much hassle."

"I have a washer."

"Seriously, I don't want to cause you any more trouble. I mean, you've had a rough night already."

"If you don't feel comfortable, I'll be glad to take you home," Lukas said. "But this just seems to be the best option. We can both be back in here early tomorrow, and it will give us some time to talk about a plan."

"Can I wear your pararescue pajamas?"

"They're sweats, not pajamas, and yes, you can wear them."

"Okay, but I'm starved, too. A girl's gotta eat."

"We'll pick up some take out on the way."

They picked up some food, drove to Lukas's, and ate. When they were finished, Lukas straightened up the house while Brooke took a quick shower. She came back out wearing his pararescue sweats and one of his JCPD T-shirts

"Thanks for the duds," she said.

"They look better on you than they do on me."

There was a long pause. Finally, Brooke broke the silence. "How was Gabriele when you saw her?"

"She said she needs some time," he said after a pause. "She's angry. I think it's over between us."

"It was probably a combination of shock and medication."

"Maybe, but she just seemed, I don't know, different. Things haven't been going well lately anyway."

"Give her time."

"Let's talk about something else," Lukas said. "Dolan knows we'll be watching his place, right?"

"Unless he's a complete moron, which obviously he isn't."

"He won't go back there, so we have to think ahead. So far, he's been a step ahead of us. We've played right into his hands. Until today, that is. Now we know who he is. We have him off his game, at least temporarily. He's on the run. We have the initiative. I say we keep the pressure up, but the problem is figuring out where he'd go. Let's look through his employee file."

Lukas retrieved the file from the kitchen and laid it down on the coffee table in the living room. They both took papers from the files hoping to find something that would lead them to him. They read in silence.

"Find anything interesting?" Lukas asked after a few minutes.

"Not really. On his application, under next of kin it says none. Did he do that intentionally, or could that actually be true?"

"It's rare that someone his age doesn't have a next of kin somewhere. But I guess it's possible."

Brooke threw her part of the file back on the table and let out a sigh. "A whole lot of nothing. No disciplinary record, no next of kin or significant other. Just an address that's of no use to us."

"It's the same here."

"He'd need money," Brooke said, "so we check his financials and bank transactions."

"Hunter should have those ready when we go in tomorrow morning. He also needs somewhere to hide.

"We'll check all known associates, which at this point shouldn't take long."

"What about the nurse, what was his name?"

Brooke reached for her notebook, then remembered his name. "Tom Clifford."

"Right. Would he go there? Abby said they were close."

Brooke hooked a wet strand of hair out from behind her ear. "That's our best bet at this point. Hell, it's the only bet as far as I know."

"If he's using Clifford's place, he's probably ditched the car by now. He'd have to assume Clifford knows what's happened, so if he *is* there, we may be looking at another kidnapping situation. Or worse."

"Unless he's in on it, too."

Lukas walked to the kitchen, pulled two bottles of water from the refrigerator, and tossed one to Brooke. "Unlikely," he said sitting back down on the couch.

"Agreed."

"We could call him from a blocked number to see what he says. If Dolan's not there we haven't lost any-thing, and then we can warn him."

"But if he is there and the alarm bells go off we could put him in danger."

Lukas reached for the remote and turned on the TV. "Let's see how much press it's getting." When the picture materialized it showed Sarah Anderson from news channel 39 standing at the site where Brooke and Lukas had crashed into Dolan's car and tumbled down the embankment. He flipped through the stations and found that the same news was being reported by two other local stations as well. "Looks like there's no hiding from it now. So, if he's at Clifford's, we should assume Clifford is already in trouble or worse. I wonder if he has a wife and kids?"

"Okay, now I'm starting to get freaked out. We have to do something," Brooke said.

Lukas turned off the TV and laid the remote on the coffee table. "No phone calls. It's too risky. I'll phone Hunter and see about sending some cars by Clifford's house. If everything is on the up and up, we'll have him call us."

"I like that better."

Lukas first made a call to Donna Blalock in the ER to get Clifford's address and phone number. He also learned that Clifford was married and had two small children, both girls. Lukas asked Donna to warn the nurses on staff to be wary of Dolan. He told her that it was unlikely he would approach any of them, but he was obviously dangerous, and they needed to be careful. Next, he phoned Captain Hunter and explained the situation to him. Hunter said he'd take care of it, and for Lukas and Brooke to stand by. He received a return call from Hunter twenty minutes later who said that Clifford had been contacted and apprised of the situation.

Brooke grabbed a throw from the love seat and curled up with it. "It's hard to believe this guy has no friends or family."

"Maybe it drove him to kill prostitutes and kidnap co-workers."

"And then he disappears into thin air."

"Tomorrow's going to be another long day. I'm gonna take a shower and hit the sack."

"I think I'll call mom and check on Sierra. Then I'll sack out, too."

"There are extra blankets in the closet in the spare bedroom. Oh, and there should be an unopened tooth brush in the vanity over the sink in the bathroom where you showered."

"Thanks for letting me stay here. Appreciate it."

"No problem."

When Lukas finished his shower and put on some sweats and a T-shirt, he walked back through the house to check on Brooke. She'd left the door to the spare bedroom open, and he peeked in. She was lying on her side, facing away from him, curled into a fetal position. She seemed to be at peace. He briefly wondered what it would be like to crawl into the bed beside her, but he dismissed the thought and turned toward his own room.

Damn, what a day.

Just as he started to take a step, he heard a soft voice. "Night, Lukas."

"Night, Brooke."

"We'll get the guy tomorrow."

"I hope so."

CHAPTER TWENTY-SIX

Lukas and Brooke arrived at police headquarters at 7:00 a.m. the next morning. Captain Hunter briefed them on the previous night's progress. A plain clothes detail was set up on Dolan's apartment, but there had been no sign of him, which wasn't surprising. Search warrants had been completed for Dolan's home, vehicle, phone, and financial records.

Lukas drove downtown and was lucky enough to find a judge, one with whom he was familiar. Judge Gaston Walker always made himself available when emergency search warrants were needed. Lukas admired and respected Judge Walker, and he was always the first choice when Lukas needed a signature.

The judge signed off quickly as usual, and Lukas headed back to the station. He stopped off at a local coffee shop that served a great caramel latte and picked one up for both Brooke and himself.

Back at the station, he entered the now sparsely populated squad room and sat down at the table where Brooke was looking through the paperwork the other suits had worked on the night before.

"I've been thinking about our next move," he said, handing Brooke her coffee. "I think the secret is going to be his associates, be they here or somewhere else. Any idea where he lived before he showed up here?"

"No, we didn't talk much during the Citizen's Academy. He asked a few questions, but nothing really out of the ordinary. I can't wait to slap a pair of cuffs on him."

"He probably used Gabriele. Pumped her for information, followed the investigation. Planning his next move the whole time. I think he probably used Odell to place the bodies after he killed them. That's why we got the leads on the red car and black male as the suspect initially."

"And he planted the evidence in Odell's house. But what about the DNA taken from Razzy?"

"Not sure about that one. Maybe had sex with her."

"I don't think so. She was tortured. There was real anger behind her killing."

"Searching Dolan's place should turn up some answers."

"Let's hope."

Captain Hunter appeared in the doorway and summoned Lukas and Brooke into his office. They spent the next thirty minutes going over theories. Hunter seemed to think Dolan had left town. Lukas wasn't sold on the idea. Either way, they all agreed that Dolan wouldn't show up at his apartment. They knew he'd need money, transportation and a place to stay. It had taken all morning, but Hunter's *ad hoc* task force had located Dolan's bank. They were watching his accounts for any activity, but none had been detected. Lukas had Hunter contact the ICAP people and pull records for stolen vehicles, which were subsequently put out to state and local agencies. The best chance of finding anything significant was most likely going to be his apartment. But they weren't ready to move on it just yet. An online search had been completed with Dolan's identifiers which had provided a few additional addresses that were currently being searched. But so far, they looked to be former addresses or different Paul Dolans. As Lukas and Brooke stood to leave, Hunter stopped them.

"You guys did good last night. There's no doubt in my mind what would have happened to that nurse if you hadn't stopped him. We've got him on the run. Let's finish this thing."

Lukas said, "We will, Captain."

"I have one question before you go. Did you know there was someone else behind this the night we found Odell?"

"We didn't lie to you, Captain. We had doubts, sure. And there were loose ends just like I told you. When we pulled on those ends they came unraveled."

Hunter sat back and looked at Lukas, then at Brooke over his reading glasses. After what seemed like an eternal silence, Hunter took off his readers and tossed them on his cluttered desk. "Next time fill me in. And I mean totally. Dismissed."

Lukas led Brooke back to the squad room. Dolan's name had been run through all the department's databases, including his NCIC record. The guy was squeaky clean. All Lukas could find was a traffic ticket and a shoplifting charge as a juvenile. He also noticed that Dolan was a part-time nurse for the county detention center. He called and spoke to a supervisor over the medical department, but they didn't have any additional information on possible associates for Dolan.

"Nothing," Lukas said to Brooke. "He's vanished into thin air."

Brooke squeezed Lukas's arm. "Lukas, I just thought of something. When cadets come into the Citizen's Police Academy, they fill out an application and there's a mandatory section that requires them to list a next of kin. He might have written something bogus, but it's worth a shot."

She put a call in to the community relations office at the Kingsport Police Department. She was put on hold for a few minutes while the person on the other end found the records. She ended the call and looked over at Lukas. "He listed a Pam Wilcox. She lives on H Street here in Johnson City. I have a phone number, too. Right now, it's all we have."

"I say we take a shot."

"Don't you think we should tell Captain Hunter?"

"We'll tell him if something pans out. Let's go. I'm driving."

"Makes sense, since I don't have a car."

They headed out. Lukas felt his pulse quicken as he brought his Crown Victoria up to speed. Dolan being at Wilcox's house was probably too much to hope for, but it was possible. Regardless, it felt good to finally be on the guy's scent.

CHAPTER TWENTY-SEVEN

Lukas picked a vantage point that gave them a relatively unobstructed view of the house from about two blocks away. It was a single-level structure with blue siding and white shutters, situated in the middle of the block. The shades were pulled. There was a silver Volkswagen Jetta in the driveway. Lukas called in the location and requested backup.

"What's our play?" Brooke asked as she watched the house through binoculars.

"I'll take the front, and you get the back."

"What about the backup?"

"We go now. I don't want marked units or uniforms to spook him if he's there."

They got out of the car, jogged across the street, and walked through yards to avoid detection. The crisp snow crunching under their feet made a silent approach impossible. Lukas waited for Brooke to get into position, then stepped up on the porch. He stood to the side of the front door and knocked. He heard footsteps from within. "Open the door! It's the Johnson City Police Depa—" His announcement was cut off as three shots slammed through the door inches from where he stood.

He dove from the porch, crouched beside a bush, and prepared to return fire.

Brooke came running around the side of the house holding her gun. "Are you hit?"

"No! Get to the back!"

Brooke ran back around to the rear of the house with Lukas close behind her. Just as they cleared the side of the house, Lukas noticed movement beyond a hedge thirty feet away. Brooke indicated she'd seen it, too. He motioned for her to fan out to the left. He moved to the right and forward. Brooke and Lukas inched along with their weapons trained on the hedge.

Lukas felt tension in his neck, and his arm still ached from the stab wound. When they cleared the hedge, they noticed an alley that ran behind the houses. An engine started from somewhere to their left. They broke into a run and saw a green Ford pickup truck turn left onto the main road from the alley and disappear.

Lukas grabbed his radio and called in the description of the vehicle, direction of travel, and the fact that shots had been fired. He could already hear sirens in the distance.

"We should clear the house," Lukas said.

They walked to the back door, which was standing open, and made entry just as marked and unmarked units began to arrive. Lukas and Brooke cleared the house methodically. The last room they entered turned out to be the bedroom. They swung into the room and found Pam Wilcox lying on the bed with her throat cut. Her eyes were wide open and her face was pale. There was no doubt she was dead.

Noises were now coming from other parts of the house as officers made entry.

"In here! It's all clear!" Lukas yelled at the approaching officers. "Lock it down and call CID and CSU. He's killed another one." Lukas walked out of the room and outside.

The cool air helped, but he felt a tightening in his chest. Another dead woman had been added to the ledger. Brooke was just a step behind. He looked up at the gray, overcast sky. There was more snow in the forecast, and he wouldn't be surprised if it started any time.

At that moment, a car pulled up, and Captain Hunter got out and walked straight toward Brooke and Lukas.

Lukas looked at Brooke and shrugged. "This should be interesting."

Lukas told the captain what had happened and was surprised when he didn't get a lecture. Hunter said he would assign the scene to someone else and insisted they continue to chase Dolan. "I want you to stay on top of him, keep pressure on him. Go get this murdering bastard."

Lukas and Brooke drove over to the complex where Dolan lived, arriving just as the teams were staging to execute the search warrant. They walked to the temporary command post, which amounted to the tactical team's striker van, three unmarked cruisers, and an ambulance.

A plain clothes detail had been watching the apartment since Dolan came onto their radar. There hadn't been any sign of him. At the staging area, the respective teams were briefed while Brooke and Lukas waited for the green light. The wait was excruciating for Lukas. Brooke seemed to sense his mood.

"Are you nervous?"

"I'm anxious. You?"

"Same. I can't wait to get in there. I know there's going to be something that will give us a clearer picture of where he'd go or what his plans are."

"I hope you're right."

Finally, the tactical team entered the apartment and the clear sign was given. Lukas walked into the apartment and immediately noticed the police scanner sitting next to a recliner. He stopped to look at it while Brooke checked an adjoining room. Lukas had no doubt that Dolan had been using the scanner to try to stay on top of the investigation. Along with the information he likely picked up from Gabriele and the police academy, Dolan had a pretty deep pool of resources.

Lukas looked around the living room. There was nothing of interest besides the scanner.

"Lukas, in here."

Lukas made the short trek down the hall and joined Brooke. He walked into a bedroom. There was a twin bed in the corner. The room was small and sparsely furnished, probably intended as a spare bedroom before the occupant's psyche took a nosedive into hell. On the wall over the bed were newspaper clippings about the murders that told the whole morbid story. Going from left to right, the order matched the killings. Mingled in among the clippings were photographs of Lukas and Brooke, some of which were taken while they were at the various crime scenes.

A curio table was near the bed. Lukas pulled open a drawer. Inside was a single scrapbook. It contained the arrest records from the county lockup of all the girls who had been killed and a few that hadn't. Attached to each of the records were photographs of the women that appeared to have been taken on the street while the girls were working.

"He stalked them," Lukas said to Brooke. "Watched them while they were working so he'd know best how and when to go after them."

Lukas continued to flip through the book. It contained more articles about the killings. The last article in the book seemed out of place, though. It was dated July 15, 1995, and was a story about the death of a local prostitute named Marjorie Atkins. The death was ruled a suicide, the story said. He held the book out to Brooke. "Hey, look at this."

"That's old. Who is Marjorie Atkins?"

"No clue. It was before my time. But the article says she was a prostitute. Are you thinking what I'm thinking?"

"I have no idea what you're thinking."

"Dolan's killing prostitutes, and here's an article about the suicide of a prostitute from 1995," Lukas said. "How old was he? Twelve, thirteen? This can't be a coincidence. When we're done here we'll have to see what connection there is between him and this Marjorie Atkins."

"We'll tag this for CSU."

"In here, you guys need to see this." An unfamiliar voice came from an adjacent room.

Lukas and Brooke walked down the hall and into the room where the voice came from. There was a cot in the corner with a small refrigerator beside it. A large wooden desk sat against the far wall and held a computer and monitor. The desk was tidy, with only a clean ashtray, a keyboard, a mouse, and a coaster.

On the monitor were three images of a house.

"These are live feeds," the officer who had called Lukas and Brooke said. "Look at the time stamps in the corners."

All three cameras were pointed at the same house from different angles. The house looked familiar to Lukas, but he couldn't quite place it.

Brooke stepped up beside Lukas. "Oh my God, that's my house! He's been watching me!"

Lukas could see terror in Brooke's face as the realization set in. She glanced back and forth from image to image as if she couldn't believe what she was seeing. Lukas didn't know what to say. He glanced around at the others in the room. They all looked stunned.

Lukas reached for Brooke's arm.

"It's okay. We'll have him in a jail cell soon. Or on a slab at the morgue."

They stood there watching the computer screen. Suddenly, the images changed. A man walked out of the French doors and onto the deck. It was Paul Dolan. He was just finishing a cigarette. He reached down and put the butt out in what appeared to be a flower pot. He walked back into the house and emerged seconds later carrying a little girl.

Sierra appeared to be sleeping.

Dolan smiled and waved at the cameras while Lukas felt Brooke's knees buckle.

PART III

CHAPTER TWENTY-EIGHT

L ukas started to bend over to offer a word of comfort, but Brooke recovered quickly, stood, and made a dash for the door. Lukas was right behind her. It was obvious she wasn't thinking clearly. She still didn't have a vehicle.

They made it to Lukas's car at the same time. Lukas jumped into the driver's seat, and seconds later they were on their way to Brooke's house. Lukas called Captain Hunter and told him what had happened.

"I'll call Chief McConnell in Kingsport and the sheriff. I'm sure they'll get there in a hurry. A BOLO has already been issued for a green Ford truck, but we'll also get an Amber Alert out as soon as we can."

"Thanks, Captain."

"Watch her closely, Lukas. She needs a compass right now. And get that little girl back."

"I will. Listen, could you do me one more favor? Could you call Special Agent Daniel Smart at the FBI and let him know what's going on?"

"I know Smart," the captain said. "Will do. Stay in touch."

"Yes, sir."

Lukas disconnected the call and glanced at Brooke. She had to be in shock. Her face was pale, but there were no tears. She looked like she was trying to process what was happening, but things were coming at her too fast. Lukas wished there was something he could say to offer some comfort or hope, but he knew there was nothing. There would be no comfort until Sierra was safely recovered.

They pulled up to Brooke's house among a large group of marked and unmarked police cars. An ambulance was pulling out of the driveway, siren blasting. Another ambulance sat in the yard. Brooke bolted from the car as though there was still time to keep Dolan from taking Sierra. She ran through the front door with Lukas on her heels and was met by a slightly overweight officer who was wearing captain's bars.

"Any news on my daughter?" Brooke said.

"Nothing yet. I'm sorry."

"My mother?"

"We found her in one of the bedrooms."

"Oh, please God, no," Brooke said. "Is she dead?"

"She'd been strangled, but she's alive. She's already on her way to the hospital."

"Is she going to stay alive?"

The captain put his hand on her right shoulder.

"The paramedics didn't say. They intubated her and got her into the ambulance. We've notified your father. He's going to meet them at the hospital."

Lukas's phone rang. He looked at it. Danny Smart.

"Danny, thank God. How far out are you?"

"We have a full team headed to Detective Stevens's house. I'll be there in twenty minutes. I just got off the phone with your captain. Has anything changed?"

Lukas stepped outside. "I'm at her place right now, and it's not good. Dolan didn't just kidnap Brooke's daughter. He also strangled her mother. Whether she lives is hit or miss. Dolan left in a green Ford pickup, but we don't know where he is. Did the captain tell you about yesterday? About Gabriele?"

"He did, and I'm sorry."

"Did he tell you he killed another woman earlier today?"

"Yes. You guys have busted a hornet's nest wide open."

"You guys are the kidnapping experts. What can we do to get her daughter back? What should *I* be doing?"

"Not much you can do other than try to stay calm until we find him. The alerts have already gone out. We'll help you all we can. Be there soon."

Lukas went back inside. He saw Brooke talking to the Kingsport police chief, David McConnell. Lukas wanted to find out what else, if anything, the folks in his department had found in Dolan's apartment, so he walked through the house and onto the back deck for some privacy. He called Rafe Carrizales, who had just arrived at Dolan's when Lukas and Brooke left earlier.

"Hey, Lukas," Rafe said. "How's she holding up?"

"Not good. Are you still at Dolan's?"

"Yeah, along with the majority of CSU. We're going over the whole place."

"Have you found anything yet?"

"We're still working. I'm not sure what all we have."

"What about the computer?"

"We shut it down right after he took the girl. Forensics will analyze it, but that will take a while."

"Come up with something we can use to find the guy, Rafe."

"We're trying."

Lukas turned around to walk back into the house and nearly ran over Brooke, who was coming out the door.

"Sorry, Brooke. I was just seeing if anything had turned up at Dolan's."

"And?"

"Nothing yet, but they're still in the early stages."

"Lukas, we have to get her back." Her eyes filled with tears and Lukas reached out for her. She fell into his arms, and he gave her a gentle hug.

"We will. I'll do whatever it takes. What's the plan with your department and the FBI?"

Brooke took a step back and composed herself.

"The chief said they're setting up a small detail here at the house until we find her. The FBI is on the way with a team who'll set up a command post here."

"Yeah, I talked to Danny Smart. He's coming with them."

"What could this possibly be about? First, he takes Gabriele, and now Sierra. Why would he take my child?"

"He's deranged, Brooke. A psychopath. Who knows what's motivating him? At this point, though, I don't really care about his motivations. I just want to get Sierra back and remove him from the gene pool in the process.

Listen, I'm not doing anyone any good here, so I'm going back to Johnson City in case they find something at Dolan's. I'll check back in with you later."

"I can't just sit here. I need to be out there looking for her. I need to *do* something." She wrung her hands. "Anything. I can't let my baby down."

"You won't. *We* won't. But we need some kind of lead first. Once we get it, we'll go find her. I promise."

Thirty minutes later, Lukas walked into his squad room and was immediately reminded of an assembly line at an automobile factory. The room was full of people, and each one was busy. The mood was serious, almost ominous.

Lukas was angry. They'd seized the momentum from Dolan, only to let him get it back. It was frustrating to be waiting again. Lukas made his way through the crowd to his desk and sat down. The murder files were still there. A familiar voice came from behind.

"Has anything turned up?" It was Rafe. He looked worried. Everyone looked worried. A cop's child had been taken by a serial killer.

Lukas shook his head slowly. "Nothing new. What about at Dolan's?"

The detective hung his head. "I'm sorry, man. I just left there. Our people are still going through everything, but it doesn't look promising. I brought that scrapbook you found with me. You want to look through it again?"

Lukas went to Rafe's desk and picked up the book. He took it to a conference room, sat down, and fished out the article about the Atkins woman. Who was this woman, and what did she mean to Dolan? He turned on a computer and entered his password. Once he was into the system, he completed a search for the name Marjorie Atkins. He found the case involving the suicide from 1995 and wrote the case number down on a legal pad.

Lukas walked up the hall to the evidence custodian, signed out the key to the case file archive room, then took the elevator downstairs. He unlocked the door and walked into the climate-controlled room. He located the 1995 section and started the painstaking task of locating the file.

Twenty minutes later, he found the case file on the suicide of Marjorie Atkins. He flipped through the crime scene photos. It appeared she died from a self-inflicted gunshot to the head. The news article had mentioned that it was a suspicious death that was ultimately ruled a suicide. He came to the report that was written by the initial responding officer, a patrolman named Lockner.

Lockner wrote that he was able to determine from the victim's son, Paul Dolan, that the victim was right handed. The gunshot wound was on the left side of her skull. The boy also told the officer that he had moved the gun when he found his mother.

"Damn," Lukas said aloud. "She was his first victim, and he got away with it."

He continued through the file and came to the statement taken from Dolan. It said he was in his room watching TV and heard a loud pop. He ran into the living room and found his mother dead. He picked up the gun and moved it away from her body, placing it on a table nearby. Lukas continued through the file to the forensic records. There was no mention of gunshot residue tests on either the victim or her son, who was 13 at the time. The medical examiner's report noted that the wound wasn't a contact wound but was instead a close proximity wound. Big difference there. He looked through the notes and reports in the file from the investigating detective. There was no mention of a canvass or statements from neighbors or family members other than the son.

Lukas closed the file and placed it back in the box. Paul Dolan had killed his mother by shooting her in the head, and then he set the gun on the table. The fact that she was a prostitute probably caused the detectives to be a little less aggressive than they might have been. And because the detectives who worked the case didn't do their jobs, the community was now littered with bodies and a five-year-old girl had been kidnapped.

Lukas felt sick to his stomach as he walked out of the room and came to a realization.

Dolan was killing his mother.

Over and over again.

CHAPTER TWENTY-NINE

Brooke sat staring out the window at nothing in particular. It was as gloomy outside as it was in the house. Her stomach was churning; her mind had gone numb.

The five-member FBI team, including Danny Smart, had already set up in the living room. They brought with them an array of computers and other equipment and were in constant motion. She prayed the equipment and the people using it would help get her little girl back.

She'd spoken briefly to her father on the phone. He was on his way to Brooke's house. Her mother's hyoid bone was fractured, and they were going to keep her for observation for at least one night, but she would be fine. Dolan must have been in a hurry. For that, at least, Brooke was grateful.

When she called Alex and told him about the situation, he went ballistic. He was in Greeneville, Tennessee, attending some kind of seminar, but he would, of course, be leaving for Kingsport immediately. Not that there was anything he could do. Brooke knew when Alex showed up, he'd only make things worse. He would blame the job. The job had always been his go-to when a problem came up. He'd even had the audacity to blame their divorce on her being a cop. He said it had changed her. But *he* was the one who had an affair. That was what broke up the marriage.

Brooke heard the front door open and saw her father walk in. She ran to him and fell into his arms. "Dad! I'm so sorry." Tears were streaming down her face again.

"It's not your fault, honey. It's nobody's fault. We need to discuss some things. In private, okay?"

Brooke and her father walked down the hall. It was adorned with family photos of happier days. They went into her bedroom. He shut the door and stood waiting for her to compose herself before he began.

"What I'm about to say to you is going to be hard to hear. But please, at least try to listen to me. I know your world has turned upside down, and I know how devastating this must be for you. But you have to find a way to put aside the guilt you're feeling and look at this through the eyes of an investigator. You have to try to remain positive and try to think as clearly as possible. She's out there somewhere. You have to believe she's still alive."

"I hear you. I do. But—" She choked back a sob. "Dad, I don't know if I can do this."

"The last thing you want to do is sit here being a victim. If you do and something happens to Sierra, you'll never forgive yourself. Use your resources. All of them. Your mother and I raised you to be independent and strong, and you're both. So, stop feeling sorry for yourself and start thinking like a cop. Evaluate the situation, look at the facts, trust your instincts. Hunt down leads and follow them. Get my granddaughter back."

She breathed in and slowly exhaled. "Okay, Dad," she said. "I'll try."

As they emerged from the room, Danny Smart approached them.

"Can we talk?"

"Sure."

Danny introduced Brooke to the team that would call her home theirs until the situation was resolved. He explained in detail what she was to do in case of a ransom call, or if Dolan contacted her by any means. She knew the drill. She just never imagined she would be on this side of it.

"Let's cut to the chase," Brooke said. "What's this guy's agenda?"

"I can't be sure. But off the top of my head, I don't think we're going to be hearing any ransom demands. I know this is going to sound a little strange but think about who we're dealing with. I think he took your little girl because he knows you'll come after him hard. I think he wants you to find him."

"Why would he want me to find him?" Brooke said.

"So he can kill you."

"And why would he want to kill me?"

"Because you've gotten in the way of him doing what he needs to do, and he wants revenge."

"What does he need to do? Kill hookers?"

Smart nodded. "Exactly. He was just getting revved up, and you got in the way. He thinks you have to pay for what you've done to him."

CHAPTER THIRTY

Brooke walked over to the French doors and stared into the back yard. The tire swing that her dad had tied to the large oak near the back of her property for Sierra last spring was swaying slightly in the breeze. It seemed like an eternity since she'd sat on the deck and watched Sierra swing.

Her mind skipped to the cameras that Dolan had used to spy on her. She opened the doors and walked through the yard to the tree line.

It took her a while to find them, but she eventually located all three. Before she thought it through, she was smashing them on the ground. She stood there looking down at the broken cameras, breathing heavily. How long had they been there? How many times had he sat there in the comfort of his own place watching her and Sierra? The more she thought about it, the angrier she became. She heard a noise behind her and spun around to see her dad walking through the field. She had to get hold of herself.

John Stevens looked down at the smashed cameras and then back at his daughter. Brooke knew the cameras were evidence and should have been processed, but she didn't care. He didn't chastise her. He didn't say anything. Instead he walked up to her, put his arm around her, and walked her back to the house.

As they entered, Brooke heard some type of argument going on, and quickly realized Alex had arrived. Apparently, he had started an argument with the first available person he could find, which turned out to be one of the FBI agents. It was getting heated, and although she could tell the agent was trying hard to keep his composure, he was starting to lose his temper.

Her father broke away and walked up to the two of them.

"Can we try to remain civil, please?" he said. "I understand you're upset, but—"

"Don't tell me to remain civil. How would you feel if it was your daughter?" Alex's tone was demeaning.

"Alex, that's enough!" Brooke said.

"Shut up. I'll deal with you in a minute." Alex took a step toward her, and John Stevens moved to block him.

"Tell her to shut up again, and I'll break your jaw," Brooke heard her father say. "Lay a hand on her and I'll kill you with my bare hands, right here, right now."

The look on her father's face and the tone of his voice froze Alex in his tracks. It surprised Brooke, too. She'd never heard that tone from her father. There was genuine menace in his voice.

Danny Smart came to the rescue. "Look, we're all upset. Let's try to remain calm. The man to blame is out there."

Brooke sat down on the love seat. She felt exhausted. She looked up as her dad walked over.

"I'm sorry honey. You shouldn't have had to hear that with everything else that's going on."

"Alex was out of line, and you're a genuine badass."

"He's upset. He's right about Sierra being his daughter, too."

Brooke looked around the room. Danny had returned to his task force. They were standing close together in the corner of her living room among the computers, tracking devices and other equipment. It was a scene right out of *Criminal Minds*.

"I can't believe it, Dad," she said. "How? How could this happen?"

CHAPTER THIRTY-ONE

L ukas needed to keep moving. He left headquarters and drove back to Dolan's apartment. He checked in with the undercover units that were assigned to watch the house and headed inside.

The apartment was dark. He flipped the light switch next to the door, and a small lamp in the corner of the room switched on. *Dark rooms for dark minds*, he thought. He took out his mini MagLite and used it to supplement the abysmal lighting so he could take some pictures with his phone. He started with the table the scanner sat on. He found an assortment of pens and scrap papers and a partially-completed crossword puzzle.

A large bookcase was positioned in the back of the room with a mismatched selection of books. He shined his light on the spines of the books. There was a collection of short stories by Edgar Allen Poe, along with several true crime books, all of which dealt with serial killers.

"Does this tell me anything I don't already know?" Lukas said out loud.

He stepped back and looked at the bookcase. There was something a bit odd about it, he thought. He remembered a couple of training seminars he'd taken that dealt with searching residences. One of them dealt with a tactic some people used to hide things in false compartments. The top of the bookcase was much thicker than the shelves. He began to tap at it, and it sounded hollow. An ornamental lip protruded from the front and Lukas pushed up on it with the heel of his hand. The thing lifted. Lukas shined his flashlight into a large compartment and whispered, "Whoa. This dude was ready for a shootout if it came down to it."

Inside the compartment was an AR-15 assault rifle, five thirty-round magazines, five hundred rounds of ammunition, a stack of hundred-dollar bills, a K-Bar knife, and a driver's license. Lukas picked up the license. The photo was of Dolan, but the name on the license was John David Danson. The address was in Chattanooga. There was also a book of matches from a place in Gatlinburg called The Woodbriar Inn.

Lukas called CSU and told them to get someone to Dolan's place to collect what he'd found. Then he called Danny Smart and told him about Dolan's alias and asked him to have someone check on the address that was on the license. Danny said they'd start a search on the alias and get banking and property information as well. Lying beside the license was a key with a blue plastic tag that read *Anytime Storage*. The number 515 was inscribed in gold on the tag. Bingo.

Lukas dialed Rafe's number and told him what he had found. He asked him to start an application for a search warrant for the storage facility, and to have someone keep an eye on the place until they could get the paperwork completed.

Lukas walked through the apartment one last time and found nothing else. He left and drove the short distance back to headquarters. Snow was falling again.

He walked into the station and went straight to the intelligence analysis office. The office was staffed twenty-four-seven to assist in any investigative matter that demanded immediate attention. Analyst Hana Fujimoto was on duty.

"Well, look what the cat dragged in. What brings you to my humble place of business?"

"Hey, Hana. Would you run stolen vehicle reports and see if anything comes up regarding a green Ford pickup?

"Sure, no problem."

"And could you possibly look at the traffic cams from between say 4:00 p.m. and 6:00 p.m. to see if there are any green Ford pickups coming into Johnson City on any of the routes from Kingsport?"

"That'll take a little more time."

"Thanks. I need it as soon as possible."

Lukas walked back to the detective's squad room. He looked through the evidence sheets to see if CSU had turned up anything at all. Nothing really jumped out. He turned on his computer and searched for John David Danson. Not a single entry. He wondered how long Dolan had had that alias. If he'd had it for a while, he'd been extra careful about using it.

His cell buzzed. It was Hana.

"Hey, Hana that was quick."

"I have something you need to see."

Lukas hurried to her office, and Hana wasted no time giving him her chair as she cued the video on the monitor.

"Here's a green Ford truck coming in on State Route 36 from Kingsport. It's not clear enough to see the driver." The screen changed to the traffic cams at a different intersection that Lukas didn't immediately recognize. "But here is the same vehicle leaving the city ten minutes later on Highway 11-E."

Lukas moved closer to the image on the screen. He still couldn't see the driver, but it had to be Dolan. There was no sign of Sierra, but that didn't mean she wasn't in the truck.

"Can you get the tag number from this video?" Lukas said to Hana.

"Hmm, not sure. I might be able to clean it up some."

"Okay. I'll relay the information that a green Ford pickup was seen leaving Johnson City, heading west on 11-E, at 5:15 p.m. See what you can do about getting a tag number and call me when you get more details."

Lukas turned his attention back to where Dolan might be as he walked out of Hana's office. He didn't think Dolan could get far in the truck. Every cop between Johnson City and Knoxville would be looking for it. An Amber Alert had been issued, which meant every *citizen* would also be looking. Halfway back to the squad room, he ran into Rafe, who waved some papers at him.

"Got the warrant for the storage building. Ready to roll?"

"Let's go."

The drive to the storage units took less than ten minutes. The owner of the property met them there in the event they needed access, but the key Lukas had found at Dolan's fit the lock on the door. Lukas opened the door and flipped on his flashlight.

"Holy shit!" Rafe said. "What is this place?"

The room was large.

"It looks like a torture chamber," Lukas said.

There was a wooden bed in the middle of the room that had chains suspended from the head and foot boards. A pair of stocks were in the corner, and from the looks of them they had been used recently. In the other corner a leather chair swing was suspended from a wrought iron fixture.

On the left side of the room sat a wooden table with a fluorescent light hanging from the ceiling. There were tools lying on top of the table stained with what appeared to be dried blood. The table had numerous stains that Lukas couldn't identify, but it didn't take much imagination to figure out what they were. There was a putrid, almost rotten, smell to the place.

"Looks like we found where he tortured and killed them," Lukas said somberly.

"I'll get CSU down here," Rafe said.

"I'm going to head over to Brooke's and see what's going on."

"I'll stay outside here and wait for CSU. No way I'm staying in this place alone."

The snow was starting to come down harder. Big, soft flakes fell lazily through the darkness as Lukas began the drive to Brooke's. Snow had covered the roads.

He decided to drive to his house and pick up his Jeep. He tuned the radio to his favorite classic rock 'n' roll station and waited for a weather report. Just before he got home, the station got around to the snow report. More snow was on the way, maybe up to six inches.

He made the trip back to Brooke's where he was let into the house by Brooke's father. He found Danny bent over a laptop, squinting at the screen with his reading glasses pulled down low on his nose, and walked over to him.

"Any news?"

Danny stood and looked over his glasses in the direction of Brooke, who was lying on the love seat. "I don't want to sound the general alarm just yet. Is there somewhere we can talk?"

"Sure, follow me."

Lukas walked out of the living room, down the hall, and into a spare bedroom with Danny in tow. Danny pushed the door shut behind them.

"When we were called in on this, we started watching the financials for Dolan and Pam Wilcox in the event he used bank or credit cards from the accounts. Just a few minutes ago, the bank card that belonged to Wilcox was used at an ATM just outside of Gatlinburg to withdraw five hundred dollars."

"So, he's on the grid."

"We don't have a location on him. Just the ATM transaction. We're not absolutely sure it's him, but the good money says it is. We have a security officer from the bank heading in now to pull the footage to see if it's him, and we should know something within the next couple of hours. He probably needed money and thought if he used her card instead of his, nobody would notice. In any event, at least now we know what direction to start looking. I contacted the field office in Knoxville and they're on high alert along with the TBI, the Highway Patrol and the locals. Oh, and we're up on the financials on his alias, too."

"That's great, Danny."

"We don't know if he's just passing through there or whether he's thrown out an anchor. And we're still trying to get some information on cell phones and a possible vehicle description."

"I may be able to help with the vehicle," Lukas said. "I had our intelligence people pull up the traffic cams, and we found a green Ford truck leaving the city headed in that direction. Couldn't see the driver, though, and couldn't make out a tag number."

"It's still worth putting out," Danny said. "Have you found anything at all in his background that linked him to someplace else?"

"I was at Dolan's place earlier looking around and found a book of matches from a motel in Gatlinburg. The Woodbriar Inn, I believe. It seemed inconsequential, but with the ATM hit it might be important."

"We might just be closing in on him," Danny said. "I'll call and have the locals check it out."

"Make sure they know who they're dealing with."

"What about his co-workers?" Danny asked. "Do you think they would have any information?"

"The ones I talked to didn't seem to know him very well."

"What about Gabriele? Would she have any ideas?"

Lukas contemplated the question. He didn't think he could talk to Gabriele right now. She'd made it clear that she needed space. And deep down, he knew the relationship was in trouble. Probably over.

"Maybe you should call her."

Danny gave Lukas a sympathetic look. "What happened?"

"I don't want to get into it. Let's just say things aren't good between us right now."

"Okay, I'll talk with her to see if she knows anything that might help. Meanwhile, you look like you could use some rest."

"No way, man. I'll hang around here in case something breaks."

Danny smiled at Lukas. "I figured you'd say that."

Lukas followed Danny down the hall and out to the living room. He looked over and saw that Brooke had stirred and was sitting up on the couch. She had a strange look on her face, one that told him something was up. He walked over to her just as she stood.

She took him by the arm. "Hey, let's go out and get a coffee."

"Are you sure? It's pretty bad out there."

"Yes. I'm sure."

Lukas picked up his jacket and watched Brooke as she bypassed the FBI people and headed straight for the closet in the foyer. She grabbed her service pistol and a thick parka that had POLICE emblazoned on the back and chest. The road in front of Brooke's house had recently been plowed, but a new film had already started forming. Lukas started the Jeep and knocked the snow off the windows while Brooke went to her cruiser and retrieved a water-resistant parka, her ballistic vest, and a go bag she used for general investigations. Lukas wasn't sure what she was doing, but it didn't take long for him to find out. Satisfied that he could see through the windows, he jumped in just as Brooke climbed into the passenger seat and tossed her things in the back.

"Lukas, I heard everything that you and Danny said earlier," Brooke said. "Sound travels well in my house."

"Okay, well, Danny didn't want to wake you up until we knew for sure it was a lead on Dolan."

"I was never asleep." Brooke shook her head. "I couldn't. Just the thought of closing my eyes gives me nightmares. I know you and Danny meant well, everyone does, and I appreciate it. But this is my daughter we're talking about. We have to *do* something. I can't just continue to sit here. Not when I know where she is."

"We don't *know* where she is, Brooke."

"Let me make sure I have this straight. You saw a green Ford pickup heading out of town toward Gatlinburg on a traffic cam. Then Danny Smart tells you that a credit card owned by a woman Dolan killed was used at an ATM near Gatlinburg. Then you tell Danny you found a matchbook from a place in Gatlinburg in Dolan's apartment. All true, correct?"

Lukas nodded.

"Then what are we waiting for? To hell with the FBI and everybody else. Screw protocol and regulations and screw a cup of coffee. *I need you to help me get my baby back!* Let's go to Gatlinburg. Right now."

"It's a long shot, Brooke. There's a very strong possibility that he's still on the move, probably in a different vehicle. If it was me, I'd be getting as far away from here as possible."

"It's the only shot we have right now," she said. "Are you with me or not? Because I'm going, with you or without you."

Lukas paused, watching the snow fall, not sure what to do. Heading out on their own could cost them their jobs. He turned and looked over at Brooke. He saw Sierra looking back at him.

Lukas fired up the Jeep and headed for Gatlinburg.

CHAPTER THIRTY-TWO

Paul Dolan pulled the silver, all-wheel-drive Honda Civic up to the front of his cabin. On his way, he'd stopped at a small piece of property he owned in rural Greene County and switched vehicles. Dolan had purchased the used Civic for cash, registered it under one of his aliases, and stored it in a barn along with some stolen tags. He'd bought the vehicle solely for the purpose of evading capture if the need ever arose, and the need had definitely arisen. He knew taking the child was a risk because of the Amber Alert system, but he'd managed to avoid detection and had made it safely to Gatlinburg. Once he'd gotten to Gatlinburg, he'd made one quick stop at a motel called The Woodbriar Inn. He'd checked in, but only went into his room for a second. He left a breadcrumb for Brooke, went back out to the Civic, and drove up the mountain to his cabin.

Dolan started hauling some equipment he'd kept in the barn along with the Civic into the cabin. Sierra remained sedated in the car. When he was finished carrying his equipment inside, he walked back out to the car, pulled Sierra from the back seat, and carried her into the cabin. He laid her on a bed in a room just off the den.

The child was a dead ringer for Brooke. Dolan found himself wondering what her father looked like. He reached down and pushed a strand of hair from the child's forehead.

He knew her mother would come after him soon. He counted on it. Brooke, the perfect, beautiful, all-American girl who was supposedly keeping society safe from the "bad guys." But Dolan knew that was a façade. She was as bad as the whores he'd killed. No...she was worse. At least they knew what they were. They didn't fake being someone decent.

Dolan reached up and closed the blinds. He continued standing over Sierra, watching the child sleep. Gradually, his thoughts turned to his own childhood. He closed his eyes, and he could hear his mother's bed squeaking. He could always hear that damned bed. It was constant. He began to sweat, and his breathing quickened as he thought again about the time his drunken mother tried to kill him.

Dolan opened his eyes and saw that Sierra had started to stir. He reached into a backpack and pulled out a syringe, some rubbing alcohol, and a vial.

"Just a small dose for a small girl," he said, drawing some clear liquid from the vial into the syringe. "Think of it as magic juice." He rolled Sierra onto her side and injected the drug into her shoulder.

"Sleep well," Dolan said. "I have to get you changed, and then I have to get ready for Mommy Brooke."

***

Lukas and Brooke were rolling down I-81 toward Gatlinburg. Brooke noticed the Jeep had little trouble dealing with the snow.

"The way I figure it, it's normally a ninety-minute drive to Gatlinburg, but with the condition of the roads, it'll probably take us two hours," Lukas said.

Brooke checked the time. Two hours was a lifetime. "What's the first stop?"

"The Woodbriar Inn. I guess I better call Danny Smart and tell him what we're doing."

Brooke listened to the one-way conversation and appreciated the way Lukas handled it. Calm but confident. It seemed to be going over better than she expected.

"That seemed to go okay," she said once he'd finished the call and disconnected.

"If we get a lead down there, the FBI will come running. Listen, I looked up an old file about a prostitute being murdered. Remember the newspaper story we found at Dolan's? It turns out she was Dolan's mother. I can't prove it, but I think Dolan killed her. He was only 13 years old at the time. All the prostitutes Dolan killed had kids. I think he's been killing his mother over and over because he hates what prostitutes do to their kids. Danny reached out to the behavioral analysis people in Quantico. The profile is complicated, but they agree with the theory. He sees his mother in each one and in his mind, he believes he's saving the children from a life of oppression, disappointment and failure."

"Where does that leave me?" Brooke said. "I'm not a hooker, I'm a cop."

"But you're also a woman, and a mother. Plus, you're trying to keep him from doing what he thinks he has to do. Killing prostitutes is his mission in life now, it's his purpose. You're trying to take that away from him."

"That's what Danny said."

Brooke typed the address of The Woodbriar Inn into the GPS on her phone. They were still more than an hour away.

"Go faster," she said.

"I don't want to wreck."

"This thing could climb a tree. It isn't sliding at all. They've done a good job on the roads. Pick it up, please."

"Okay, lady. But we're screwed if we wind up in another wreck."

CHAPTER THIRTY-THREE

After what seemed like an eternity, Brooke's GPS app announced that they had arrived at their destination. She couldn't remember a ride ever seeming to take so long. Moments later, the Jeep crunched to a stop in front of the motel. The parking lot was full of cars, most of which were probably travelers who decided it would be better to seek sanctuary than brave the storm. A quick trip around the lot did not reveal a green Ford truck.

"It doesn't look like his vehicle is here," Lukas said.

"He could have changed again."

"True. Let's check with the office."

Brooke followed Lukas across the parking lot. The man behind the desk appeared to be busy with paperwork. He was gray-haired and looked sleepy.

"How's business?" Lukas said.

"Booming. It happens every time there's a snow storm. People can't make it to the cabins up in the mountains, so they end up here. You folks need a room?"

"No, thanks. We're here on business. I'm Detective Miller, and this is Detective Stevens. We're working the kidnapping of a little girl from Kingsport and were

THE SINS OF THE MOTHER

wondering if you've seen this man." Lukas pulled up Dolan's driver's license photograph on his phone.

The man put his glasses on but still squinted at the picture. "Looks kind of familiar, but I can't say for sure. The Gatlinburg police were already here about this, you know."

"Sorry, we're just being thorough and following up. He would've been accompanied by a five-year-old girl." This time Brooke showed him a picture of Sierra she had on her phone.

"No, but she's adorable. I think I'd remember her."

"Would you care if I looked at the register?"

"No, by all means. Come around the counter, and I'll set you up in the office."

Brooke and Lukas entered the office and took seats in swivel chairs. Lukas combed the guest register while Brooke studied the vehicles the guests had registered. About a minute into the search, Lukas asked Brooke, "What's Dolan's middle name?"

"I think his driver's license said Alan."

"There's no Dolan or Danson here, but there is an Alan Atkins."

"Another alias?"

"Maybe. There's an Alan Atkins registered here right now."

"What room?"

"Room one-eleven, bottom floor. Do you think it's him?"

"Cross the vehicle listings."

Brooke found the entry for the matching room. "Here it is. Silver Honda. It doesn't match, but he could have switched cars again."

"Agreed," Lukas said. "We have to hit the room no matter what the vehicle register says."

"Should we call anyone?" Excitement and anticipation were starting to build up inside of Brooke. It was a long shot, but maybe...

"I'll call the locals. Meantime, we watch the room."

Lukas was on his phone for five minutes.

"They're sending their Tactical Response Team. Should be here in twenty minutes."

It was closer to a half-hour than twenty minutes, but eventually a black tactical van rolled into the parking lot along with a marked and an unmarked cruiser. Lukas and Brooke had kept a close eye on the room, but they'd also searched the parking lot for a silver Honda. There wasn't one in the lot. No one had gone into or out of the room.

Lukas, Brooke and the Tactical Response Team commander talked for ten minutes and devised a plan for entering the room. The first step would be evacuating the people in the adjoining rooms. After that, the TRT would blast through the door using a battering ram. They would clear the room, and if Dolan was in there, they would either arrest him or – if he resisted or threatened to harm Sierra – kill him. Each member of the eight-man team was shown photos of Dolan and Sierra.

"But we're not sure he's in there, correct?" the TRT commander said. He was a skin-headed, tough-looking man named Deakins who looked to be about forty.

"We're not, but we can't take a chance on him being there and us doing nothing. If he's not in there we need to focus our energy elsewhere."

"Why don't we just wait until morning? Wait him out."

"What if he kills her during the night?" Brooke said. "We've already told you what we're dealing with. He's unpredictable and dangerous. We called you out of respect because we're in your jurisdiction. We can't wait."

"I have to call my chief and cover my ass," Deakins said.

"Do what you have to do, but my daughter might be in that room. We're going in with you or without you," Brooke said.

Deakins put his phone to his ear and walked away for a few minutes. When he returned, he said, "Let's do it." He began giving orders to his men, and within minutes, the rooms adjacent to room one-eleven were being evacuated. It was nearing midnight, and people were clearly not happy about being hauled out into a snowstorm. They were all directed to the lobby.

Once the rooms were clear, one of Deakins's largest officers, followed closely by four others, walked up to the door carrying a battering ram. Brooke and Lukas moved in behind them, but the looks they received from the other officers told them their presence wasn't appreciated.

"On three," the second officer in line whispered. "One...two...THREE!"

The door exploded, and the officers rushed in, shouting instructions for the occupants to get on the floor. The flashlights attached to their assault rifles lit up the room, and when Brooke stepped in, her heart sank. The two beds in the room were neatly made. There wasn't a sign of anyone.

He was still one step ahead.

Brooke walked through the room slowly, taking note of everything. She stepped into the bathroom. On the counter next to the sink was something that seemed out of place. It was a white, cardboard coaster that advertised "Smoky Mountain Cabins, Inc." She was taking a photo of it with her phone when Lukas walked in.

"What is it?" Lukas said.

"He left it for us. He's telling us where he is."

"Are you sure?" Lukas looked down at the coaster.

"Why would that coaster be sitting there? He probably knew we'd find the matches at his place and knew we'd eventually show up here. He must have figured we'd catch onto the alias. He's playing games, Lukas. He's enjoying this."

"I'll get an evidence bag and seal it up," Lukas said.

Brooke went outside and told Commander Deakins what she'd found. She asked him about the business.

"They've got a bunch of cabins and chalets scattered around Gatlinburg, Pigeon Forge and Sevierville," Deakins said. "Pretty big operation. They rent some and they sell some."

"The coaster says they open at eight in the morning," Brooke said. "I guess that's our next stop."

"You'll have to call the Sevier County Sheriff's Department if you need tactical help," Deakins said. "That's out of my jurisdiction."

"We appreciate you helping us out here."

"When they send us a bill for the door, we'll forward it on to your department," Deakins said, and he turned and walked off.

CHAPTER THIRTY-FOUR

L ukas had rented a room, and Brooke walked in to find him staring at his laptop. She took off her windbreaker and hung it on the back of a chair. She was bone tired, but there was no way she was going to sleep. She walked over to the kitchenette and brewed a pot of coffee.

"Lukas, do you think Dolan bought a cabin here somewhere?"

"I do, and I think he wants us to visit."

"He wants *me* to visit," Brooke said. "He wants to kill me and my child."

"He probably wouldn't mind bagging me, too, at this point," Lukas said. "I've been a pain in his ass, too."

"Sierra's close," Brooke said. "I can feel her."

"I need to call Danny and tell him about the coaster and this new Alan Atkins alias."

Brooke walked over to the bed while Lukas called Danny. She fell onto it and closed her eyes. She knew she couldn't sleep even if she wanted to, but closing her eyes, even for just a minute, kept them from burning so much. She heard Lukas talking to Danny but didn't pay attention to what he was saying.

"Brooke, you okay?" Lukas asked a few minutes later.

She got up and walked to the window. The snow had already painted a fresh coat on the landscape and cars in the lot. "I know you don't like to talk about it, but when you were in pararescue, did you ever feel helpless? I mean completely helpless."

"I don't know if anything that happened to me can compare to what you're going through, but yeah, I guess there were times I felt like I had no control over anything. It's a terrible feeling."

"I feel like Dolan is controlling everything," Brooke said. "I feel like a puppet on a string."

She stood there looking out the window thinking about happier times and wondering if she would ever experience happiness again. Lukas's phone rang, which caused her to jump. Lukas answered it and turned on the speaker.

"Hey Danny, you're on speaker. What did you find?"

"Good news. It looks like Dolan is using Alan Atkins as an alias. He's been very careful about how and when he's used it, so we don't have much, but there's enough to link the alias to Dolan."

"And if he bought a piece of property using that alias there'll be a record."

"We're looking, but the Sevier County Register of Deeds hasn't entered the twenty-first century. None of their records are online, which means we have to go there to search. They're obviously not open. We can get to the sheriff and have him roust the Register of Deeds, but I don't know how long it'll take. The business opens at 8:00 a.m., which is in five hours. The best bet for you two is to go to the office of Smoky Mountain Cabins as soon as they open and see what you can learn. We'll keep working the digital side, and if you don't come up with anything, we'll send an agent to the courthouse in Sevierville to search deeds."

"Sounds like a plan," Lukas said.

"Good luck, guys."

Lukas ended the call. He looked at his watch and then to Brooke. "Three hundred minutes," he said. "Let's try to get some rest and be there when they open."

CHAPTER THIRTY-FIVE

The next five hours seemed like five years to Brooke. Finally, just after daybreak, they were in Lukas's Jeep. Brooke Googled Smoky Mountain Cabins, Inc. and typed the address into the GPS app on her phone.

"It's eight miles from here," she said. "Turn right going out of the parking lot."

The trip to the company's office took half-an-hour. They climbed steadily, negotiating switch-backs and treacherous roads. Snow was still falling.

The office was a cabin. It looked cozy from the outside, especially with snow on the roof. "How quaint," Brooke said. "All it needs is smoke coming from the chimney."

Brooke walked past a new, silver Mercedes AMG SUV and an older, red Dodge Durango as she approached the snow-covered steps. She pushed through the front door at precisely eight. A bell announced their presence, and a petite, gray-haired lady who appeared to be in her late sixties emerged from a room behind the counter. She had a pleasant smile and a charming air about her. Three walls were adorned with paintings and photos of cabins. The fourth was covered by a huge quilt.

"I'm sorry," the woman said, "but all of the cabins are rented. Even most of the people who own cabins are here. Everybody wants to go skiing when it snows like this."

Brooke held up her badge. "We don't need to rent a cabin," she said. "I'm Detective Stevens, and this is Detective Miller. What's your name, ma'am?"

"Clara Ogle."

"We were wondering if you could give us some information about the people who own or rent cabins from you."

"You should probably talk to the owner," she said. "She's back in the office. I'll get her."

Clara returned a few seconds later followed by a dark-haired, middle-aged, attractive woman. *Has to be the owner*, Brooke thought. The woman was not smiling.

"How can I help you?" she said.

"I'm Detective Stevens, and this is Detective Miller," Brooke said. "As we were telling Ms. Ogle—"

"Yes, she told me you're detectives looking for information about our customers. I don't want to come across as uncooperative, but I'm afraid you'll have to go through our corporate attorneys to get any of your questions answered or look at our records."

"Can I have your name, ma'am?" Brooke said.

"It's Gloria Winn, with two ns."

"Mrs. Winn, we're investigating a series of murders and the kidnapping of a five-year-old girl. We think the killer and kidnapper is most likely in this area based on information and evidence we've recently discovered. We need to know whether you have any information on a man named Paul Dolan. He also goes by John David Danson and Alan Atkins. He's our suspect, and he has the child with him. I'm sure you wouldn't want to withhold information about something so serious. We're talking about a dangerous man and the life of a young girl."

"Detectives, I'm terribly sorry, but like I said, we have a policy against giving out any information regarding our renters or owners. But I would be glad to provide you with our attorney's name and number. Now, if there is nothing else?"

"Actually, there is something else," Brooke said. "The child he has is my daughter, and I think she's nearby, so here's how this is going to go. We've identified ourselves as police officers and stated our business. We've told you the seriousness of the situation. It's urgent that we find this man. So, having said that, you are now going to provide us with records regarding the people who own theses cabins."

"Detective, are you threatening me?"

"I'm telling you that withholding information related to this case could put you in danger of being charged as an accessory after the fact and/or obstruction of justice. And I'm sure you don't want the media to learn that you refused to provide information regarding a serial killer and kidnapper. Imagine how it's going to look if something happens to that child and you could have helped but refused. Just show us the records. If he's not here, we'll be on our way."

Brooke noted the incredulous look in the woman's eyes. She was clearly not used to being talked to in such a manner.

"I'm not afraid of you," she said. "Get out, or I'll have my attorneys on you so fast it'll make your head spin."

Brooke stuck her finger within an inch of the woman's nose.

"Listen up, lady. You have no idea the kind of shit I'm going to bring down on you. We'll be back soon with a warrant. In the meantime, I suggest you call those attorneys you mentioned, because you're going to need them. I look forward to slapping the cuffs on you myself. Oh, and when you finally realize the gravity of the mistake you've made, don't bother asking for sympathy. You won't get a damned bit from me. Ms. Ogle, do you have any information for us?"

The woman shook her head. Brooke handed her one of her cards.

"Call my cell if you think of anything," she said. "Ms. Winn, we'll be seeing you very soon."

Brooke turned to leave. Lukas was in front of her. As she reached the door she gave one last look back. Ms. Winn had moved around the counter toward the door. She looked conflicted. She spoke before Brooke made it out the door. "We have an owner by the name of Alan Atkins," Ms. Winn said. "But he's a nice man. I don't believe for one second he's capable of the things you mentioned."

"I don't care what you believe," Brooke said. "Where's the cabin? Give me the address and tell me how to get there."

"Number One Rhododendron Circle. Turn west out of the driveway. It's less than a mile."

Brooke turned and hurried outside to the Jeep. Lukas jumped in, started the engine and pulled out of the lot.

"You're scary when you're pissed," Lukas said. "So what's the play? Do we go in now or wait for Danny's guys? They'll scramble a SWAT team out of the Knoxville office, but it'll take them a while to get here."

"Call Danny and see what he thinks," Brooke said. Brooke's phone buzzed. She didn't recognize the number. The screen said it was from an unknown caller.

"Detective Stevens."

"You finally made it, Brooke."

"Who is this?"

"Really? Come on now, let's not play games. You know who this is."

"Dolan! Where's my daughter? Let me speak—"

"You can call me Alan Atkins if you want. I have to give you credit. I mean, you caught a couple of breaks along the way, but it looks like we're finally going to get the chance meet in a more intimate setting."

"I want to talk to Sierra!"

"Shut your mouth. Sierra and I look forward to seeing you soon."

CHAPTER THIRTY-SIX

Brooke could feel the blood draining from her face. Her hands began to tremble. A tingle ran down her back, and for a second, she was afraid she might not be able to speak. Lukas pulled the Jeep over to the side of the road.

"Brooke," Dolan said. "Are you there?"

"I'm here," she said, trying desperately to keep her voice from trembling. "Do you have any idea what I'm going to do to you if you've hurt my little girl?"

"Our little girl is fine. But she won't be if you involve anyone else. If I see so much as a mall cop, you'll never see her alive again. This is between you and me. Is that clear?"

"This is between you and your mother."

"Shut your filthy hole! I swear to God, you dump the boyfriend and come alone or Sierra will suffer."

"I'll come alone, and I'll bring hell with me."

"That's perfect. The devil is already here, and he has eyes everywhere."

"Let me talk to my daughter," Brooke said. "I want to hear her voice."

The line went silent.

"That bitch Gloria Winn must have called him and warned him," Brooke said. "It's the only way he gets my cell number. It was on the card I gave to Clara."

"What did he want?" Lukas said.

"He's taunting me. He's ready to kill me. He said he has eyes everywhere and that he better not see you or any other cop. If he does, he'll kill Sierra."

"Let me call Danny and get their guys in motion," Lukas said. "In the meantime, you and I are going in."

Brooke sat there watching the snow fall hard and fast. The wind had picked up and was blowing the snow horizontally in spots. The mountain roads were covered. Lukas put his phone on speaker after dialing Danny Smart.

"We know where he is," Lukas said. He gave Danny the address. "How long before you can get a SWAT team up here?"

"What's the weather like?"

"Heavy snow. Windy."

"At least an hour. Can you hold on that long?"

"Not a chance. Brooke and I are going in."

"If we come up there and find your bodies, I'll be answering questions all the way to Washington. I'll get the SWAT team mobilized. Just hang on. Our guys know what they're doing. We can handle this and get Brooke's girl back."

"Can you guarantee her safety while we wait?" Brooke said.

"You know I can't."

"Then we're going in. Now. She's my daughter."

There was a long pause.

"Hey Danny," Lukas said. "Could you pull up some satellite photos and send them to my phone? I'd like to do a little recon."

"Will do. You watch each other's asses out there."

CHAPTER THIRTY-SEVEN

Lukas disconnected the call and looked at Brooke. Her face was flushed.

"Are you ready?"

Brooke nodded.

"Are you sure?"

"Dammit, Lukas, I'm ready. Stop trying to coddle me."

Lukas slammed the Jeep into gear and pulled back onto the road. It took less than five minutes to get to the street where Dolan's cabin was located. Lukas stopped the Jeep about three hundred yards short of Rhododendron Circle and opened up the photos Agent Smart had sent. Brooke watched as he studied the terrain leading up to and surrounding the cabin.

"What are you looking for?" she asked.

"High ground. Some kind of tactical advantage. Dolan's expecting you, but he has to know I'm coming, too. I'm looking for a way in that he wouldn't expect."

"And which way would that be?"

"The most difficult way."

Brooke watched Lukas study the photos. She thought about what was about to happen and how she would handle it. Dolan wanted her alone. Was she up to this? She'd done a lot of things during her time as a police officer and detective, but killing a man wasn't one of them. Could she kill him if she had to? Could she pull the trigger? She thought about Sierra, and the doubt went away. She'd blow his head off his shoulders if it got Sierra back unharmed. She found herself hearing her father's voice: "Remember your training," he'd always said. "Remember your training."

She glanced over at Lukas, who was still looking over the photos.

"Come up with anything?" she said.

After what seemed like an eternity, Lukas said, "Looking at the way the terrain is laid out around the cabin, I have a plan. Tell me what you think."

"Lukas, I'm not ashamed to tell you that I'm out of my league here. I've never been in a gunfight, never been in special ops in the military. Just tell me what to do."

"He's expecting you to come alone. And you will, to a point. I'm going to swing around to the right flank. It's a difficult, steep approach and he won't expect it. It'll give me the high ground, a good vantage point to cover you. Give me a fifteen-minute head start to get into position, then walk straight up the drive. Utilize whatever cover you can. There are plenty of trees. By the time you get close to the cabin, I should be there, too."

"What do we do when we get to the cabin?"

"We wing it."

"You won't let him see you? He made it clear he wanted me alone."

"I hope the way I'll be going in will surprise him and give us an edge. We'll shift the tactical advantage from him to us. Are you good to go?"

"I'm good."

"Then let's gear up."

CHAPTER THIRTY-EIGHT

The snow was coming down in a virtual wall now, which Lukas believed could give them at least somewhat of an advantage during their approach. They went to the back of the Jeep and started to assemble their gear. Lukas decided against his usual tactical ballistic vest and instead pulled out the new ghost body armor the department had issued to the detectives. It was t-shirt thin and unnoticeable. The shirt was made of Kevlar and was brand new to the market. Ghost body armor was relatively untested in the field, but Lukas felt like he would be able to move better since it was less bulky than the traditional vests. The way he would be going in, he needed as much mobility as possible.

Once he was ready, he helped Brooke into her gear and made last minute adjustments. While he worked, he maintained a steady conversation to help calm her nerves and assess her mental condition. She appeared to be doing well.

Lukas brought up the satellite photos of the area and moved closer, so she could follow along as he explained.

"Okay," he said. "Like I said, you walk straight up the road to the cabin, using the trees for cover.

Eventually, you're going to come to a clearing where the cabin sits. I'll be coming in this way circling around to the east. It'll be a tough climb, but it'll get me to the high ground with a good view of the cabin. I think it's our best chance. Make sure you have easy access to your phone. Put it on vibrate. I'll text you if anything changes."

"Okay, got it."

Lukas called Danny again and put it on speaker.

"Speak, Lukas."

"Hey Danny, I have you on speaker. Give us a last-minute sitrep."

"The situation is pretty much the same as before. We have a team scrambling. They'll be there, but with the weather, it'll take some time."

"Any last-minute advice on Dolan before we go in?"

"It's complicated, but the tactical version is less so. Dolan is a control freak, and he'll want to maintain that control. He's calculating and smart, and he'll be ready. But I don't think he wants a shootout. He'll want to manipulate you. To taunt you and show you he's won, rub it in your face."

"What about my daughter?" Brooke asked.

"I think she's alive. I could be wrong, but I think he needs her for bait and I think she's safe for now. This is about you right now, Brooke. He's using her to lure you in. If he gets you into a bad situation, be strong. Don't let him dominate you."

"You said he'd be ready," Lukas said. "Any advice?"

"You're only going to get one chance at ending this. Make the most of it."

Lukas ended the call and looked at Brooke. She looked ready. He'd seen the look on the faces of his fellow soldiers during his years in the field.

"One last thing," he said.

"Remember my training," Brooke said.

"You got it. Let's do this."

Lukas began to climb while Brooke waited by the Jeep. He needed the head start because of the distance he would be traveling. He turned and looked back at Brooke as he went over the first ridge, wondering what destiny had in store. How would it play out? Would he ever see her alive again? Would he be alive? He was worried. Dolan was smart, and he'd had some time to plan. Lukas assessed the ridge, checked his gear one more time, headed down the back side.

The snow was a blessing in one regard and a hindrance in another. On one hand, it helped hide him. On the other, it made climbing the ridge slick and dangerous. He continued at a slow but steady pace, stopping periodically to check his progress on a topographical map Danny had sent him earlier. It was important that he get to the top of the ridge before Brooke approached the cabin. His shoulder ached as he climbed up a rock face, and he was breathing heavily. He glanced at his watch. *Pick up the pace.* He pulled out his phone and texted Brooke. The text told her he was moving slowly and to take her time.

He resumed his climb toward the summit of the ridge. As he grew close, he was tired and soaked with sweat. He reached what he thought was the top and cursed under his breath. False summit. In front of him was yet another rock face that would need to be quickly negotiated. He set his feet, dug his gloved fingers in, and pulled. It took nearly every ounce of energy he had to get himself to the top.

He saw the boots a fraction too late.

And then he saw nothing at all.

CHAPTER THIRTY-NINE

When Lukas regained consciousness, he was being dragged. He looked up at his assailant, knowing before he saw him that it was Dolan. How could he have let this happen? Brooke and Sierra's lives were at stake. Lukas was dazed, but he did his best to understand his situation. He was handcuffed. His head was throbbing. He figured he'd most likely been disarmed. He'd screwed up, made a mistake, and now he had to figure out a way to regain an advantage. Adapt and overcome. The mantra of a Special Forces operator. He tried to focus, but the blow to his head had left him addled and made it difficult.

The texture of the snow beneath him changed. He could see ice along the shoreline of a pond or lake. Was he being dragged onto a dock of some kind? When they reached the end of the long, wooden walkway, his captor dropped him. Lukas rolled over and sat up.

Dolan was looming over him.

"I've been watching you from the time you started up the ridge," he said. "Surveillance cameras. Remember the ones I used at Brooke's? They're hidden well, but a smart detective like you should have figured I'd have some kind of surveillance at my own cabin. I enjoyed those cameras. I've actually seen Brooke naked. Have you? The woman is built like a brick shithouse. I hope you got a chance to sample the goods, because I'm afraid this is the end of the line for you, Detective Miller. What's that old saying? Life's a bitch and then you die?"

"Screw you," Lukas said. "While you're out here gloating, she's getting Sierra out of the cabin. And then she'll come out and park a bullet in your brain pan."

"You underestimate me, as usual. Stand up."

"Go to hell."

"Stand up or I'll put a bullet in *your* brain pan, right where you're sitting."

Lukas struggled to his feet. He noticed that the pistol in Dolan's right hand was his Sig Sauer. The blow to the head must have been worse than he originally thought. Now that he was standing, blood was running into his left eye, obscuring his vision. He tried to think of something, anything that would get him out of his situation. He decided to talk. He had to try to buy some time.

"I have a question, Dolan. What was your plan with Gabriele?"

"It was simple. I was going to have some fun with her, and then I was going to kill her."

"And Razzy? Was that directed at me?"

"Razzy? You mean Kimberly Raznovich? You give yourself too much credit. She was just another whore that needed to be exterminated. But I knew her death would really ramp things up when she showed up at the mayor's house. Not that I have anything against the mayor. I just thought it would be fun, and Rodney would do anything for a fix. She was a fighter, though, I'll give her that. A scrappy whore. She actually thought she could get away from me. What a joke."

"Joke's going to be on you," Lukas said. "The only way you're getting off of this mountain is in a body bag."

Dolan laughed. "Good for you, Lukas Miller. Defiant to the end. Well, as much as I'd like to stand here and trade threats and insults with you, I have other things to do."

Lukas glanced around, taking in his surroundings, desperately looking for some way out of his predicament.

"Before I go," Dolan said, "I want you to know I learned in the Citizen's Police Academy that a cop's worst fear is to be shot with his own gun, and I have to say this Sig Sauer Legion of yours is a nice piece. Expensive, well-made firearm. I think it's fitting that you should wind up on the wrong end of it. Goodbye, Lukas."

He raised Lukas's pistol and pointed it straight at the center of his chest. Lukas saw the flash, felt the searing pain as the bullet struck him in the chest, and fell backward into freezing, black water.

CHAPTER FORTY

Brooke heard the shot as it echoed through the trees. It sounded as though it came from the direction Lukas should be heading. What the hell? Was Lukas in trouble? Had he killed Dolan? She waited, hiding in the trees behind snow covered branches. It took every bit of restraint she could muster not to run for the cabin. It was only thirty yards away. Smoke was coming from the chimney. Someone was in there.

Something moved behind her. She spun and noticed a branch bobbing up and down from snow that had fallen to the ground. The wind? No. She was in an area that was relatively sheltered from the wind. *"Hold it together."* She continued watching the cabin and the surrounding area.

She heard footsteps approaching from the ridge where Lukas was supposed to be. She leaned against the tree until she saw movement. It was Dolan. Fear gripped her. Where was Lukas? The shot she'd heard earlier suddenly took on ominous possibilities. *"My God, Lukas, where are you?"* Dolan trudged through the snow moving closer to the front of the cabin. It was now or never.

She emerged from the trees with her Glock in hand.

"Hold it, Dolan. That's far enough. Take another step, and I'll drop you where you stand."

Dolan stopped. He was holding what looked like Lukas's gun in his right hand.

"Brooke," he said. "It's good to see you. Lukas sent his regards, right before I shot him with his own gun."

She couldn't believe what she was hearing. Lukas was dead? He couldn't be. She refused to believe Dolan.

"Drop that weapon and lace your fingers behind your head," Brooke said. "Do it. Now, Dolan!"

"Don't think so," Dolan said. His left hand slid into his coat pocket and he pulled out a small, black plastic object that looked very much like a fob for keyless entry to modern cars. He pushed a red button on the device and held it in. "Guess what this is?" he said. "It's a detonator. Have you ever heard of a dead man's switch, Brooke? I just pushed the button. The button just armed a little vest I have on Sierra. If I let go of this button for any reason, that vest explodes. There won't be anything left of her."

Brooke felt a wave of terror run through her. She wasn't sure what to do. She decided to stall. "You're lying. Where is she?" Brooke said.

"Sleeping inside. Don't worry, she won't wake up anytime soon. I've made sure of that."

Dolan raised the Sig Sauer and pointed it at Brooke's head.

"Time to make a decision, Mommy," he said. "Drop your weapon and come inside with me or listen to the explosion that blows your precious Sierra to bits."

"I want to see her," Brooke said. "Prove to me that she's alive."

"First of all, you're in no position to be dictating terms. Secondly, you reneged on our deal. You were supposed to come alone. That makes me angry. So, what do you say we do this old school? I'm going to count to three. If you haven't dropped your weapon, I'm going to start shooting and release this button. You've seen me shoot. You know I hit my target."

Brooke's mind was whirling. If he was telling the truth and she shot him, the vest would explode, and Sierra would be killed. Was she willing to take that chance? My God, where was Lukas? Was she alone on this mountain with this maniac?

All her training had told her to never surrender her weapon.

Never.

"One," Dolan said.

She needed more time. God, she needed more time.

"Two."

Lukas, where are you? She couldn't risk Dolan blowing up Sierra.

She dropped the gun.

CHAPTER FORTY-ONE

The freezing water had a numbing effect that decreased the pain in Lukas's chest. He was sure he had a broken rib, maybe worse, but the icy water would slow the bleeding if there was an open wound and keep swelling to a minimum. His immediate problem was that he was handcuffed and sinking into a black abyss.

When Dolan shot Lukas, he must have had no idea Lukas was wearing the ghost vest. Otherwise, he would have shot him in the head. But center mass was always what was taught, and Lukas figured Dolan had used his Citizen's Police Academy training to aim for center mass. As it turned out, the damned vest worked.

His military training kicked in as he sank downward. He knew from his distance to the shoreline that the chances were good the water wouldn't be more than fifteen, twenty feet deep at the most. He didn't lose consciousness, not even for a second, probably because the water was so brutally cold. When he reached the bottom, he kicked his way to the surface. Memories of the pool exercises from when he was going through the pipeline at Lackland Air Force Base came back to him.

Surfacing, he took in a long, life-conserving breath. He took a quick look around but didn't see Dolan. He'd worried that Dolan would still be there to make sure Lukas was dead.

As he sank a second time, he arched his back, curled his legs, and worked his cuffed hands over his boots until they were in front of him. Reaching the bottom, he kicked off once again. He angled toward his right, changing directions to surface under the dock. He wanted to make certain he remained undetected and to keep a barrier between himself and Dolan in case Dolan was still there.

He slowly surfaced and listened. The only sound was the wind rustling through the trees. He struggled into a modified breast-stroke, pushing through the cold water and finally onto the shore. He hurriedly removed his handcuffs with the key from the ring in his front pocket.

Lukas knew it wouldn't be long before he became hypothermic. He stripped off his jacket, shirt, and vest, leaving him bare-chested. Next, he took off his boots and socks. He put the boots back on, knowing they would provide some much-needed body heat once they drained completely. He checked his chest, which was throbbing, and found a nasty bruise but minimal bleeding.

He reached down to his ankle where he kept a Glock 42 backup. Thankfully, it was still there. Dolan had missed it.

Dragging himself to his feet, Lukas began to hurry toward the cabin. He hoped he wasn't too late.

CHAPTER FORTY-TWO

Brooke sat in a chair in front of the fireplace, her hands bound with thick black zip ties.

The cabin would have been cozy under different circumstances. Quilts and afghan throws were draped over the back of the various chairs and couches. A fire was burning in the fireplace, warming her back. Up and to her left was a loft. Was that where Sierra was? Dolan disappeared down a hallway and answered her unasked question as he came back with Sierra in his arms. He'd set the detonator down on a table in the kitchen right after he'd bound Brooke.

"I didn't lie about the detonator. I've disarmed it. See? You made the right choice. Now, here's our baby girl. Sleeping like she doesn't have a care in the world."

Brooke's throat tightened. She could see Sierra was breathing, but she could also see the vest. It looked like one of those suicide vests used by terrorists. There were four pipe bombs in the vest's pockets, all attached by wires.

"Say goodbye, Mommy," Dolan said, and he turned and disappeared back down the hall. When he returned, he went to the kitchen table, grabbed a chair, and walked over to within five feet of Brooke. He turned the chair around backward and sat down.

Dolan smirked at Brooke. "I think you know how this ends, don't you? It's what you deserve."

Brooke needed to buy time. Maybe Lukas had survived and would show up. Maybe the FBI team would arrive sooner rather than later. Could she stall him that long?

"I understand your hatred for the hookers," Brooke said. "You were killing your mother. But why me?"

"You really don't know? You don't have any idea? You're a single mother who neglects her child for her job. You're a whore to it, like the others were to men. How much time has your child spent alone while you were out chasing me? Where were you when I took her? That alone proves my point, doesn't it?"

Brooke immediately felt a pang of guilt. There was some truth to what he was saying. But he was clearly psychotic, and she needed more time. She needed to keep him talking, maybe stroke his ego a little. "So, you killed the women to save their children? Is that how you look at it?"

"I killed them because they deserved killing. I'm going to kill you because you deserve killing and because you and Lukas were trying to stop me from doing my work. He's gone now, and you will be soon. I imagine you probably have some more friends on the way. The vest I have on Sierra should give them pause. And if it comes down to it, I'll hold our baby girl in my arms as I blow us both to hell. Neither of us will feel any pain. But I can't say the same for you."

Brooke knew that Dolan was in control, at least for now. She couldn't see how this could end well for either her or Sierra. Lukas was her only hope, and if Dolan was telling the truth, he was dead. She had to buy more time. "What about Pam and Gabriele?" Brooke said. "What did they do to you?"

"Pam was collateral damage. Gabriele betrayed me. Look, I'm not a monster. I'm for justice, just like you. Can't you see that? And remember this. You wouldn't be where you are now if you'd just left me alone and allowed me to do what I needed to do. I'd never heard of you until you started chasing me."

"How did Rodney fit into the picture?" Brooke said. "You almost had us fooled there. The way you set that scene up was… well, it was smart. I have to give you credit."

"Rodney was just a pawn. I needed help luring women, staging bodies after I'd killed them, things like that. I met him at the hospital when he came into the ER trying to get drugs. It was easy to find him after that. All I had to do was keep feeding him morphine, and he'd do anything I asked. I even let him have a little fun with Lukas's pet Razzy before I did away with him. Addicts are ultimately unreliable, so I had to put him down. And you're right, I almost pinned everything on him. But you and Lukas had to interfere."

"So, now you kill me and maybe Sierra and yourself, then what? You'll just be remembered as another nut job. You'll be in the news for two days, and then you'll be forgotten. You strike me as someone who would want more."

"Shut your mouth," Dolan said. "Time to have a little fun."

Dolan stood up and walked over to Brooke. He picked up a hunting knife that was lying on a coffee table just to his right.

Brooke's skin tingled. She could feel her heart pounding in her chest. He stepped close to her and ran the blade across her left arm beneath the elbow, cutting her just enough to make her bleed. She flinched but refused to cry out. Next, he cut the straps on her Kevlar vest and pulled it off. He breathed in deeply, like an animal trying to catch a whiff of prey. He cut off the buttons on her shirt. She tried to look him in the eyes, but he turned away. Was it a weakness?

"Look at me, Dolan," Brooke said. "If you're going to torture and rape me, at least be man enough to look me in the eyes."

"Who said anything about raping you?" Dolan said. "I'm not a rapist."

"Ahhh," Brooke said. "Now I get it. You're impotent. Can't get it up?"

Dolan, who was still behind her, slapped her hard across the side of her head. Her right ear began to ring.

"So, I'm right. You're nothing but an impotent coward."

Dolan touched the knife to Brooke's side and placed his arm around her neck, pulling her up from the chair.

"This impotent coward is about to show you what real pain is," Dolan said. He pushed her a step forward, and suddenly, the front door burst open. Brooke turned her head to see a snow-covered, shirtless Lukas, holding a gun. His teeth were chattering, and his hands were trembling. Brooke couldn't believe her eyes. He was alive. She watched the gun in his hand and wondered if he could shoot well enough in his condition to hit Dolan. She looked around, looking for an edge, something to help.

"Back away from her and drop the knife," Lukas said.

"Why the hell are you still alive? You really are a pain in my ass."

Brooke winced as the knife edged under her ribs. She could feel blood soaking through her shirt. At least she knew Sierra was safe, at least for now. And Lukas was alive.

"I suggest you drop that weapon before I put this knife in your girlfriend's liver," Dolan said. "From the looks of you, you couldn't hit anything anyway."

"Are you willing to bet your life on it?"

"Are you willing to bet hers?"

Brooke could see that Lukas was suffering. Hypothermia was setting in now. His lips were blue and his skin had a ghostly pallor to it. It was now or never.

"Go ahead, *Big Boy*." Brooke slammed her right foot down onto Dolan's instep as hard as she could as she said it. She twisted to her left and dropped with all her weight. She felt a searing pain in her right side as she fell and knew the knife had pierced her. She heard half-a-dozen deafening gunshots as she hit the floor. The chair she'd been tied to broke and came apart under Dolan's weight. Brooke strained against the pain and looked toward the door where Lukas had been. The acrid smell of gunpowder stung her nostrils. The air was thick with blue gray smoke. She gathered herself and rolled over. Paul Dolan was lying on his back. His eyes were open, staring at nothing.

Lukas was standing over her almost immediately. He helped her to her feet. He took the knife Dolan had dropped and cut the zip ties. She threw her arms around him and gave him a fierce but brief hug. The pain in her side caused her to moan.

"Brooke, you're bleeding."

"I'm fine. I need to get to Sierra." She almost ran down the hall to the room she'd seen Dolan take her daughter into. She burst into the room. Sierra was lying in the middle of a large bed surrounded by stuffed animals. She appeared to be sleeping peacefully.

"He put an explosive vest on her," Brooke said to Lukas. "There's a detonator on the kitchen table, but I don't know anything about these things. I don't want to remove it and take a chance on setting it off."

Brooke felt Sierra's pulse. It was slow but steady, and her breathing was shallow. She wanted to take her daughter into her arms and never let her go. Tears were starting to well up now, but she had to keep herself together. The nightmare wouldn't end until she knew Sierra was safe.

Brooke felt Lukas's presence as he walked up behind her. She turned. He was holding up a vial.

"I think she's been sedated," he said. "It's Lorazepam."

Brooke turned her attention back to Sierra and ran her fingers gently through her daughter's hair. "Is it dangerous? How much do you know about it?"

"It can be dangerous, but not if it's given in the right dosage. Dolan was a nurse, so he most likely knew how much to give her. Her color is good, but we need to get a bomb tech in here to remove the device and then get her to a hospital. You, too. Turn around."

He lifted Brooke's shirt where blood was seeping through the fabric. He walked to the bathroom that adjoined the room, emerging seconds later with a wet rag. "Hold pressure on it. It's doesn't look life-threatening, but it'll need stitching."

"I thought you were dead," Brooke said.

"So did I. I'm going to secure the detonator and call Danny and advise him of the situation. Give me your phone. Mine drowned."

"Dolan took it. It's on the kitchen table next to that detonator."

Brooke stayed with Sierra as Lukas went for the phone. The moment was interrupted by sounds coming from outside the cabin. Brooke followed Lukas as he hurried out of the room and walked quickly toward the open front door. She heard a commotion and then shouts from someone outside the cabin claiming to be with the FBI. The feds had arrived. Brooke breathed a deep sigh of relief and hurried to the front door, holding up her badge.

"Dolan's dead," she yelled. "Please tell me you have a bomb tech and an EMT with you."

After a brief argument, the agent in charge convinced Brooke to go to the command vehicle for first aid while a bomb tech worked on Sierra.

"What happened?" Brooke pointed to the ugly bruise on Lukas's chest.

"We'll talk about it later."

Brooke's eyes were beginning to tear up. The adrenaline was fading, and shock was starting to take over. She looked up into Lukas's eyes as he moved closer. He placed his hands on her face, wiped a tear away, and gently kissed her on the forehead.

Brooke noticed a parka hanging on the driver's side mirror of the idling FBI command vehicle. She picked it up and put it over his shoulders.

"Thanks," Lukas said. "I'm freezing."

Just then an EMT came into view from the road that led to the cabin carrying a small child in a blanket toward a waiting ambulance. The vest had been removed.

It was almost over.

CHAPTER FORTY-THREE

I t had been more than a week since Lukas's encounter with Dolan on the mountain. He was having nightmares, which was something he wasn't used to. He dreamed that he was drowning in cold, black water. He would wake up soaked in sweat and wouldn't be able to get back to sleep. It was good that he was off on vacation, because he didn't know how he'd make it through a work day on as little sleep as he was getting.

He hadn't heard a word from Gabriele. Not even a "Hey, glad you're alive" in a text. There had been calls from Brooke, but for some reason, he couldn't bring himself to talk to her.

Lukas knew what was going on. He was suffering from Post-Traumatic-Stress Disorder and depression. He wasn't eating well. Couldn't sleep. Hadn't shaved in a week. Was drinking more beer than he should. He'd been through it before. The nightmares he'd endured after leaving the Air Force had lasted for a year, but with the help of a psychiatrist at the Veterans Administration and some group therapy, they'd finally stopped. He knew he might have to call the VA shrink and set up an appointment, but he hadn't yet been able to bring himself to do it.

He'd gone to the mandatory session with the police department psychiatrist after killing Dolan. But killing Dolan wasn't the issue. Dolan deserved to die, and Lukas had no regrets about sending him to hell. He was bothered more by nearly allowing Dolan to kill *him.*

But what was at the core of this depression, he believed, was that even if Dolan had killed him, who would have mourned him? His mother was dead, murdered by his father. His father was in prison. His grandparents had all passed away. His brother had been killed. He had no one. Had he spent his life being so selfish that no one would care if he left this earth? Had he poured too much of himself into the job? He had his cop buddies and his Little League teams where kids came and went, but those were all superficial relationships. He had Brooke, but he wasn't sure where they stood. He hadn't ever really given of himself, and because of that, he was alone.

He was sitting in his den, the blinds drawn, as darkness was falling outside. He heard a soft knock on the front door. His first inclination was to sneak into the bedroom and lock the door, but he forced himself to get up and see who was knocking. He looked through the peephole.

Brooke.

Shit.

"Lukas? Are you in there?" he heard her say through the door. "Lukas?"

"I don't really want to talk right now, Brooke," he said.

"Open the door, Lukas, please."

"I look like hell."

"I'm sure you do. Please let me in. I'm your partner, remember?"

"That case is over."

"That case will never be over. For either of us."

She was probably right about that. How many female detectives wind up getting their own daughter kidnapped during the course of an investigation? There was plenty of trauma to go around, courtesy of the psychopath Paul Dolan.

"Sierra says hello."

Lukas dropped his forehead against the door. Why did she have to come now?

"Lukas, please? It's cold out here."

"You can get in your car and get warm."

"I'll stand out here all night if I have to. I'm not leaving until I see your face and we sit down and talk."

Lukas sighed and unlocked the door. He opened it and stepped back into the room. He began cleaning pizza boxes and beer bottles off the table in front of the couch. He looked up to find Brooke staring at him.

"Wow," she said, "you weren't kidding. You look pretty bad. I have to admit I kind of like the beard, though."

"Sit," Lukas said, motioning to a chair at the dining room table.

Brooke was wearing tight blue jeans and a black turtleneck sweater underneath a denim jacket. Her blonde hair was down, and it shimmered beneath the dining room light like golden thread. Damn, she really was easy on the eyes.

"Want a beer?" Lukas said.

"Sure, a beer sounds great."

Lukas pulled two beers out of the refrigerator and sat one down in front of Brooke. He took a seat across the table from her.

"How's Sierra doing?" he said.

"She's good, remarkably good considering what happened to her. She's so young, though, I don't think she's able to really process how bad it was or could have been. Thank God that psycho sedated her and didn't abuse her in any way. Haley took her out to eat and to do some shopping because I wanted to come over here and check on you. You won't return my calls."

"We were lucky," Lukas said, ignoring the remark about the phone calls. "Give Sierra a kiss for me."

"Why don't you give her a kiss yourself? Come to my house tomorrow for dinner."

"I don't know…"

"We can't let this get the best of us, Lukas. Are you having nightmares?"

"I've had a few," he lied.

"Me, too. More than a few."

"Mind describing them?" Lukas said.

"They're vivid, as though it was all happening again. The one that recurs most often is of Dolan's arm around my throat with that knife pressed against my side."

"Those are PTSD nightmares," Lukas said. "Are they in color or black and white?"

"Black and white."

"Mine, too."

"What happened out there, Lukas? How did Dolan get his hands on your Sig?"

"It doesn't matter now. We were warned, and I failed. It's a lesson learned."

Brooke smiled. "Lessons we walk away from are good ones."

"Seems like I've heard that before."

"It must have been terrifying," Brooke said. "Have you heard about Mrs. Winn, the owner of Smoky Mountain Cabins?"

Lukas shook his head.

"A federal grand jury in Knoxville indicted her for calling Dolan and warning him we were coming. She's facing half a dozen charges. My guess is she's going away for a while, no matter how good her attorneys are."

"Karma's a bitch."

"So why are you sitting here alone, in the dark, depressed?"

"Honestly? I've been thinking about how self-involved I've been all my life. I've never made any real connections with people. It stems from something that happened when I was a kid."

"What happened when you were a kid?"

Lukas looked at the beautiful woman in front of him. He could count on one hand the number of times he'd discussed the incident. Did he trust this woman? Did he want her knowing his deepest secrets?

"It stays in this room?"

"I promise."

"I was six, my brother, Ben, was seven. We were living in Dalton, Georgia, just south of Chattanooga at the time. My dad was a long-haul trucker. He'd be gone for two weeks at a time. My mom started seeing this guy. He was a few years younger than her, and she started bringing him home once in a while. She said he was her cousin, but Ben and I knew better. We spied on them, which was easy because they were usually drunk and snorting this white powder that I later learned was cocaine. Over the next couple of months, when my dad would come in, he and my mom would get in these big fights. I heard her threaten to kill him, or have him killed, if he tried to take her boys from her. Anyway, one Friday night when he was supposed to be on the road, he showed up at home around midnight. Mom and her boyfriend were there, partying in the den. Ben and I were awake upstairs, playing video games. They didn't care. I guess they were too high to care. I don't know exactly what happened when he walked in, but I think they were having sex, and he just lost it. He had a Smith & Wesson 686 revolver that he carried with him on the road for protection, and he just opened up on them with it. Ben and I dived into the closet. I'll never forget those shots. It seemed like they'd never stop.

"So, after they were both dead, he called 911 and came upstairs to make sure we were all right. The police came, took him to jail, and he wound up pleading guilty to two counts of first-degree murder. He got life without parole. I haven't seen him since."

"I'm sorry, Lukas," Brooke said. "Do you think it would help to see him?"

"He doesn't want to see me. My grandmother wrote to him all the time and she and my grandfather went to visit him, but he told them not to bring Ben and me. He didn't want us to see him locked up in prison. I wrote to him a few times, but he never answered. I eventually just let it go."

"So his parents raised you and Ben?"

"Yeah. My mom's parents were divorced and had both moved away. They were always fighting anyway. My mom used to say terrible things about her parents. I don't think my mother was a very good person. She wound up paying an awful price."

"I had no idea."

"It's not something I advertise. But my dad's parents were good to Ben and me. We both went into the military right out of high school – Ben into the Marines and me into the Air Force. Ben was killed in a training accident not long after he got into a Marines special ops unit. I was discharged from the Air Force because I beat the hell out of a civilian in a bar in Anchorage, Alaska, shortly after Ben was killed. They didn't burn me, though. Gave me an honorable discharge, didn't mention the fight in any of my separation papers, didn't charge me with any crime. They just sent me packing.

"I wound up being interested in law enforcement, probably because of what happened between my mom and dad. I got a degree in criminal justice from the University of Tennessee at Chattanooga, and then got a job with the Johnson City Police Department. And yes, I told them about my dad, but they gave me a shot anyway. I've been here ever since, but I haven't really *lived*. Do you know what I mean? If Dolan had killed me, nobody would have really cared. I haven't made a real difference with anyone because I haven't connected with anyone. I haven't really loved anyone."

"You've made a connection with me."

Lukas looked at her and she held his gaze.

"So, you don't think it was just professional?" he said. "Just a man and a woman, both of whom happened to be detectives, thrown into a desperate situation who wound up relying on each other?"

"I've been calling you, Lukas, and I didn't come over here just to talk about the case."

"Why did you come?"

"Because I miss you. Because I care about you. Because we *have* connected. I feel closer to you than I have to any other man in my entire life. What you're sitting here torturing yourself about is right in front of your face. You just refuse to see it."

Lukas took a long pull from his beer. His stomach was tingling. He felt as though the fog that had been surrounding him the past several days was lifting.

"Are you telling me you want to give us a try?" he said.

"If you don't mind taking a chance on a woman who works too hard and has a daughter."

"Stay right there," Lukas said. "I'll be right back."

"Where are you going?"

"I'm going to take a quick shower and shave. And then I'm going to come back out here and give you a kiss if you'll let me."

"I have a better idea," Brooke said.

"What's that?"

"How about you let me wash your back?"

CHAPTER FORTY-FOUR

ukas knelt behind home plate again to receive another pitch from Timmy. He was truly surprised at how much stronger the little guy's arm had gotten since June. What was even more surprising to Lukas was Brooke's athleticism. She was standing near first base receiving throws from both Lukas and Timmy. Her movements were smooth and graceful, her hands quick, and her arm strong. If Lukas ever started a coed softball team, he knew exactly who his first pick would be.

He looked out into the outfield where Sierra was happily pedaling along on her bicycle. The day was unseasonably warm, nearly seventy degrees, making the recent snows seem like a distant memory.

Lukas winced as another fastball smacked the palm of his mitt. It was getting to the point where he would need to bring a proper catcher's mitt if he was going to receive pitches from Timmy. He thought this would be a good time to take a break, so he motioned for Timmy to follow him to the dugout for a bottle of water. Brooke wandered into the outfield toward Sierra. Lukas sat down on the concrete bench in the dugout and pulled a bottle of water from a cooler they'd brought.

"Timmy, I think you're right about being a pitcher for me next year. You're really throwing the ball well, and it'll only get better between now and next spring."

"Thanks, Coach," Timmy said, sitting down beside Lukas. "You really think so?"

"Sure do." Lukas handed him a bottle of water.

"I can't wait until next baseball season is here. The winter is so long. And this year it'll be even longer since… well, you know."

"I wanted to talk to you about that," Lukas said. "How do you like staying with Ms. Clay?"

"I like it fine. She's really nice. I have my own room and everything. And she just bought me a bike. It's the first one I've ever had, and it's cool."

"It sounds like you're doing great."

"I guess so. But I miss my mom. I try to be strong like you asked me to but sometimes at night I get to thinking about her and I… I just start crying and can't stop." The boy dropped his head and his shoulders slumped.

"You *are* being strong Timmy, and I'm proud of you. It'll get easier as time passes, I promise. You won't ever forget your mom and you shouldn't. I don't want you to, and I know she wouldn't want you to. Your mom would be proud of you, you know that, right?"

"You really think so?"

"I sure do. Listen, I was wondering what you'd think about the two of us spending more time together."

"I'd like that a lot, Coach."

"As a matter of fact. I was wondering whether you'd like to come and live with me."

Timmy paused. Lukas searched his face for some clue as to what he was thinking. "You mean like all the time?"

"All the time. You'd just come live with me. Would you like that if I can work it out?"

"That'd be great. I'd love it. Would you be my dad? I've never had a dad."

"I'd do my best."

"But you'd still be my coach, too, right?"

"Sure would. Nothing would change except you would come and live at my house."

"That would be awesome." Lukas could see excitement building in Timmy's eyes.

"There's a lot involved. I have to file some papers in court, some lawyers and a judge will have to get involved, and it'll take some time. But if you think you'd like to come stay with me, I'll see what we can do. Okay?"

"Yes! I'd love it."

Lukas and Timmy sat in the dugout talking over the possibilities of Timmy living with him and watched Brooke and Sierra play together in the outfield. Lukas marveled again at the resemblance. It was as though Sierra had been cloned from her mother.

"Ready to throw a little more?"

"Yes, sir."

The two spent the next ten minutes with Timmy back on the mound. Brooke eventually meandered in from the outfield.

"Watch this one, Miss Brooke." Timmy let go of one that Lukas really felt.

"Wow, Timmy. That's great."

"Thanks."

"Hey, Timmy, do me a favor please," Lukas asked.

"Sure."

"Would you take my glove out with you and see if Sierra would like to play a little catch? Don't throw the ball too hard to her."

"Sure, Coach." He looked at Brooke. "Can she catch?"

"I think she'll surprise you, but like Lukas said, don't throw it too hard. She's only five."

When Timmy was safely out of hearing distance, Lukas walked Brooke over to the dugout, and the two sat down on the bench. Lukas playfully grabbed her right arm and squeezed it.

"That's some arm you've got there, Nolan Ryan," he said. "I'm impressed."

"Wait till you see me hit."

Brooke picked up a baseball that was lying on the bench beside her and looked at it. "I played softball in high school. Made all-conference my junior and senior years. Played basketball, too."

"A regular jock, huh? How are you, anyway? Holding up okay?"

"I still have the occasional nightmare, and if Sierra gets out of my sight for more than a minute I get panicky. But I'm trying to cope. Lukas, since our talk a few weeks ago I've gone back and examined a lot of things, too. I've learned a lot about me, both good and bad, and I owe a lot of that to you. I feel like I've changed, like I've grown. I feel like I'm a better mother, a better friend, a better daughter and a better cop."

"You've done the same for me," Lukas said. "I wake up in the morning with a different attitude these days."

They started back toward the field. He glanced over at her. "You know," he said, "our relationship was so complicated, or at least I thought it was. Now it seems easy. Where have you been all of my life?"

"My dad always said the best things are worth waiting for."

"Your dad's a smart man. Speaking of which." He reached in his pocket, took out some papers and handed them to her.

"What's this?" she said as she looked them over.

"It's something I'm going to try to do."

"Lukas, this says 'Petition for Adoption.' For Timmy? Are you sure?"

"I don't know. How can I know until I try?"

"You're just full of surprises, aren't you? I admire you. Very few men would do something like this. Just be sure about it, for your sake and for his."

Lukas allowed her words to sink in. "I know I can't save them all, but I can save this one."

Brooke looked out at Timmy and Sierra. Both seemed to be enjoying each other's company. She turned to Lukas with watery eyes and said, "Actually, Timmy makes two. You already saved a little girl, and her mother will never forget it."

Thank you for reading, and I sincerely hope you enjoyed *The Sins of the Mother*. As an independently published author, I rely on you, the reader, to spread the word. So if you enjoyed the book, please tell your friends and family, and if it isn't too much trouble, I would appreciate a brief review on Amazon. Thanks again. My best to you and yours.

-Scott

ABOUT THE AUTHOR

Scott Pratt was born in South Haven, Michigan, and moved to Tennessee when he was thirteen years old. He is a veteran of the United States Air Force and holds a Bachelor of Arts degree in English from East Tennessee State University and a Doctor of Jurisprudence from the University of Tennessee College of Law. He lives in Northeast Tennessee.

www.scottprattfiction.com

ALSO BY SCOTT PRATT

ABOUT THE AUTHOR

Mark Stout was born and raised in East Tennessee. He joined the United States Air Force after high school and attended the University of South Carolina while stationed at Shaw Air Force base. Mark has been a police officer for over twenty-seven years, twenty of which as a detective. He lives in rural east Tennessee with his wife, two sons, and two dogs.

www.markstoutbooks.com

ALSO BY MARK STOUT

Lukas Miller Book 2 (Fall 2019)

Made in the USA
Columbia, SC
14 August 2021

43638350R00172